Debt

Debt o

Book 11 in the Border Knight Series
By
Griff Hosker

Debt of Honour

Published by Sword Books Ltd 2021

Contents

Prologue

Shadow Of The Past

Birger Persson was dying. He had enjoyed a good life, but he was not dying the way he wished to; he would not enjoy a warrior's death with a sword in hand like his wild warrior ancestors. Instead, he was dying piece by piece as whatever worm lay inside him devoured him. He had no appetite and he was losing weight on a daily basis. He would be on this earth for but a little while longer. *Wyrd.* He had but one son and his wife had died giving birth to him. His brother Petr had died childless. Was the family cursed? Such things happened even in a Christian country. He should have been a rich man but he would be dying almost penniless and, even worse, taking any hope for a future from his son. It had to be a curse.

He had been on a crusade to the Holy Land and he had fought in Bishop Albert's crusade against the Estonians, but it seemed it was not enough for God. Each day was worse than the one before and Birger wanted it ended but he was a Christian and could not contemplate taking his own life. He would have to endure it. The priests and the doctors ministered to him every day and that did not please him. The latter cost money and did not appear to make a difference. Money was not important for its own sake but he had little enough to leave to his son as it was. Hermann Balk was the only friend he had left in this part of the world and he lived across the sea his ancestors had called, Østersøen, the Eastern Sea. His old friend had left the Livonian Knights when he was rewarded with a castle and a manor. Of course, it entailed constantly fighting barbarians but his old comrade in arms was happy enough and had made enough coin for Birger to be envious. Perhaps he should have stayed that little bit longer in Estonia. Who knew?

The doctors left and his old retainer, Sven Loyal Sword, said, "What do you need, lord?"

"That which none can give me, Sven, a dignified end."

Sven had been a warrior who had served with Birger Persson, becoming the leader of his warriors, and he had also fought in Bishop Albert's wars. He was the last survivor of the Swedish lord's men and had loyally stayed with the almost penniless Swedish warrior. "I am ever your man, lord, and I can put a sword in your hand and send you on your way."

"And I know that you would, but some would call it murder and I have enough enemies who will seek to destroy every memory of me. Fetch my son."

The old warrior was still as fit as he had ever been, and Birger watched him walk as easily as a young man. Perhaps there was a curse for Sven was older than he.

His son, Petr, opened the door and entered. Petr was a knight but there was not enough money to give him anything but the most basic of hauberks. He was a good knight for Birger had ensured that he had been trained well and the old warriors who had fought alongside Birger in the wars against the Estonians had made him as good as any Teutonic Knight. Had Birger thought more of himself and less of other causes perhaps he would have more money and would not be living in a hall which had changed little since his ancestors had sailed dragon ships and raided Christian churches. His son, however, lacked many qualities which Birger knew that a knight needed. He was an arrogant young man and for that Birger blamed himself. He had indulged him. Had there been a sibling as a rival then who knows what might have been. Perhaps he should have sent him to England. It was many years since his great friend Sir Thomas had returned to England but over the years Birger had heard of great deeds done by his friend and his family. He would have made a better man of Petr. He would have eradicated those flaws which the doting father recognised.

"How are you, today, father?"

Sven turned to go but Birger said, "Stay, Sven. I need you to hear this." The Dane nodded and stood apart. He still had good hearing. "Son, I am dying, and my doctors do not think that I will see the week out. They have submitted their bill which is never a good sign. I wish to speak with you whilst I am still lucid and while the drugs the leeches have given me ease my pain. There is no money when I am gone, and I fear for your future. Folki is a good squire but there is no money for mail. You both have horses but I fear they are not war horses. It is a sort of begging, but I have two old friends on whom I can rely. Herman Balk lives in Estonia and is a rich warrior. You can go to him and serve as a sword for hire. He has luck and skill. You will prosper."

5

His son nodded. Everyone had heard of Hermann Balk, but Petr had also heard that this was not the same man who had fought with his father. He said nothing.

"The other is Sir Thomas of Stockton." The Swede smiled at the memory. "We were young crusaders in the Holy Land and then he came here to help us rid the land of pagans. I have heard that he is a well-respected knight who guards England's northern borders. Seek one of those as a master. Both men promised me that they would help me if ever I needed it. I am calling in that debt now." He nodded towards Sven, "Sven I charge you with watching over my son when I am gone."

Sven just nodded but father and son knew that the nod was as good as a blood oath. The three then sat and just spoke the way people do when they know that they may never get the chance again. Birger and Sven spoke of the campaigns and battles in which they had fought. Petr spoke of his hopes for the future. Both Sven and Birger knew that they would never see the young man become a father and that was sad. Birger was dying and Sven was getting old.

When Birger Persson, Crusader and defender of Christianity, died, there were just four people at the graveside: Petr, his squire Folki, Sven Loyal Sword and the priest. That was not the saddest part. There were more people at the hall than at the grave but those at the hall were creditors come like crows to strip the dead of all that they possessed. The four mourners were, truly, the only ones who mourned the passing of a knight whose greatest fault was generosity. Petr determined that he would not be the same as his father.

The hall was sold and the small chest of coins which remained was barely enough to fit the three of them out as warriors, but Petr had decided that the three of them would become mercenaries. He was too proud to beg and besides he had heard that Hermann Balk was not the same man who had led the fight against the pagans and Sir Thomas seemed a lifetime away. They would hire out their swords, make money and simply not give it away on irrelevancies. More, he chose to leave Sweden for his father had been abandoned by all his Swedish friends. When times had been hard none had rallied around. His father had never been successful in managing land. He had been a warrior. He had sailed away to make his fortune. Perhaps he should have stayed away and never returned. The world was wide and surely a good knight could earn a crust by using his sword. Sir Petr determined not to repeat the mistakes his father had made. The three took ship.

After three months of unsuccessfully seeking a paymaster, they found themselves in Norway where the Norwegian King and his jarls were recruiting knights to serve in his war with the Scots. Sven was not sure about the prospect, "Sir Petr, your father would not approve. These Norse are little better than raiders. There will be no honour in what we do. Better we seek to serve the King of Denmark. He makes war on the Wends and the Pomeranians."

Sir Petr snapped angrily, "And as we have had no honourable work for the last months and I am eating into the small number of coins left to us, I care not. I have heard the pay is good. We are here now, and the ships gathered in the harbour tell me that they may be going to war. We can sell our horses and fight as foot soldiers. That will save us the cost of feeding horses which are not warhorses!"

Both men were right; it was good pay but the work they undertook was banditry rather than upholding a just cause. The days when Norse warriors had crewed huge dragon ships and rampaged through the seas taking what they wished were long gone. The Norse who remained in Norway were farmers. The young envied their ancestors, and they sought a life at sea. There were still enough wild young men who had a sword and shield, sometimes a helmet, and were willing to throw themselves into battle with little hope of survival. If a leader wished to take and hold then he used professionals. These were the Norse and Danes who did not relish the life of a farmer or the crew of a knarr. They liked the bonds of the oar brothers and the shield wall. They cared not who paid them just so long as they got to draw sword. The dregs of the warrior world were drawn to the ports on the west coast of Norway as those, no matter what nationality, sought pay and a warlord.

Jarl Bergil Beer Belly had a crew to row his drekar but when he saw the three men approach, he knew he had a hard core of warriors to go with his hearth weru, his bodyguard. There were just six such men, but they were mailed and had sworn a blood oath. They just took a share of the profits. He could afford to pay for three more swords. The knight had good mail and the other two had short byrnies. All had a helmet and the oldest one looked as though he knew his business. The Scots they would fight were not, in the main, knights and his crew could handle almost all that came their way but if there were knights then it would be his hearthweru who would have to face them. If he had a knight then the odds were that his hearth weru would survive and he would not have to pay for the hire of three swords!

He met them in the inn in Stavanger where the small fleet which would sail to join the other ships ready for the war was gathering. The jarl went over to their table and took a large jug of ale with him, "Can I offer you three warriors a drink?"

The old one, not the knight, nodded cautiously, "So long as there is no commitment with the drink."

"Of course not, but you will hear my proposal, will you not, and at least consider what I have to say?"

The young knight, Sir Petr, nodded, "Yes, Jarl. Ignore Sven, he is an old man and does not understand such things."

The Jarl had the measure of the young knight. He had been fitted out well and had good equipment. What Jarl Bergil did not know was the skill level of the knight. That would be the gamble. He poured the ale and leaned in conspiratorially, "Our king is sending ships to reclaim his islands to the west of Scotland. Scottish knights are poor and ill-equipped. I propose to hire the three of you. I will take you on for three months. There will be five crowns now and a further twenty at the end of the six months. I will find your food too. If, at the end of that time you tire of my company, then feel free to leave me with the twenty crowns in your purses."

It was an attractive offer and the sceptical Sven accepted that it would be hard to find a better one. Even so, he had a question, "And whatever we take in battle is ours?"

Petr frowned for he had not thought of that.

"Of course, and if we take other treasure then you and the rest of my crew share a third between you. Sir Petr, you could make your fortune in six months."

Sven shook his head, "That is not true Jarl Bergil. Be honest with Sir Petr,"

Bergil Beer Belly laughed, "I can see that you know your business. The old one is quite right. You may make good money but not a fortune."

Petr looked at Sven who, reluctantly, nodded. It was not a perfect solution to their problem, but it was work and Sven did not think that some wild-eyed Scotsmen would be a threat. When they had sought work he had been asked to show his skills and he had beaten everyone they had sent to fight him. He wondered why none of them had hired them. He did not doubt his own abilities and this, while neither honourable nor glorious was, at least, a start.

The voyage out and the first week were easy for they did nothing. Others rowed and when they arrived on the island they would use as their base they were housed in a longhouse and fed well. There they met other mercenaries. None had mail as good as Petr and when the leaders watched them practising then Petr's superior skill was clear. Sven, however, knew that things might change when they did begin to raid for then there might be fights and squabbles. He had to watch over Petr and Folki for these were treacherous men alongside whom they fought. He had sworn to Birger Persson that he would watch over his son and he would do so.

Their first raid was easy and the small port on the north coast of Scotland they raided was quickly taken. They landed at dawn and had secured the village, slaughtering all the men by the third hour of the day. It was then that Petr had his first lesson in the men with whom he was fighting. They behaved like animals and took the women, regardless of age. It was as they sailed to their next fight that Petr began to anger and annoy his comrades. They had seen him fight well but none of them liked to be told that they were animals. Sven shook his head as Petr kept speaking of his connections in Estonia and England. Hermann Balk and the Earl of Cleveland had their names bandied about as though they were personal friends of the young knight when, in fact, he had never even met either of them.

That did not, however, impair his ability to fight. In fact, he fought even better the second time, when they landed on the west coast of Scotland for he had learned from his first fight and the opposition was better. A Scottish knight led the local villagers as they marched to the slightly larger settlement. It was Petr, with Folki and Sven at his shoulder who took on the Scottish knight and his squires. Petr had been taught well and he knew how to angle his shield to minimise damage from a sword and also to give himself an opening. The Scottish knight had a long, heavy sword but Petr's skill lay in using his shield and his feet to dance out of trouble and to tire the knight. Sven soon despatched one of the squires by hacking into his leg. The squire was out of the battle and would never walk properly again and that allowed Sven to watch Petr's side. Sven did not interfere in either combat for he knew that combat was the best way to hone Petr's skills and he knew the old knight could be beaten. If there was danger, then he would interfere. Folki, too, was learning and while he did not yet have the measure of the other squire every blow they traded helped Folki to learn. Sven noticed that Petr had yet to use his sword to strike with the edge of the blade. He was using the flat of it to hurt. That skill had been drilled into him at the pel. You kept your blade sharp until you needed to make a killing cut. When the sword was brought around to smash into the side of the Scottish knight's helmet then Sven knew the end would not be long. All around them the Norse and their Irish mercenaries were eating into the sides of the clansmen who fought for their lord. but none would flee while the knight stood. The Scottish knight tried to do the unexpected. Instead of bringing his sword around in a sweep he punched with his shield and brought his sword over his head. Petr had good reactions and even though the Scot's shield had made him reel he had enough balance to lunge at the open-faced helmet and the strength to drive through the nose and into the Scot's skull. Petr had to take two steps back but when the Scottish knight fell then the Scots fled.

Sven sheathed his own sword and clapped the young knight on the back, "That was as well fought as I have ever seen and this time, we have treasure. He has mail and a good sword." The other squire had fled, and Sven said, "Folki, search them. They will have purses."

Jarl Bergil Beer Belly was delighted for they had barely lost men and while they had not taken as much treasure as they might have hoped King Hákon would be delighted that they were taking settlements.

Petr began to appreciate Sven and the training he had enjoyed but he also began to behave even more arrogantly towards the other mercenaries. He boasted of his skill and that it was he who had won the battle for them. He could not see that he was antagonising them. Sven tried to tell him, when they ate around their own fire, that he had to be part of the warband. He could not do it on his own. Sven spoke the words, but someone had to listen to them for them to take effect. Petr just nodded politely as though Sven knew nothing. They were moving away from the coast and there were castles ahead. Other crews arrived and the warband swelled. Sven advised Petr to bury some of their treasure. "Better we hide it so that if things go against us, we can always find it."

"Sven, I know you mean well but I have seen nothing yet which suggests we are going to lose. More and more men are joining us. Our numbers are growing. Bury yours if you wish but I keep mine. We are one third through our contract and when it is over, I have a mind to ride to England and seek a lord there. This taste of money is just that, a taste and I would bathe in coins. The Earl of Cleveland is rich, and he is the one we shall serve and become rich men." Petr had changed since he had dismissed the voyage to England. The three months of unemployment had done that.

The name of Sir Thomas of Cleveland had been spoken by some of the Irish Gallowglasses who talked of the man who was close to kings and was so rich that all his men wore mail! From what they had said of the wars on the Scottish borders and the Welsh marches, he appeared unbeatable. Sven knew it was snobbery on the part of Petr. The Norse were wild and uncouth men, but Sven had come to like them for they fought well and they had heart.

The warband did grow and after another month had managed to build an enclave in Scotland which was as large as some of the islands ruled by the Norse. They avoided the castles for everyone knew that storming a castle led to death for too many men. Instead, they struck at small towns without walls. Their coins grew and even Petr had to agree to bury some. It was just after they had done so when they met, for the first time, a large enough army to test them properly.

The Scots cleverly arrayed themselves on the other side of a river. There was no bridge, but the river was fordable. The Scots had mailed men in the centre protected by long spears brandished from behind them and they were shielded along their front and their side. As Sven lined up, once more in the centre, close to the jarl and the other leaders, he reflected that Norse had fewer archers than they used to, and it was archers they needed. This would be a bloody battle. He and Folki were behind Petr and Sven saw another problem, the Norse on either side of him had round shields. They could not lock them as effectively as they ought. Petr was confident and standing a little taller than those around him would draw attention, and in a battle that meant danger.

As they stepped into the river the Scottish boys began to hurl their river pebbles. Men fell and that caused gaps. Sven ignored the icy water and kept his shield protecting Petr's side. The old retainer was not concerned that he ought to use his shield to push both men before him. He had sworn an oath to protect Petr. The Scots were shouting, and the Norse replied with a chant. Of course, being Swedes they did not know the words and could not join in but the beat helped them to keep in step. Clambering out of the river was difficult as the Scots had deliberately muddied it. Petr, wearing good boots, was surefooted and that was a mistake for while the others slipped and slid on the slick mud, he was pushed up the bank by Folki and Sven. Unwittingly they had created a wedge and they were facing mailed men. Even though he sensed imminent disaster Sven could not help but be proud of the young knight who, despite the long wooden spears lunging towards him, managed to deflect a sword and find the thigh of the Scottish man at arms. He also had the wherewithal to step forward and catch the next spearman unawares. With no mail, the man was gutted and for Petr this was encouragement. He felt invincible as swords and spears struck his mail but did not penetrate. He was young enough to shrug off the bruises they would cause. Long spears work best when there is no swordsman an arms' length from the spearman. All three of them were able to stab and thrust with impunity as they carved a hole deep in the Scottish line. That was their undoing for what they could not see was that the rest of the attack had faltered on the muddy bank. The three were alone and when Jarl Bergil sounded his horn three times there was no escape for the two Swedes and the Dane. The three were brave men and they fought on not knowing they had been abandoned. Had they turned around then they would have risked death. The Scots did not kill them;

they did not need to. Instead, they rendered them unconscious with their hammers and axe heads. The three fell in a heap while their warband abandoned them. Petr's first foray into the mercenary world had ended badly. He was now a prisoner and who knew if, or when he would escape.

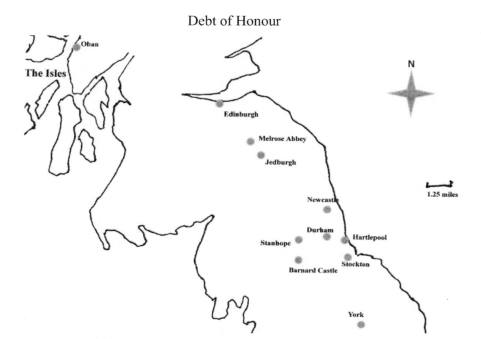

The North 1250

Author's work
Griff 2021

Chapter 1

The Spectre From The East

When we returned from the wars in Wales it felt good to be back in my father's valley. We had lost men but far fewer than we might have anticipated. The war still went on and Sir Gerard had stayed there. My squire, Geoffrey had merited his spurs and I had knighted him upon our return, Dick, my son, was not yet ready to be my squire but he had shown that he had skills and soon I would begin to train him as such.

Back in the north, we were at peace and here we feared no enemies. This was a land without treachery. My father had made it so and as I feasted with him and the rest of his knights as we celebrated, some months after our return, the marriage of Henry Samuel and the Welsh girl we had saved, Eirwen, I saw the pride in his careworn face. He would never go to war again for he was old, and he looked it. He appeared to have shrunk since I had left for Wales. My mother too showed the ravages of time and yet both of them still looked younger than some of those we had seen on our travels. I smiled to myself as I looked at my sisters and brothers in law. They too had, like me, grey flecks in their hair. In the case of Sir Robert of Redmarshal, the hair was also thinning rapidly. Sir Robert was another who seemed to have given up on war for he had not come with us.

I was suddenly aware that my father was speaking to me, "Is your mind elsewhere, my son?"

Shaking my head I said, "Not really but I was reflecting that age is catching up with us all. I see thinning and grey hair and on this last campaign I wished nothing more than to sleep in my bed!"

My father laughed, "And that is as it should be. It has taken some time, but I now accept that when the King calls and the knights of the valley go to war I have to stay here and watch them go. I am now used to it but it took some time before I was able to sleep peacefully. That will happen to you. Henry Samuel and Alfred are now knights, both, and have acquitted themselves well. Take credit for that, William, you trained them. Not only is Henry Samuel a knight but your squire, Geoffrey, is also now a knight and a worthy one too. Perhaps your days of fighting are gone for the borders are now quiet."

I shook my head and, as I spoke, lowered my voice, "I was cursed by the witch Angharad!"

My father's face creased into a frown, "You do not believe in such things, do you? She had no power. It was words only!"

I was not sure, "I do not know but I have not slept well since she cursed me."

My father was the wisest man I knew. He leaned into me, "Then ride to Durham and seek the advice of the Bishop. This prelate knows his business."

"I had planned on doing that for I need to present my new knight to him."

My father nodded towards the isolated figure at the end of the table. Thomas, Isabelle's eldest, had been named after him, "I would deem it a favour if you would take Thomas with you."

"There is a problem?"

"I know not for of all my grandchildren he is the one who is distant." He shrugged, "It may be because... I do not know. I think I treat them all the same but..." I saw that rarest of looks on my father's face, doubt.

I smiled, "You are fair, but we all know that my dead brother's son, Henry Samuel, is the one you are closest to."

"Perhaps but that may be because I was trying to make up for a murdered father. This could be because of a rift between Thomas and his father, I do not know but I do know that Thomas resented being left here while his cousins went to war."

"You would have me make him my squire?" I suddenly felt guilty for I had not even thought of asking my nephew to go with us.

"You need one and you have trained the others well. Henry Samuel, Geoffrey, all show your influence."

"But what of his father? He may not wish that."

"Leave that to me. You will not be leaving for a day or two, will you?"

I shook my head, "No, there are matters I need to deal with in Hartlepool."

"Good, then I can speak to all the interested parties." That was my father; he cared about his family but he would not rush like a wild bull into a tricky situation. He would scout it out and investigate. I would travel to Durham but there was no rush.

The two of us then turned to speak to the rest of the table who had, no doubt, wondered at the closeness of our heads and the content of our words. As I chatted to Rebekah's husband, Sir Geoffrey, I studied Thomas. Until my father had spoken, I had not noticed that he was silent but now I did, and I saw that his face was creased with a frown. What story was behind the frown?

The next day the newly knighted Sir Geoffrey and I headed home to Hartlepool. My wife was keen for me to be back in my hall. I think she felt I was safer there. I could understand her feelings. Matthew was still too young for a pony, but I allowed him to sit on my cantle. Precariously placed he giggled and laughed all the way home. I wondered how Sir Robert could have allowed a void to open up between him and his son. It would not happen to me. Dick and I were still close, and it would be the same between Matthew and me.

We passed Newton Bewley and then Gretham. In the distance, I could see the walled town that I had been given by the Bishop. My manor controlled the main port of the Palatinate, Hartlepool, and I knew was considered more important than my father's. If the tides were wrong, it could take days for a ship to navigate all the bends from the estuary to Stockton. The journey by road from Hartlepool to Durham was almost the same as the one from Stockton and so Hartlepool had grown more than Stockton. I also knew that there was a Scottish family, the de Brus, who also claimed the port. This Bishop had given it to me but if another was given it then I could lose my home. I was unworried for Stockton had enough room for my family. The de Brus family also had other irons in the fire. They had a claim on the Scottish crown. Scotland, even more than England was filled with malcontents!

When we reached my home and after I had stabled my horse I went to speak with the Bishop's representative. I had been on the King's business, but I had been absent for some time. There had been no issues in my absence, and I felt relief for I hated to be seen as a lazy lord. I knew many lords in my position would choose to delegate. I did not. Once I had dealt with those matters, I went to the hall and spoke to my steward. Edward was an efficient man and the only problems he brought to me were the ones which had to be determined by a lord. "We will hold an assize at the start of next month."

"Ay, my lord. A good time for this time of year always brings its problems."

I nodded, "And we need to make arrangements for Sir Geoffrey. Now that he is no longer my squire, he should have quarters which reflect his status, and he will also need quarters for his squire. I will need one also."

I knew I was making hard work for him, but he merely nodded and said, "It shall be done, my lord."

16

I returned to the stables. There I found Geoffrey who was doing what he had done since I had rescued him from the Holy Land, he was grooming my horse. "You know that there are others who will do that now, Geoffrey?"

He smiled, "Old habits, my lord."

"Come, walk with me." The hall had a walled garden which was filled with herbs and crops for our table. It was pleasant and sheltered. "You shall need a squire."

"Can I afford one, my lord?"

I knew what he meant. "You are part of my lance now, Geoffrey, and that means I pay you and your squire. That is, of course, until you have a manor."

"Lance, my lord?"

The term had grown in the last few years and was a way for a mighty lord, or a king to gather an army quickly. I owed my father, as Earl of Cleveland, fealty and he could demand of me, men to serve him. I used that as an example to explain to Geoffrey. "Father can call upon me to provide him with warriors. The same is true of Sir Robert, Sir Geoffrey, Sir Peter, Sir Fótr, Sir Richard, Sir Mark and so on. I owe him six men at arms, ten archers and fifty spearmen. I also owe that to the Bishop of Durham and to the King. It is true that we rarely have the need to call upon the spearmen but as we showed in Wales our archers and men at arms are required."

"How can you serve three masters, lord?"

I smiled, "The King has the first call and then the Bishop. We have just served the King and given him far more than the forty days we owe. We were paid for the extra days and you shall have your share of that. Spend it wisely, Geoffrey. My father was a sword for hire for a while and there you have no choice over your master. Eventually, you will need your own retinue. Your squire will be the first. When you are not practising the art of being a knight you should be on the look out for likely men. The ones I lead, as you know, were all chosen by me. They will be loyal to you and, in battle, protect you."

"And will there be a war soon?"

"It may be tempting fate to say so but I would say no. Since King Alexander signed the Treaty of York a few years past, the Scots have been relatively quiet. That is largely down to my family. Now King Henry has tightened his grip on Wales I think that, unless he has ambitions in France, then there will be peace, but we will need to be vigilant to maintain that peace."

"Then I will use this time to hone my skills, find a squire and men who can follow me."

17

I pointed towards the sea, "Here you will often find men who travel to England seeking an employer. Sometimes you can find a jewel amongst the cobbles and rough rocks which pass through." I knew as I said it that this would be a test for the young man. He would have to judge the men who sought to serve him. Perhaps this was as much a test of a knight as the vigil in the church!

It was then I took Dick to one side, "Dick, you served me well in Wales."

"Thank you. And am I ready to be your squire?"

I shook my head, "You have learned much but I need a young man and not a boy. I would have you spend the winter becoming ready for your training as a squire. Do not worry, that day will dawn soon. You will work with my men at arms and use the pel and you will not neglect your studies. I took you away from your reading and writing, not to mention languages. I wish you to work exclusively on them. Even if I am to ride to war then I shall not take you. There is no criticism in this for I am looking forward to the day when you shall carry my banner and ride behind me, but it will not be yet."

He showed that he had grown for he nodded, "I understand, and I will apply myself in all things. I will make you proud of me."

"I am always proud of you."

"And who will be your squire, father?"

"There is time enough for that."

A few days later Thomas, my nephew, rode in. He was alone and rode a simple palfrey with a lightly laden sumpter behind. He reined in and dismounted; my men knew their business and his horses were led away. I smiled and nodded for I knew that my father had spoken with him and his arrival meant something. He would begin the conversation and I would judge him on that.

"Thomas, it is good to see you."

He gave a bow and kissed the back of my hand, "Sir William, your father sent me. He thought that you might provide an answer to my dilemma."

It was a simple and honest statement and it endeared him to me for it told me there would be honesty and that was what warriors wished.

"Will you be staying long?"

He smiled and said, "That depends upon you, uncle."

"Come let us talk where the sea breeze which brought my father from the Baltic can make our cheeks redden." We said nothing until we stood on the sea wall and I spoke, "First, tell me of the rift twixt you and your father."

He stopped and stared, "How…?"

"I am close to my son and, indeed, my other nephews. I have fought alongside them and yet you are almost a stranger to me. That tells me much. You have the blood of the Warlord in your veins and I know that you are a warrior. What is amiss?"

He sighed and sat on the sea wall. "I do not know. I am eighteen summers old, and my father has never taken me to war. I have trained at the pel and with lance and shield, but I am not a squire. When you went to Wales and I was not chosen to follow you I felt slighted. Then I wondered why my father did not make me his squire. Does my father not trust me?"

He stopped and I knew that he was awaiting a comment, "I do not know. I can only speak of Henry Samuel, Alfred and Geoffrey. I have helped to train all three, but I never sought that role. Your grandfather was the one who asked me to train them. Had I known that you wished to be a warrior then I would have taken you under my wing."

There was silence. He nodded, "I know. I wanted grandfather to ask me to be his squire, but it did not happen. My father... I know not and you always had others as squires, and I wondered if you wished to elevate Dick to be your squire."

"Do you wish to be my squire?" I put my hand up. "Do not answer yet for there is another alternative. My new knight, Geoffrey, seeks a squire. He is a good knight, and you would learn much with him."

"Thank you but I would wish to be trained by you. Grandfather will not go to war and if I cannot be trained by him then I would choose you. He said that you were the best and if I am to be a knight who is worthy of the blood of the Warlord then I need to be well trained."

I studied him, "Ah, so you are happy to have second best! You cannot have Sir Thomas and so you would have me."

He had the good grace to smile and shake his head, "Perhaps this is why my father did not offer me the chance. I am not witty like Henry Samuel and I can be clumsy when I use words."

"You are honest and that is not a bad thing in a knight." I looked east and saw winds blowing scudding clouds towards us. This felt right. As Fótr or Erik might have said, it was *wyrd*. "I will take you on but if you find it is not for you then tell me. I would not waste my time on a lost cause."

He gave a half-smile and nodded. I could see that he was a troubled soul. I suppose that would have been the moment to question him a little more, but we were interrupted. Margaret, my daughter, was no longer the babe of the family and Matthew demanded more attention from my wife. I heard shouts and turned to see Margaret running and squealing towards us with her nanny, Sarah huffing and puffing behind

Debt of Honour

her in hot pursuit. Margaret ran fearlessly towards me and hurled herself at me. I barely caught and held her.

She laughed, "Sarah cannot catch me!"

I saw the distressed look on Sarah's face and held my daughter at arm's length, "That was naughty! Sarah is here to look after you! This is a dangerous place for a child. Wagons arrive daily and you could have been crushed." I saw Sarah nodding as she gasped for breath,

Margaret looked contrite, "Sorry Sarah, but I wanted to speak with my father."

I sighed, "Come, the four of us can walk back to the hall and you can speak on the way." That was not as easy as it sounded. The townsfolk waved and called to me as we walked. I nodded and waved back so that the conversation was a little truncated.

"I want a pony."

"A pony? Can Sarah ride?"

"Why should she need to ride, father? It is I who needs the pony."

"And who is the one who watches over you?"

Margaret stopped and turned to look at Sarah, "Sarah does not ride! Then you will ride with me and Cousin Thomas when he next visits."

"Thomas is to be my squire and he will be living here."

She squealed with delight, "Then he can be my protector."

Thomas smiled and I shook my head. Little Margaret was going to be a handful when she grew up. Events conspired to delay my departure for Durham and the Bishop. I had pressing matters concerning the port and Thomas needed to be accommodated and fitted out as my squire. I had learned over the years to maintain a good supply of surcoats. Battle and journeys took their toll. I wondered how many had been discarded on battlefields! I took just two of my men along with Thomas. These days the roads to Durham were safer. I also took with me the documents from the port. The Bishop did not concern himself with such trivialities, but his clerks would need them.

Nicholas Farnham had been at Durham for seven years, but I had barely seen him. When I did, I wondered if he was dying. He looked ill. I wondered if this would mean a new Bishop who might favour the de Brus claim. One of his priests confided to me, as we were escorted to his chamber, that his health had deteriorated of late. Despite his illness, the Bishop greeted us warmly. "It is good to see you, Sir William, and your father is well?"

It was on the tip of my tongue to say compared with you he is ready to go to war! I did not, "He is hale, my lord."

The Bishop nodded, "You and your family have served the king well. I have also been working on his behalf negotiating a marriage

20

between King Henry's daughter and the future king of Scotland, Alexander, but you did not come here for that, did you?"

"No, my lord, I need advice which is more religious rather than secular," I told him of the war in Wales and the curse of Lady Angharad.

He listened and then, after folding his hands and closing his eyes, he was silent for a while. He opened them and spoke, "Such curses have nothing to do with the church. I frown on the burning of such creatures for they are deluded but the church does not have any recommendations for dealing with curses." He smiled, "As you know I was a teacher in a former life. I taught in Paris. If I cast my mind back to my time there I remember other teachers who came from lands with more recent pagan traditions. They spoke of quests; deeds which would eradicate the curse and the memory of the one who cursed." He shrugged and spread his arms, "Perhaps, in ending the life of this creature you have already performed the deed. I am sorry I could not be of more help."

I nodded, "Your words have helped me. I shall seek a cause to champion."

The Bishop made the sign of the cross and said, "And, of course, it goes without saying that you have my blessing."

"As we rode back Thomas asked, "What kind of quest, uncle? There are no dragons. What of the Holy Grail? Perhaps we could seek that!"

I laughed, "That is a legend too. If the cup that Christ used to drink exists, then it is more likely to be in the Holy Land rather than in this land. My father is right, and I should put the curse from my head. We have a time of peace and we should enjoy it. Tomorrow we begin your training. We have the luxury of knowing that we will not be called to war any time soon."

Perhaps I had tempted fate. A month after our return a rider came from Stockton with a message to visit with my father. The strange thing was that a day or two earlier a ship from the Baltic had docked and Geoffrey had found three or four warriors for hire. He had asked me to help him speak to them but, of course, my father's request took precedence. I was torn for swords for hire always had interesting stories to tell. Thomas and I headed for Stockton leaving Sir Geoffrey the task of sorting the wheat from the chaff!

Without a family feast, Stockton Castle always felt empty. My parents rattled around the great house. Sir John was my father's household knight but he was unmarried. I know that my mother preferred it brimming with grandchildren and family. It was she who greeted me and made a fuss. "William, you live just hours away and yet

we never see you! Matthew and Margaret need their grandmother!
Bring them next time."

I smiled, "Yes mother."

"And you, Thomas, you hid away at Redmarshal which is even
closer; come and give your grandmother a kiss!"

"Yes, grandmother."

He had to lower his head to kiss her cheek. My mother seemed to be
shrinking and yet she was younger than my father.

"Your father is in his solar. He has an intriguing visitor, and I must
organise food and a bed for him." She turned and said, "You will both
stay the night!" It was not a request; it was an imperious command and
we both nodded.

Part of Thomas' training was to be party to all of my life. A squire
was trusted completely by his knight and Thomas needed to learn all
that he could about the life he would face. Perhaps this was why his
father had not offered him the same opportunity I had given to my son,
Richard. My father's favourite room was the solar. It had a wider
opening than it once had for it had been fitted with shutters to keep out
the cold when necessary. With a good fire in the corner, it had the best
views west. We would not see the best until later in the day. My father
never bothered with guards in the corridors, nor even on the walls. We
were at peace and Stockton was safe. I knocked on the door and my
father said, "Come!"

When I entered, I saw that he had a visitor. It was a warrior. He
looked to be in his twenties and had suffered. His face was scarred, and
his boots looked as though they were held together by hope alone. His
lank hair and the state of his hands told me that he had not had an easy
time of late. He was patently not a knight and yet my father treated him
as though he was important.

I also saw that my father appeared thinner and smaller. Like my
mother, they were getting old.

My father smiled, "Thomas, fetch your uncle and yourself a chair
and then pour a couple of beakers of wine. You are going to hear an
extraordinary tale."

Intrigued I sat and when I had the beaker of wine, I toasted my
father, "Sir Thomas!"

He held his beaker up too. I noticed that the visitor had not smiled.
My father said, "I will speak for our visitor. His English is not the best,
yet, but I hope that it shall be. This is Folki Eriksson, and he is a
Swedish squire. I knew his grandfather, but he does not come to me for
that reason. I have a debt of honour to pay."

Both Thomas and I sat up in our chairs for my father's voice was as serious as I had ever heard.

"You, William, I think know the story of my time fighting for Bishop Albert." I nodded, "Thomas, you may not. When I left this land I went on a crusade to the Baltic and there served with Birger Persson. It is his son, Petr who has asked for our help." He spoke some words to the Swede who nodded. "Sir Petr did the same as I did and hired himself out as a sword for hire. He served King Hákon Hákonarson of Norway and they fought with the Scots amongst the islands to the north-west of Scotland. Their fortunes rose, fell and rose again. Then, a year since, the three of them were taken along with other swords and imprisoned in the castle Macmaghan. Their captor was a powerful lord, Sir Cailean Mór, Sir Colin Campbell in our language, who is a Scot loyal to King Alexander. Folki was sent, with other squires, to ask for ransom. They returned to Norway. Folki told me that my old friend was penniless when he died but he had told his son that there were two men who would aid him, myself and Hermann Balk. It seemed that as he was in Norway he would travel to Pomerania and seek the five hundred gold marks required to pay the ransom."

"Five hundred marks?" I could not help myself from interrupting. It was a ridiculously high sum and you could fit a ship out for the crusades for less.

My father smiled, "That was my thought. I shall continue with the tale, eh?" I was duly chastised. "Hermann Balk is dead and his sons, it seems, do not honour such old allegiances. Worse, Folki was treated like a vagabond and thrown out. He had to work his passage to England, and it was not a swift journey. He finally took a ship which landed him at Hartlepool, and he walked here." I was about to speak when my father saved me the bother, "He did not know that you were my son and his master had asked him to seek Sir Thomas of Stockton. There is the tale. That Sir Petr chose a bad master is neither here nor there for the debt still remains." He drank more of the wine. I had many questions I wished to ask but there were so many that I remained silent.

It was my new squire who asked them for me, "Grandfather, I am unfamiliar with these matters, never having been to war. Tell me is it usual to ask for such a large amount and to hold prisoners for so long?"

My father nodded, "Sadly, yes, especially amongst the Scots. I can imagine that mercenary knights from Norway, Sweden and Denmark might be seen as having a higher value than mere Vikings and the prisoners could always be held as a threat."

"And will you pay?"

"Of course! This is a debt to an old friend. We saved each other on more than one occasion. It will take a week or more for me to gather the money and then I can leave. I wished you to hear the tale William, for you will command my knights during my absence."

I shook my head, "No you shall not. I am guessing that my mother would stop this foolish gesture."

"Did you not hear me, my son? This is a debt of honour."

"I did not say that the debt would not be paid although I think it is too high a price, you will not be the one to pay it."

"Why not? It is my debt!"

I would have to be blunt, "For the simple reason that you are too old and the journey too great for a man of your age. You would put in jeopardy the lives of those who went with you." I wondered if I had gone too far and then I saw in his eyes that he thought I was right.

Folki said something and my father answered. Immediately I saw a problem. I could not talk with the Swede; my father could. Then I thought of another problem; speaking with Scots around Elsdon had been one thing but those in the north-west spoke a language I did not know. I could not allow my father to go on this perilous quest and so I would have to deal with these problems. He smiled at me, "Folki seems to think you do not want to help his knight, William. Is that true?"

I looked at the Swedish man for he was no longer a youth. I saw care in his eyes, and I thought back to the squires my father and I had trained. Had we been in Sir Petr's situation then our squires would have done as Folki had done. I could not imagine the trials and tribulations he would have endured to reach us.

I sighed, "Of course I want to help him, but I do not want you to have to do this. Is that so hard to understand?"

He smiled, and after speaking to Folki turned to me, "As I said we have a week, but each day's delay puts Sir Petr in even greater danger. Come let us join your mother." We descended and as we approached the hall my father said, "Thomas, see if there are clothes in the warrior hall which might fit Folki."

"Aye, grandfather."

The Great Hall was in the process of being prepared for the evening meal. It would hardly be a feast for there would just be a handful of us there, but my mother was a real lady in every sense of the word and if there was a visitor then all would be done well. Edgar, one of the servants left what he was doing to fetch a jug of wine and beakers. He hurried to the table close to the fire and placed them on it.

"Thank you, Edgar." As we sat, my father said, "What troubles you, my son?"

"There are too many unknowns, father. Where is he held? Why the high demand for gold? Will he still be alive after all this time and, most importantly, if this is the north-west of Scotland, then how do we get there through a land which, in the main, hates us?"

He laughed and, seeing the puzzled expression on Folki's face spoke in Swedish. The Swede smiled too. "You have used the word we and that tells me that you are going to help. That pleases me for whilst I may not be able to complete this quest alone, you are the lord who will rule this land when I am gone, and I have the utmost confidence in you."

I realised that my father planned on going on this quest. He was in no condition to do so and that meant I would have to take it on myself. I drank my wine and waved a hand as though to dismiss the flattery which hung in the air. "And the language? I cannot speak Swedish and you, father, are not going. What about the land of the Gaelic speakers? These are practical matters and are there regardless of the virtue of the task. I agree that Sir Petr should not languish in some Scottish castle, but it is the how."

Thomas appeared, "I have clothes for our guest."

"Take Folki with you and help him." He spoke Swedish and our visitor left with Thomas. "Now I shall answer your questions. Folki speaks neither English nor Gaelic and so his directions are a little vague." I sighed and my father smiled. "Do not put obstacles in the way, William. Let us look at what we know. The castle to which they were taken was in the middle of a lake not far from the coast. He said it was called Innis Chonnell and although I have not heard of it, I know that there are many such places in that part of Scotland. It is the land controlled by the Campbell clan and that makes sense for he said that the knight who held him was Cailean Mór Caimbeul. That is the Campbell clan and we know which are their clan lands." I nodded for that made sense. "To answer your other questions it seems to me that if the Scottish knights we fought on the borders are poor then how much poorer would be those on the west who have Vikings for neighbours? It would not cost much for this Cailean Mór Caimbeul to keep a knight a prisoner for a long time in the hope of rich reward. Birger Persson was related to Birger Brosa and his family were amongst the richest in Sweden. This knight may not have realised that my old friend fell on such hard times."

My father stared into the fire as though lost in his memories. My mother entered, obviously satisfied that the food was on its way. We stood and she asked, "So who is this mysterious guest, husband?"

"He is the squire of the son of Birger Persson and he is here to ask me to pay the ransom for him. He is held in Scotland."

My mother was a strong woman, but I saw, in her eyes, the pain as she realised what her husband was saying. She nodded, "You will, of course, have to pay it. We owe Birger." The look of triumph on my father's face lasted but a heartbeat for she added, "Of course you cannot go, you are too old. I fear we must put my son's life in jeopardy. You shall take it, William!"

And so, not by any real consultation I was to be sent almost three hundred miles to ransom a man I did not know.

Chapter 2

The Road to Jedburgh

Of course, my father argued but we both knew that when my mother made up her mind there was no going back. The rather one-sided debate continued through the meal and I knew that the Swede was confused. We had just finished the lamb my mother had ordered cooked when my father finally accepted the decision. I could see that he recognised the arguments, and it was mine that he might put others at risk which persuaded him. Once the lamb was taken away and the cheese, ham, pickles, and bread were brought in he became more positive.

"King Alexander likes you, William. He and Queen Joan arranged your marriage."

"The Queen is dead, and she died childless. He has a new wife and a son who, I believe, although only seven is about to become engaged to be married to King Henry's daughter." When the Bishop of Durham had told me that it had seemed almost irrelevant.

"That matters not. He likes you. Go to Jedburgh and seek his help. At the very least he could give you the authority to travel through his land."

I nodded for it made sense.

My mother was a practical woman too. "You need someone who can speak the language. There are but two, Ridley the Giant and Sir Fótr for Erik Red Hair has still to fully recover from his wounds."

My father shook his head, "Not Ridley! If I am too old, then he is more so, besides he has not been to war these many years."

"Neither has Sir Fótr."

"True but Sir Fótr has kept up his practice and his son is ready for knighthood. That would please Sir Fótr and he may be ready for one last adventure."

I laughed, "You make it sound like we are all doomed. Do you think so, father?"

He smiled as my mother shook her head, "No, but I am used to being the one who takes these risks. I do not like sending men to do that which I should do. I will ride with Folki to speak with Sir Fótr tomorrow and you will need to tell Mary. I will help you to select the men you lead."

"You know that it cannot be many."

He nodded, "You need enough to protect you but not enough to create a threat."

We left early in the morning and we went with my father and some of his men to Norton. Sir Fótr was older than I was, but it had been some time since he had risked his life. He was, however, one of my father's most loyal knights, more than that he came from Sweden, and when he was told of the situation he volunteered before he was asked. I saw the relief of Folki's face when Sir Fótr conversed with him. Sir Fótr turned to me, "William, I am not a young man anymore, but this should be a peaceful journey. I am happy to follow your banner."

He was telling me that I would lead despite the disparity in our ages. I saw his son looking eagerly at me as though willing me to invite him. My father dashed his hopes, "And you Thomas, shall be knighted so that Norton has a lord while your father is away." He was being given that which he desired but I wondered if he would have taken the adventure rather than the spurs.

Once my squire and I headed along the road through Cowpon towards my home, Thomas asked me all the questions which had been on his mind for the last day. "How can this be a debt, uncle? The stories I heard were that it was my grandfather who was lauded by the Swedes."

"And that is true but when my father left England after the death of the Bishop it was sanctuary he sought, and it was Birger Persson who gave it to him. Without that welcome and that home then who knows, my father may have been in the same situation as Petr Birgersson." The rest of his questions, once the moral ones had been answered, were practical ones about the journey and they were useful. We would need sumpters and, as we could not guarantee to find shelter, then tents too.

We reached my hall and while I sent Thomas to find Sir Geoffrey, I bearded my wife for this could not be delayed. She paled when I told her. She was Scottish and knew better than any of the dangers we would face. As I told her the tale she nodded and came to accept it. "I knew when I married you that you were not an ordinary knight. None of your family is and I would be lying if I said that I was happy about this, but you need to do it. I pray that you take care."

I kissed her, "You know that I shall."

She would worry while I was away and there was nothing that I could do about that. At least this was not the King's business. This was for my family and family honour: she understood that.

When Thomas fetched Sir Geoffrey to me, I saw that he had with him his new squire. As much as I needed to tell Sir Geoffrey what I intended and to hand over the manor to him in my absence I felt honour bound to speak about the men he had found.

"This, Sir William, is John son of Walter. He is an English soldier who was serving in Frankia. His master was a knight who was killed along with his squire and most of the other men when they fought the Danes."

I could see that Geoffrey was satisfied but I was curious not to say suspicious, "And you were mightily lucky to have survived when the others all perished."

He nodded, "I know it sounds like I was and perhaps it is true but the reason I survived was that although I was wounded, my comrades all died around me. I was unconscious and when I came to, my body was about to be thrown on to a fire. When I rose from the pile of corpses the men charged with burning them fled for they thought I was a ghost. I thank God and my dead comrades daily."

Satisfied with his miraculous answer I nodded and turned to Sir Geoffrey, "Did you find any others?"

"Two, Carl the Dane and Will the Sword. They are both young and have little."

"And that was all?"

He hesitated and then said, "There was one I considered but he was a wild man, a Hibernian, Calum of the Isles. He was older than the three I chose, and I feared he would be set in his ways."

"Then that was wise." I addressed Sir Geoffrey's squire, the English youth, "And what do you know of this wild man?"

John son of Walter looked nervously at Sir Geoffrey and said, "I did not wish to speak until asked, my lord, which is why I have not added to this discussion, but I know a little of this man. He is from the islands to the west of Scotland and he fought for the Vikings. I know of him for when we were waiting for this ship, he stopped me from being robbed of the little I had. He is a wild man, my lord, but he has honour. It is just a different sort of honour to that of a knight. He fights for his own kind."

Sir Geoffrey said, to his squire, "Why did you not say when I spoke to you all yesterday?"

"I was just grateful to be chosen and knew not how many men you wished."

Sometimes events happen and there is no explanation to them. An idea crept into my head even as John was speaking, "John, go and find this Calum of the Isles and ask him to come here."

He looked happy as he nodded and said, "Aye, lord."

I then told Sir Geoffrey about the quest, "Then it is good that I chose a Dane. He might be able to converse with this Folki."

I shook my head, "You stay at home and watch my manor." He was disappointed but he accepted my commands. It would be good for him to learn how to be the Lord of the Manor.

When Calum was brought to me, I saw recent wounds upon his face and hands. I frowned. John son of Walter also looked a little embarrassed. The Irishman had a haughty look but, from his build, he was a powerful man. I saw no sword at his side but he had a wicked-looking dagger. Wearing just a leather jerkin he had little else to mark him as a warrior.

"Calum of the Isles, I am Sir William, and I am the lord of this manor, what is your tale?"

There was no obeisance in his demeanour as he shrugged and said, "I am an Irish warrior and I have left Norway to make my way back home where I can fight amongst men that I like." Both Thomas and Geoffrey looked shocked, but I put my hand up in case they were going to say something.

"And where is home?"

"The islands to the west of Scotland. It is where I was born!"

"And how did you end up in Norway?"

He grinned, "I went a-Viking with some comrades. We heard of a treasure in Roskilde and decided to take it." He shrugged, "There was no treasure, and the others were all killed. I managed to hide away on a ship which went to Norway. I thought to return to the isles and have a glorious death like my shield brothers."

"You do not seem put out that your comrades lost their lives."

"They died like men with swords in their hands. What other end is fitting for a warrior?"

I liked him but I knew that if I took him on it would be liking a wild horse and I would need to learn how to manage him. "Do you speak the language of those who live in the west of Scotland?"

He nodded, "You wish to go there?"

"I do and I would be willing to fit you out as a warrior and pay you to act as a translator for me."

Sir Geoffrey said, "My lord, is this wise?"

The Irishman appeared to be considering my words and then he grinned, "You are going to take back the Swedish warrior, lord!"

I was stunned, "How did you know?"

He said, "I am not a witch, Sir William, but I keep my ears open. I saw the Swede on the ship and spoke enough of his words to know that he is the squire of a knight taken by the Norwegian King. He looked like a warrior. I will do it!"

I had my Gaelic speaker and with Sir Fótr then two obstacles were gone. I spent the rest of the day working out who I would need and what supplies we would take. With Calum fitted out and mounted, I left the next morning with my family and the men I hoped would choose to follow me to the west, for Stockton Castle. My mother would ensure that while I was gone my family would be looked after. I wanted to get back to Stockton in case the money for the ransom was gathered earlier than I expected. Sir Geoffrey would guard the port and the manor.

When we reached Norton Sir Fótr did not come from his hall to greet me. Instead, his son Thomas came out. "My lord, my father has had an accident."

Leaving Thomas and my men watching the horses my wife and I raced indoors. Sir Fótr had a heavily bandaged and splinted leg resting on a stool. He shook his head, "My lord after you had left, I decided to go riding. It is some time since I have ridden for a long period. My horse slipped and I fell. I have broken my leg."

I smiled sadly, "What is that word your people use when they talk of Fate, *wyrd*? This is *wyrd*. I pray you recover quickly, and it does not lame you."

"The word is the perfect one lord. It tells me that I should no longer ride to war. Your father knighted my son, and he can take over the martial duties. Even if it heals the leg will never be the same. Sir Fótr of Norton will go to war no longer."

It still left me the problem of a Swedish speaker although the presence of Calum meant that some of the words would be understood. My father, when I told him was philosophical about it all, "Some things are meant to be."

We went to the outer bailey where Folki was practising swordplay with some of my father's men. He stopped and my father explained the situation. I saw Folki nod and then he saw Calum. He frowned and spoke to my father. "Folki says he recognised this man. He sailed to Hartlepool with him."

"That is true and he can speak the language of the isles and that part of Scotland. More he has some Swedish words too." Folki listened to my father and then nodded. My father said, "Folki says that the three sisters have spun, and we are all in their spell."

Calum made the sign of the cross, "Aye, and I can see that I was meant to be here. I swear, Sir William, that you will reach this man's knight and master!"

I do not know why but his words made me feel better.

We spent another two days selecting the men. All were given a choice and could have refused. None did. Alan Longsword was an obvious choice. He had made it clear when we had headed for Stockton that he wished to come. Tom of Rydal came from the west and he too was an easy choice. Eric the Dane almost chose himself. I took just four archers, but they were all easy choices. Idraf, Robin Greenleg, Alan Whitestreak and Ged Strongbow. The day the money was gathered and placed into four small chests we met in the Great Hall so that we could plan the journey effectively. It was one thing that I had noticed when travelling and serving alongside other lords, my father's castle was the only place I had seen men at arms, archers, squires and knights treated equally. It was made all the more obvious by the reactions of Calum and Folki. The Swede could now both understand and speak the odd word of English. That was something else. In the castles of other lords, only the common people spoke English. Nobles still spoke Franco Norman as though it excluded the native population.

We had worked out our route which was largely dictated, in the early stages, by the need to visit King Alexander and in the latter stages by the glens and lochs of Western Scotland. It was Calum who was of the most use. Folki merely had the name of the castle where Sir Petr was held. He had never been there. He also knew many of the men we might encounter. It was a complicated picture as the islands off the coast were ruled by King Hákon Hákonarson yet many of the lords who ruled in that area owned lands on the mainland as well as the islands. One, Ewen MacDougall appeared to be an ally of the Norwegian and that made him an enemy of King Alexander. It seemed to me that this was as complicated as the ownership of lands in Gascony and Normandy. His most disappointing news was that it was on an island and any rescue attempt was doomed to failure before it could be considered. We would pay the ransom. It had not impoverished us. Indeed my father had not had to ask any of us for money.

We had almost finished when Erik Red Hair entered. He had been recovering at Stockton for my father had better doctors than in Hartlepool. I said, "Yes Erik?"

"My lord, I hear you travel west and have yet to invite me."

I smiled, "Erik, you were badly wounded! Stay here and recover."

It was almost as though he had not heard me, "And you have a need for my language skills. I can still fight but if I can serve in another way…"

"Erik…"

"Lord, you gave me life and hope when I had none. I know that I have wounds, but they are almost healed, and the journey will complete the process. If you need me then I would ride with you. Let me go as a translator. Where is this Swede?"

We all looked at Folki and Erik gabbled out a torrent of words. When Folki smiled I knew that we would have to take Erik. Folki had frowned at Calum who was the only other choice we had. My father smiled, "This is for the best, William. This selection has been made by other powers and I believe it bodes well."

That night I lay in the bedchamber with Mary in my arms, "I hope that my countrymen do not bear you ill will, husband." Before we had wed, I had been the bachelor knight at Elsdon and had only met Mary through the good offices of the King and Queen of Scotland. "To that end, I have written to King Alexander to remind him that I am still a landowner in Scotland and that he bore my father his own debt."

"Thank you, my love but it should not be necessary."

"It cannot hurt."

We left before dawn for I wished to be beyond Durham and closer to the Roman wall by dark. I knew that it would test the fitness of not only Erik but also Calum and Folki. I stopped in Durham merely to dismount and speak with the Bishop. My men watered horses and drank ale.

The Bishop hurriedly wrote a letter for me to give to King Alexander. Since he had arranged the marriage of the King's son he was held in high esteem. He also gave me what I considered to be bad news, "Sir William, I have written to King Henry. I can no longer function as Bishop, I am unwell. I have asked if I can spend my last days in a Durham manor."

"That is sad, Bishop for I believe you are a good man."

"Thank you but my bouts of illness have already taken me close to death. This way King Henry has the chance to find a replacement. As you know this can take time."

Two days later, as the sun was slipping to the west, we reached Jedburgh Abbey and the residence of King Alexander, his wife, Queen Marie and his son, Alexander. I felt a little nervous as we approached the ford across the river. I knew that King Alexander had liked me and that we were at peace but crossing the border was not something I had done often in peacetime. There was peace and so no trumpets or bells sounded the alarm as we approached. Instead, guards and officials came to the gate to greet us. I recognised none of them and that was no surprise. Those I had known had served the King and Queen Joan. His French Queen had replaced them with her people.

"Yes, my lord?"

I handed the knight the Bishop of Durham's letter and the one my wife had written. "I pray you to give those to the king. We seek shelter for the night."

He nodded and waved over his squire, "Take Sir William and his men to the abbot, ask if they can be accommodated."

"Aye, my lord."

I had not recognised the knight, "You know me?"

He smiled, "When I was a squire, I was one who fought along the border. I came to recognise your livery. I was glad when you moved south." There appeared to be no malice in his words, but it was a warning of what we might meet.

As we were led away Alan Longsword said, almost under his breath, "Do not worry, Sir William, we have the measure of these men."

I knew that one to one my men were more than capable of dealing with the Scots, but we had a long way to go and there was always the possibility of ambush.

I remembered the abbot and he remembered me but, as with the knight, there did not appear to be any ill feelings. I discovered some of the reason as we were taken to our rooms before eating in the refectory, "The last years have been peaceful and quiet in the borders. We put that down to Bishop Farnham and your father's knights. The threat of them keeps out hotheads engaged elsewhere. It is the war in the west where there is both turmoil and disruption. The Norse are evil men my lord and they even purport to be Christian, they are just a blade away from paganism. They turn brother against brother!"

It was a further insight into the mind of the Scots. The days of King William the Lion were long passed.

Abbeys, nunneries, priories and the like all provided accommodation for travellers. The rooms we were given were simple but better than a tent. We would have to make a contribution, but it was worth it. All my men were given rooms and the horses were stabled. When the bell rang, we knew it was time to eat. The food would be simple but wholesome. All this came at a price, but I did not mind the payment and the chests of gold we carried would be safe here.

The talk was of the king's son and the hope that lay therein for Scotland. Queen Joan had been popular but childless. Many said that her father, King John, had been cursed and the curse passed down to his daughter. Perhaps it was for King Henry appeared to have little luck despite his obvious penitence. I listened more than I spoke for I was trying to attune my ears for the Scottish accent. We had almost finished when a pursuivant came from King Alexander. I was granted an audience the next day. I was relieved. Had he chosen not to see me it could have been an ominous sign that I was no longer in his favour.

I was not sure when we would be leaving and so I had my men ready the horses just in case. I did not take Folki with me for there was no need. I just took Thomas. I could tell he was nervous and that reflected the fact that he had rarely been out of the valley. His father had failed him. A knight had the responsibility to prepare his son for a future following in his footsteps. Henry Samuel had turned out as well as he had because my father and I had taken charge of him once his father had been murdered.

King Alexander had aged since last I had seen him. Perhaps that was because the Queen was so much younger than he was. She did not smile at me and I took no offence at that. I was English and she was French. She had been brought up with me as an enemy. Their son, Alexander the Prince of Cumberland, was too young to form an opinion but as with all boys his age, I saw his eyes drawn to my mail and my weapons.

"Sir William, it is good to see you again." He held up the letter from my wife, "I can see that Lady Mary has prospered since you were wed. I am pleased. I owed her father much. And now, it seems, you need my help."

I nodded. My conversation with Calum had given me an insight into the situation which made me warier than had I not met the Irishman, "My father wishes to ransom a warrior, a mercenary, taken by Sir Colin Campbell." I used the anglicised version of his name for I was still wary enough to keep some secrets from the Scottish king."

"It has been some time, I believe, since the demand for ransom was made. Are you sure that this Swede is still…"

He glanced at his wife and son for he did not wish to say the word, 'alive'.

"I hope so for we have the ransom, even though it is exorbitant, and my father will pay."

"The road west is a dangerous one, Sir William, and even I might baulk at such a journey." Something in his words and his manner of delivery intrigued me. I said nothing. "Perhaps we can aid each other, Sir William."

"If I can do anything to help you, King Alexander, then all you have to do is to ask."

35

He nodded, almost absentmindedly, "I had planned on visiting Oban in the next few days. It is not far from Innis Chonnell, which is where this Swede will be held, and it may be that I can help the negotiations."

"I am grateful, my lord, but I cannot see why you need me. I have but a handful of men."

He laughed, "It is known that the men you lead are all extraordinary and whilst I have my bodyguards, I do not travel with an army. I confess that had you not come I would still have travelled west for... well that is my business, but your arrival is fortuitous. No matter what men say of you and your family, the one thing they cannot say is that you are treacherous."

"Then we will happily act as your escorts." I glanced at the Queen of Scotland and her son, "Will her majesty and your son be with us?" If they were then the journey might take an extra week.

"No, Sir William, they will stay here. I have twenty knights and men at arms to escort me as well as twenty mounted spearmen."

The thought came into my head that the number was too low and then I realised I had intended to attempt the same with fewer. All this meant we would not be leaving any time soon. That was good as the rest would help Erik to recover. My men continued to eat in the refectory, and they were happy about that. The food was good, and they were both safe and comfortable. It also enabled Erik and Folki not only to get to know one another but for their communication to improve. I needed Folki speaking our language! The sooner he could converse with me and not through Erik the better. Thomas and I were housed in the palace. It was more of a large hunting lodge than palace and Thomas and I had to share a room. He would be used to augment the other servants and squires who waited upon the knights. There was just a handful of knights and one of them was almost a neighbour of mine. Alain de Balliol was the second son of Sir John Balliol who held Barnard Castle. In the time of the Warlord that had been held by one of the Earl of Cleveland's men. Although in England it had been governed by a Scot for as long as I could remember.

Alain was alone in being happy to converse with me and as King Alexander was normally closeted with his two closest mormaers, Patrick of Dunbar and James of Galloway, it was a case of talk to Alain de Balliol or eat in silence. I also wished to learn as much as I could. Alain seemed to be open and honest but there was something about him I did not like. It was hard to put my finger on but he seemed too earnest and too keen to be friendly. He told me that the Vikings of Suðreyjar, their western kingdom and part of King Hákon Hákonarson's domain, had not only begun to strengthen their grip on the islands but also to put

36

pressure on the Argyll and mainland Scotland. King Alexander hoped to use diplomacy to achieve his ends rather than force. It explained the paucity of numbers, but I thought it a mistake. You do not try to talk to the wolf, you hunt it and the Vikings were wolves.

We left two days later and I immediately regretted the delay for the weather turned once we had left Edinburgh and we had to endure a week of heavy rain. We were sodden despite oiled cloaks. This land had been barely touched by the Roman road builders and after a day we were all the same colour, a muddy brown. In the column, we were relegated to the rear, close to the servants and baggage. It was not a place of honour but, then again, it suited me for the purpose of this expedition was to get to Innis Chonnell in one piece. Another advantage of travelling with the king was that we did not need to use our tents: Melrose Abbey, Edinburgh Castle, Falkirk, and Stirling Castle all provided comfortable accommodation. We also picked up another ten knights as well as some local hobelars, lightly armed horsemen mounted on swift ponies when we stopped at Stirling Castle, the last great bastion before we neared the disputed lands.

Alain spoke to me as we mounted our horses in the inner bailey of Stirling Castle. "The road from here to Oban is dangerous, Sir William. I know that you have good archers with keen eyes. Have them use all their skills. The road will twist and turn through forests and over ridges. It is why we have been joined by the hobelars."

"Thank you, Sir Alain. Tell me, why are you here? Your lands are so far away that you cannot be hurt by these Vikings."

He shrugged, "I am the second son and I need advancement. If there is a war here and I can catch the eye of King Alexander, then there may be a manor for me. It will not be in England, but it will be mine." There were many knights like Sir Alain.

After he left Erik Red Hair wandered over, leading his horse. I had not had much time to speak with my men and I had no idea how Folki's language had improved. Erik bent down to adjust his strap to speak with me. I attended to Destiny's cantle for I knew he wished to speak privately to me. "Sir William, I know now why Sir Petr's ransom demands are so high." I looked up. "When he sailed, he was constantly telling the other mercenaries of his great connections with important men. Folki seemed to think it was because he had lost all and wished to make himself appear more important. He kept mentioning your father's name and Hermann Balk. When they were taken it was he told Cailean Mór, Sir Colin Campbell, that he was an important man; for the Earl of Cleveland was his friend."

"Then why did Folki not come directly to Stockton?"

37

"That was just bad luck. He could not speak the language of the Scottish crew who took him and by the time they reached Norway it was too late." I nodded, "I believe that the high ransom was deliberate." He shrugged, "Your father's name is well known. He is the scourge of the Scots and you know, better than any, how much ransom the knights of the valley have taken."

"Thank you. And how are his language skills coming along?"

"He can converse with Alan Longsword and Eric the Dane now but Idraf and the archers still struggle to understand him."

As we rode from the castle I chewed over Erik's words. Perhaps this was more than an attempt to extract gold, perhaps it was an attempt to gain revenge. Was this a plot to get me? If so, I had played into the hands of... whoever it was and brought a handful of men. Had I doomed then all?

Debt of Honour

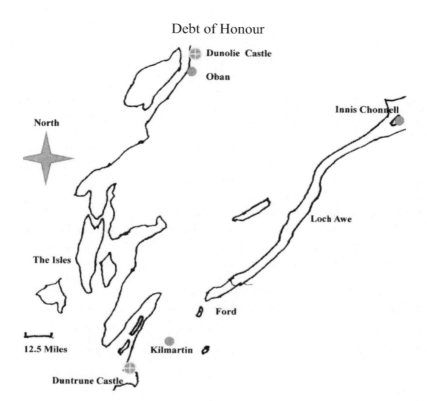

The West of Scotland 1249

Author's map

Griff 2021

Chapter 3

Norse Treachery

We were not far from the disputed lands and so we all rode with coifs, helmets and shields hung from our legs. Our archers had strung bows and we were vigilant. We had left the hamlet of Callander and were riding along the narrow River Teith when the ambush was sprung. Had my mind not been distracted by Erik's words or had we been at the fore then I might not have been taken by surprise. It was a lesson, but one bought at a cost. Arrows flew from the trees which flanked us and wild men leapt at the horses and knights with axes, swords, and spears. We had discussed such matters back in Stockton and my men knew what to do. We stopped. The four chests had to be protected and Tom of Rydal and Alan Longsword, along with Robin Greenleg, shielded the four animals which carried them. Idraf and the other two archers dismounted and strung their bows. Erik, Calum and Folki drew their weapons. The Swedish squire had a hauberk, helmet, shield, and sword. The one I was most worried about was Thomas for he had yet to fight for his life and that was likely to be the outcome of this attack.

Swinging up the shield which protected my leg I drew my sword and looked for enemies. King Alexander was surrounded by his closest knights and the wall of shields meant that it was unlikely that they would be hurt by the arrows. It was the men with axes, war hammers and poleaxes who could hurt them. Even as I whirled Destiny to face the four Scottish warriors, I was aware that the Scottish hobelars had disappeared. I pulled back on Destiny's reins and stood in the stirrups as I made him rear. I risked having him speared but I counted on the fear factor. The ones who came for the baggage would not be the real killers; they sought the king. Three of the four moved to the side but one was too slow and as my horse's hooves crushed his skull, I leaned from my saddle to hack into the shoulder of a second Scot. I need not have worried about Thomas. He had the blood of the Warlord and my father in his veins. He urged his horse to my left and his sword sliced through the badly made helmet of a third Scot. I saw the arrows from my four archers as they used them to target the most dangerous enemies who were close to us. We had been asked to defend the king, but we could not do that if we were dead. We first had to destroy those who were closest to us.

Folki and Erik were not comfortable fighting from the backs of horses, but they were both warriors and they appeared on my right so that the Scots before us had four mounted men and I saw hesitation on the ones who remained. Calum was a natural warrior and I saw how he had managed to survive when his shield brothers had all died. He fought as though he did not care if he lived or died. They hurled spears at us and loosed hunting arrows, but our mail, shields and helmets were too well made. The danger was to our irreplaceable horses and so I shouted, "Charge!" and spurred Destiny at them. We took the ten of them completely by surprise. The four who had first charged had been the bolder warriors. The ten each hurled another spear or loosed an arrow and then turned to flee. They would have to recross the river. As they jumped into the water, I launched Destiny. It was a prodigious leap and took him halfway across the shallow river. He landed on one man crushing and drowning him and as the water splashed up and a second man turned to face me, I sliced diagonally across his neck so that he fell in the river which was now reddening with the dead men's blood. The other three warriors with me had also drawn blood and there were just two men left to scramble up the far bank. I saw that they had discarded their weapons and I turned and shouted, "To the king!" Now we had the chance to fulfil my promise.

As we headed back to the bank, I saw that the chests and baggage were safe. My archers were able to target the men who swarmed around the king but there were so many men hacking and chopping at the horses of the king and his bodyguard that it struck me he was now in real danger. Destiny was the best horse, and I was the best rider. I made the bank and charged the nearest warrior. The one I spied was a Viking. He had the long byrnie which came below his knees and he had the large round shield with a metal boss. Even as I drew closer to him I saw the axe rise and chop into the flank of a courser. The horse reared and threw the rider. The Viking leapt forward, and I began my swing as he raised his axe to finish off the fallen knight. My sword hit his mail and shattered some of the links. He wore a padded undershirt and that, too, was ripped. Then my sword found flesh and bone. The man was tough, and he whirled like a wounded wild boar, slashing with his axe. Had I not already wounded him then Destiny might have suffered a wound. As it was, I was able to pull the reins to the left so that the axe head missed. I had no room for a full swing and so I stabbed at the Viking's bare arm. The tip found flesh and I pushed. As the axe fell from his arm Erik's sword smashed into the Viking's skull. He died.

The five of us, allied to my archers, meant that we had backs to fight and the men who first died were slow to react to our sudden threat.

41

They wore no mail and swords which were well sharpened and handled hacked through leather with ease. Bones were broken and flesh torn asunder. Calum used his long sword particularly well and I was able to observe that each blow was carefully aimed and struck so that the wounds were fatal and the man he fought stood no chance. I wondered how he would fare against a knight. Behind us, across the river, a horn sounded three times and immediately those that could, turned to cross the river. Erik and I had fought together before and our natural reaction was to turn and follow the men into the river. Folki and Thomas had little choice but to follow us while Calum was slightly ahead of me. As before, our powerful horses gave us an edge over the weary men, some wounded, who struggled through the icy water. This time we followed them on to the opposite bank. We slew a handful before the last two put their hands up to surrender. I had just sheathed my sword when three arrows flew from behind me and the Norse warrior who charged towards me with a double-handed axe in his hands was thrown backwards. As I looked up to view the fleeing warriors, I saw a Scottish knight, one of the ones who had joined us at Stirling. He was with some of the hobelars and it was then I knew of the treachery. This was not just an ambush but an attempt to take King Alexander. The knight, who had a blue shield with three white harts upon it, turned when he saw that our pursuit had stopped and the Scots melted into the forest.

Erik jabbed his sword into the back of one of the captives and forced them both into the river. By the time we reached King Alexander our wounded were having their wounds tended. The Mormaer of Dunbar said, "We cannot go further today, my lord. We must return to Callander. Men need to have their wounds tended and these two captives must be questioned."

I saw that King Alexander was shocked by the attack, although he must have expected something like it else why did he seek our help? I saw that my men were all whole and I rode back to the chests.

"We will return to Callander. Put our dead on the horses and take the weapons from the wounded." It was the Mormaer of Dunbar who took charge. King Alexander had not drawn his sword and yet he looked as though he had fought in a great battle. He looked drained and I wondered if we would continue our journey.

There was no hall in the hamlet and some of the villagers had fled when we returned. Had I been in command I would have suspected them of involvement but the Scottish lords seemed more intent on having a roof over their heads. The largest building was a farm, and we took that over. The Lord of Dunbar organised food and his voice told me that he was angry. It became clear that at least four of the knights

42

who had joined us at Stirling had been involved in the treachery as well as the hobelars. We had used the light horsemen as local scouts and they had led us into the trap beautifully. King Alexander had lost four of his household knights as well as twelve spearmen. It mattered not that twenty-five of the ambushers had been slain, they had very nearly succeeded. This was not my command and I was on the periphery as the two captives were questioned and then, when they refused to answer, tortured. I saw that Patrick of Dunbar was a leader who took hard decisions. I did not understand a word but when the two men were executed, I gathered that they had learned all that there was to learn.

My men had a fire going and were already cooking our supper. Alan Longsword shook his head, "Lord, this is not our fight. We are here to defend the treasure and, perhaps, King Alexander. Why be so reckless?"

"You know better than any, Alan, that to attack is always better than to defend. Besides, it is in my blood."

Folki said something to Erik who turned to me and said, "Folki recognised the warrior I slew after you had wounded him. He was with Sir Petr when they were defeated. These were part of the force with which King Hákon Hákonarson attacked Oban."

Calum shook his head, "But not the only ones. There were men from the MacDougall clan and I also saw Gallowglasses from my island. This was not an army, lord, but a carefully chosen warband. Four knights were lost and that is a larger number than the king can afford to lose."

Alan nodded, "Calum is right, lord. We should return to Stockton." He looked at Folki, "From what he has told Erik then his master deserved to be taken for he boasted too much and a good warrior does not do that."

I said, quietly, "I agree that the young knight was foolish and any who wish to return to Stockton and Hartlepool may do so with my blessing. For myself, I go on for this is a debt of honour and I gave my father my word that I would help the son of his old friend. This is for friendship's sake. Suppose this was my son, Richard, who had been taken. Would we turn back because of an ambush?"

They all loved Richard, Dick, as they called him, and their heads dropped in resignation."

A young knight, Sir James of Argyll, came to me, "Sir William, King Alexander wishes to speak with you."

I nodded, "Save me some food, Thomas."

As I approached the royal fire, I saw that the two mormaers and King Alexander were sitting apart from the rest of the knights. A priest tended the wounds of the ones who had been hurt. King Alexander smiled, "You have put me in your debt, Sir William. Despite my treacherous knights and countrymen, we have survived and that is in no small part to your charge across the river and into the backs of the men who tried to kill us. Thank you." He nodded to Patrick of Dunbar, "Some of my men did not trust you and thought you might be a threat."

The Mormaer of Dunbar gave a slight bow, "I am happy to apologise, Sir William. You and your men have heart. The question is what do we do now?"

"You are considering returning east."

He nodded, "Aye, for whom can we trust? The men we questioned told us that King Hákon Hákonarson has landed men on the west coast and they are raiding the villages. There is a castle at Oban which is holding out as well as Cailean Mór at Innis Chonnell. All the rest are suffering privations from these barbarians. We sent for riders to fetch men from the north, Inverness and Lochaber when we reached Edinburgh. Perhaps we should have brought more men from the east."

King Alexander shook his head, "We do not want a war. We are too poor for a war and it might bring on famine in those parts not threatened by King Hákon Hákonarson. I wish to bring Ewen MacDougall back to our side. With his help, we can defeat the Norse. When the time is right, next year, the year after perhaps, we can begin to claw back the islands. Let us try persuasion first."

My face was as a book which men could read and Patrick of Dunbar laughed, "Sir William is a warrior, and he knows, as do I, that you cannot speak to a traitor and trust aught that they say."

"I am king yet and so we go on but, Sir William, if your archers, who have a well-deserved reputation, could be our scouts then I would feel safer."

I nodded my agreement.

The king continued, "In one way this may have helped us. We now know that we cannot trust any except for Cailean Mór and we will be suspicious of any further offers until we have spoken to him. We go not to Oban but Innis Chonnell. We have less than fifty miles to go and there is a castle at Lochearnhead, the lord there, David of Ardveich, is loyal."

Patrick of Dunbar sighed, "King Alexander, you are too trusting. He may have been loyal but in these trying times who knows. However, a castle would be safer than the glens. We will watch him."

Calum had heard of David of Ardveich and he agreed with King Alexander. "He fought against the Norse king. I believe he can be trusted but Cailean Mór is another matter. He hates the MacDougall clan and that, I think, colours his judgement." He glanced at Folki as he spoke. There was something between the two I could see that. Had something happened aboard the ship which brought them to Hartlepool? I could have questioned Sir Geoffrey's new men, but I had been in such haste to begin the quest before winter proper that I had put such things from my mind.

"You fought well today, Calum. How is it that you are not a knight?"

He laughed, "I am afraid that I tend to speak my mind. It is men like King Alexander who make knights and I do not respect him or those who are similar leaders. His sword was bloodless today. Yours, Sir William, showed that you are a warrior a man could follow for you slew more than any!" He grinned, "Now if *you* were to offer me spurs…"

I laughed, "You have cheek, Calum of the Isles, I will grant you that!"

Ardveich Castle was not large. It reminded me of the small one the first Bishop of Durham had built at Bishopton, not far from Stockton. The hall would accommodate just King Alexander and his two mormaers. The rest of us had to make do with the outer bailey. There was, however, not only a ditch but a loch which afforded protection and we had a good wall. The knights managed to squeeze into the hall to eat, but only just. Sir David's wife Morag and son Lauren had to eat in the kitchen which was in the outer bailey. The squires too, once they had served us, had to wait without for a shout from within.

Sir David was knowledgeable about the raids, "King Alexander, you would need more than this handful of knights along with many hundreds of ordinary warriors if you were to defeat King Hákon Hákonarson. He has yet to show himself but he sends warbands to raid and suck the life from the people." He nodded to me, "I wonder that Sir William wishes to ransom a knight who was preying on our people."

I smiled, "I hear the question, Sir David, and understand it. Know that under normal circumstances I would be with you and hang any raiders, but this raider was a knight and serving his master, the King of Norway. He was, is, a little misguided, and when I have paid the ransom, we shall take him back to Stockton. I believe, even though I have never met him, that my father and I can mend his ways."

My answer seemed to satisfy him, but Lord Patrick said, "And would you be willing to fight these raiders, Sir William? Our king wishes to speak to them and persuade them to cease but you are a warrior and know that sometimes, often, in fact, a man must fight, or an enemy will continue to come."

"You are right in what you say, Lord Patrick. When I have Sir Petr safely in my charge then I will consider your request but at the moment that is four chess moves ahead. Let us say that I am sympathetic to your request."

King Alexander wiped his hands on the cloth which hung over his shoulder, "And tomorrow we ride for Innis Chonnell. Sir David, would you come with us?"

The frown told me that he was not happy about the request, but he answered honestly, I could see that in his eyes, "Your Majesty, I will come with my squire, but I will leave my handful of men to guard the castle. As I have told you, there are many raiders in this land and there are few warriors." King Alexander nodded but I knew that there was criticism in the knight's voice.

The next day we rode through land which bore the marks of violence. The glens and valleys were the only places which could be farmed effectively, and we saw more which were burnt out than were whole. I saw the effect of the arduous journey on the king. In truth, the rains and the journey had taken their toll on him. He looked weary and ill. He had begun to cough and sneeze before Callander. The rains had ceased but the icy wind from the east chilled even a well man to the bone. He seemed to shrink into his saddle; we should have brought an army! We were now in the area ravaged by war. It was not a garden of Eden and the glens were steep-sided. It was a land riddled with rivers, becks and burns. Loch Awe was not as large as some of the patches of water we had seen and passed but the castle which sat on an island looked although made of wood, to be substantial. I saw, around the northern edge of the loch, the pele towers like the one at Otterburn. They were made of stone and might explain why the farms around the loch looked to be intact and there was a jetty with a ferry waiting. Four spearmen guarded it.

King Alexander stood on the jetty and said, "Sir William, perhaps it might be better if you were to wait here while I speak with the lord in his castle."

"I have the gold, my lord, and I do not object to paying for the knight."

He leaned in, "I believe that you may be of more service to me as a warrior."

"What do mean, my lord?"

He merely smiled, enigmatically, "Camp here for the night and I will send for you in the morning. That I promise."

I was in no position to argue and I nodded. It took four journeys for the flat-bottomed ferry to take the men and horses to the island. I had enough time to observe that while the castle was largely wood there was a keep made partly of stone. While the ferrymen were away, I turned to

Idraf, "Scout the land hereabouts. If we have to leave in a hurry, then I would like the safest route out of here."

"And if we stray upon a deer, my lord?"

I smiled, "With the ransom we are paying I do not think that the Lord of the Manor will object." They rode away to the north and I said to Calum, "Scout the southern part of the loch and speak to the locals. Find out all that you can. Take Thomas with you."

My squire was eager to learn and that left the rest of us to put up the tents. I saw the surprise on Folki's face as I pitched in with my men, and it told me much about his lord and master. He would not have dirtied his hands. Before I met him and had just heard his story, I had not particularly liked Petr Birgersson and I did not relish paying gold for him but I would follow my father's commands for I had said that I would. We lit a fire and the ferrymen glowered at us. As Calum was not with us, we could not communicate with him, but I think he took offence at our language and that we had dared to camp so close to his home.

Alan was an eminently practical man and he said, "We got here safely enough, my lord, but how will we get home? We will not have the King of Scotland with us."

I shrugged, "Before we leave, I will seek authority from him to pass through his lands. Of course, that would not do us much good with the likes of those who attacked us near Callander. We trust to our own skills. At least we shall not have the gold to worry about."

It was after dark when my archers, as well as Calum and Thomas, returned. My archers had killed a deer. As soon as it began to cook then the ferryman and his family would know. It might be another bone of contention for the Lord of Innis Chonnell, but I cared not. The hot food would be welcome. Calum's news was even less welcome. Lord MacDougall controlled the lands just eight miles from the lower end of Loch Awe. We were even closer to the battleground than I had imagined. It meant we would have to set sentries. I divided us into five watches. Thomas, Folki and I, made a team of three. The Swede could now speak a little with us and, as he had fought alongside us, we all felt closer. There would be no need for silence, the ferryman had a dog. It had ceased barking at us when we had given it a cooked deer bone. When it had finished it the huge, wolf-like beast had settled down close to us in hopes of more food. The dog would wake us, but I wanted men on watch in case there was an attack.

"This has been a real experience, Uncle!"

"You speak as though it is almost over and yet we have barely begun. King Alexander wishes to use us and as we are guests in his land we cannot refuse!"

"What does he want us for? We are too few in number to be of use to him as warriors!"

"Of that, I am not certain. The attack at Callander took away some of his household knights but there are other ways we can serve him. My father and I are close to King Henry and King Alexander owes fealty to England for his manors there. Perhaps he keeps us as insurance so that King Henry might come to his aid. Norway and Scotland have ever been at war." I lowered my voice. "In many ways that has suited England by drawing Scotland's eyes north and not south."

I was doing what Sir Robert should have done but had not. I was teaching Thomas about the world he would inhabit.

I caught Folki looking over to the island. "Thinking about your lord?"

He shook his head, "No, Sir William." Those words were easy. I saw him screw his face up as he tried to conjure up the words he would need. "It is of Sven I am thinking." He rubbed his beard as he struggled to make the next sentence. "Like a father to me and to my lord."

I knew that they would keep Petr alive for the ransom, but Sven was another matter. From what Erik had told me he was an old man, and I could not see them having a use for him. I wondered if they had simply executed him. We had taken the last watch and so I had the two of them refresh the fire while I made water. As I walked back from the loch, I saw the hint of dawn in the east. Soon we would wake the men and eat for I wanted to be ready when King Alexander sent for us.

It was almost noon when the signal came from the island for the ferry to cross. I left the archers guarding the horses and the rest of us, along with the treasure, were ferried across by a silent ferryman and his sons. It was Sir James who came for us. He was not wearing mail and that told me we would not be going anywhere soon. When we reached the castle I discovered why. Lord Patrick greeted me at the substantial wooden gatehouse, "King Alexander is a little unwell and has only just risen. The damp journey did not help him. Come, he has risen now, and you are expected." He smiled, Cailean Mór is no friend of yours, is he?"

I shook my head, "Until we headed west, I had never heard the name."

Realisation dawned and he stopped, "Then I should tell you that his brother died when Elsdon was attacked. He blames you for the death even though you did not initiate the battle." He shrugged. "I gather that there was a disagreement about his brother fighting in the east. I just thought you should know."

"Have you seen the Swedish knight and his man yet?"

He shook his head, "They are alive, we ascertained that much, but none asked to see them." He paused. "That might have been a good idea."

Chapter 4

The Vengeful Plot

King Alexander was seated by the fire with a fur around his shoulders. His servants and physician were fussing around him. The other lords stood at the table picking at food and drinking wine. There were many armed men in the castle, and I could see that this was a land at war. I knew Cailean Mór as soon as I saw him. That was not because I had seen him before but because he stared and glowered at me; his hands bunched into fists. He was an enemy and as with all my enemies, I assessed him as I walked towards him. He was older than I was and had flecks of grey in his beard. He looked powerful but he was not as tall as me. If it came to a fight, he would give a good account of himself.

"Sir Cailean, Sir William come here by the fire so that I may speak with you both." King Alexander's voice sounded weary and I wondered if this journey to the west had been wise. Of course, we could not have predicted the rains but, even so, it had been a risky thing to undertake.

I realised that I was the only one wearing mail and I knew how it would look. It was too late to do anything about it. We both looked at King Alexander rather than each other. It seemed politic.

"Sir William, the two men you have come to ransom are both here and are alive. I have spoken to Sir Cailean and whilst he is unhappy about the situation, I have persuaded him to reduce the ransom to one hundred marks."

I nodded, "I thank Your Majesty and Sir Cailean, but Sir Cailean should know that we brought the full amount. I did not request a reduction as my father was keen to pay off this debt of honour."

The Scot could not resist snapping a reply and I turned as his words were showered upon me. He spattered them through angry teeth, and they were filled with venom, "Honour? What does an English Warlord, and a murderer of bishops know of honour?"

I sighed, "My father was absolved of his sin by both Bishop Albert and the Bishop of Durham but if you are determined, Sir Cailean, to impugn my family's name and my father's honour, then know that I am happy for a trial by combat to settle the matter!"

I heard the sharp intake from the audience of knights and I also saw that I had taken Sir Cailean by surprise. I knew that my men would have their hands hovering by their swords in case this came to blows. It was, however, King Alexander who spoke and the voice which had been weak a moment or two earlier was now both firm and commanding, "Sir William, there will be no trial by combat and Sir Cailean, you will curb your tongue. You rule this land with my permission and as I told you last night when we arrived, we need Sir William to wrest control of this land back from the MacDougalls."

I turned to face King Alexander, "Your Majesty?"

He coughed and a physician glared at me as he first dabbed the mouth of the Scottish King and then held the goblet for him to drink. When he had regained control he said, "I need you to come with me when I speak with Sir Ewen MacDougall. Your wife's father was held in great esteem by this rebellious lord and his family. I hope to persuade him to return to the Scottish side without the need to resort to armed conflict."

"I doubt that it will work, Your Majesty."

He gave a wry smile, "That is what the others spent last night telling me, but I would not shed more Scottish blood. The blood I wish to shed courses through Norwegian bodies. Besides, the men from Inverness and Lochaber will not be here for a week. Only then can we use a force of arms and by that time I hope to have the MacDougall clan as well as the Campbell clan to fight them." He smiled, "The handful of men you bring will not go amiss for as they showed on the journey here they are both skilled and resourceful."

"As I said, I am happy to spend the full ransom." He waved a hand as though to dismiss the idea. "Could I see the knight, Sir Petr, and his man?"

Sir Cailean shook his head, "First, I wish to see the gold, paltry amount though it is and no compensation for the loss of a brother!" He struck me as a bitter man and that he had agreed to the reduction reluctantly. He would still be an implacable enemy.

I sighed and turned to Thomas, "Fetch me one hundred marks!" He bowed and went to Erik. Each chest had one hundred and twenty-five gold marks inside.

"Fetch the knight!"

Sir Patrick brought me a goblet of wine. The air was icy in the hall and none spoke, but the mormaer gave me a smile of encouragement. That this situation was of Sir Cailean's doing was immaterial. I wondered if I could get out of the new task given to me by King Alexander and then realised that I could not. I had to obey him or risk a more dangerous journey home. This would not be the swift journey I had anticipated when I had agreed to leave Hartlepool. Thomas gave me the bag of coins and I handed it to Sir Cailean. If he had attempted to count them then I might have reiterated my challenge, but he merely nodded and handed them to his steward.

The young knight, when he was brought in, walked but he was thin and his body showed scars. He was dressed in rags. It was the other, though, the one I assumed was Sven, who caused me more concern. Folki ran to him as he was helped in by two of Sir Cailean's men. I saw that every knight was shocked. It was a skeleton whose body bore the scars of punishment that was carried into the hall. When a man was held for ransom then he was supposed to be treated as a guest. Having surrendered his sword a captured knight agreed not to escape. The same applied to those he took with him into captivity.

King Alexander shook his head, "Is this well done, my lord?"

Sir Cailean had the good grace to look embarrassed, but he was still defiant, "He was an enemy, and this is a castle at war."

I turned and glared at Sir Cailean, "And there are rules about such things or are you the barbarian and not King Hákon Hákonarson?"

"Peace!" Turning to his healer King Alexander said, "See to the injured man and take him somewhere comfortable until Sir William has finished here." As his doctor hurried to obey, the king turned to Sir Cailean, "Sir William is right Sir Cailean, there are rules about such things, and you have broken them but there are more important matters to be dealt with so let us put this behind us." He paused, "That is my command!"

Sir Cailean nodded, as did I but in my case, this was just a truce. The war was not yet over.

"Until I am fit to ride, I give command of my knights and Sir Cailean's to Lord Patrick of Dunbar. In a few days, I shall be ready to ride to Duntrune Castle to speak with Ewen MacDougall but before then I want the siege of Oban ended and the town relieved. That is a royal port and I wish it to be returned to me so that I may take a ship to visit MacDougall. You have enough men, Dunbar?"

"Aye, Your Majesty. From what I have learned there are just two hundred men at the siege works but the MacDougalls have Dunolie Castle just north of Oban and that is a threat."

Sir Cailean shook his head, "It does not have a large garrison and most of those are at the siege. If they are defeated, they will retreat there."

"And that does not matter much for by then we will have the threat of the men from the north. You buy time so that when I negotiate with MacDougall I do so from a position of strength." He began coughing again. It took another goblet of wine before he recovered sufficiently to speak once more.

"Sir William, I dare say you would wish to speak with Sir Petr. Sir Cailean has provided a building at the south end of the island close to the church for you and your men. Sir Cailean will provide men to show you where it is and to bring Sir Petr's arms and food for you." He turned to the Scottish lord, "Will you not, Sir Cailean?"

"Aye. Angus, see to it!" It was done with ill grace.

An old retainer said, "Follow me, my lord!" His accent was so thick that I had to strain to understand what he had said.

As we left the hall I said, "Alan, take Tom and fetch the archers and our horses. I will send Thomas to direct you to our new home." I turned to Erik and said, "Tell Sir Petr what is happening."

The Swede said, "I have enough of your words to understand. Thank you, Sir William, I thought you were never coming!" There was a hint of criticism in his voice.

I was irritable, I knew, and that was the fault of Sir Cailean, but I did not like the tone of Sir Petr, "Your squire Folki had a long and arduous journey to find us and we have not wasted a single moment in coming to your aid. I think, Sir Petr, that you should be a little more grateful for what has been done. This was a debt of honour but from what I can gather you have shown little of that hitherto!" He reeled as though I had slapped him, and I regretted my words. They had been spoken in anger. However, I liked Folki and knew what he had been through. Sir Petr seemed an ungrateful young man. I hurried after Angus who looked as though he wanted to be rid of us as soon as he could.

We walked through the woods along a simple track until the trees ceased and we could see overgrown land which must have been farmed at some point in the past. We arrived at a group of buildings which looked as though they had been used as some sort of granary with a house for a watchman attached. It had a roof and looked as though the walls would keep out the wind. It would do and was better than the open camp by the loch.

Angus pointed to the loch, "There is your water. Food will be fetched down for you." He grinned, "If you havna pots you will have to use the open fire!"

Calum quipped in Gaelic and the Scot coloured and then stormed off.

"What did you say?"

"I said we could always use his helmet as Scotsman always have big heads!"

The others laughed but I counselled, "We may be fighting alongside some of these men so watch your words." They looked a little abashed, but I knew that they would not heed my commands. "Thomas, go back to the quay." While my men made the building habitable, I waved Erik and Petr down to the lochside. "I know you can speak some of my words but if we use Erik to translate it will be quicker." They both nodded. "I know, Petr, that you were treated badly, and I can do nothing about that. As for the delay in getting here, we came as soon as Folki arrived and we had the gold. You should ask your squire about his journey. He was loyal and endured more than a squire should have."

Erik translated and Petr answered.

"He says he knows he should be more grateful, and he is sorry that Sven and Folki suffered for him," Petr added more. "He wants to know what will happen now?"

"A good question; I had planned on returning immediately but we must spend some time aiding King Alexander. That may not be a bad thing. It will give you and Sven time to recover."

Just then Thomas returned with the horses and servants brought food along with Sven, carried on a litter. He was carried into the house part and I waved the rest away. "Let them have some privacy and we will make this our home. We cook for ourselves, but we will not need to keep watch. Sir Cailean may not like us, but he will not risk the wrath of the king."

Calum said, "Lord MacDougall is a treacherous man, lord. I would not trust him and more than that; until King Hákon Hákonarson is defeated then he will still be a rebel. Hákon Hákonarson promises him islands to rule and that is a powerful gift."

I was pleased I had Calum. He might be a wild man when it came to fighting but I had seen him as a thoughtful one when the moment was right.

Alan Longsword shook his head, "It does not sit right with me, lord, to fight for these Scots. Defending ourselves was one thing but..."

Tom of Rydal was another who said little but when he did it was worth listening to, "Alan, we do not fight our own kind, we fight Scots, and we fight Vikings. We may not make much gold from this but if it gets us home in one piece then whatever we can take will be more than we might have made at home. We are still paid and thus far we have not been taxed, have we?"

Alan nodded but I could see that he was not convinced. "This Cailean Mór attacked us, by deliberately taking Sir Petr when we were just living peacefully and then demands five hundred marks! I would not have given him anything. I believe he took Sir Petr because he saw a way to punish your father, lord."

"There may be something in what you say, Alan, but do you really want to start a war over this?"

"No lord," he smiled, "I just thought I would get it off my chest and now I am content."

Tom of Rydal shook his head, "When did you begin whingeing so much?"

He laughed, "Put it down to age!"

His words helped us for it made clear our position. Night had fallen, and food was ready when I went in with Erik in case my words needed to be translated although Folki had improved dramatically. As soon as I entered the dimly lit house Sir Petr launched a torrent of words and Erik translated with a smile. When he did so I knew that Sven and Folki were responsible for them. "He says, Sir William, that he is a young fool, and he knows that he owes you all. He would be your man if you wish and both Sven and Folki are happy to serve you."

I nodded. "Then tell them that when we have aided King Alexander and have been released from his service we will go back to Stockton and the three of you can meet my father. I am here on his behalf. I would be honoured to have you serve me, but my father is the one you owe. We were just his messengers." When the words were translated, I said, "Erik, come and get some food for them. Sit with them and eat. See what you can learn for Sven knows more than he has told thus far."

The granary was cosy, and the food and the candles made it more so. Thomas was learning with each passing day. Serving knights at the table would seem as nothing after the foraging he had been forced to do. Cooking food in the open was easy but making it tasty was an art and my men were experts. We had been sent mutton to cook and they managed to make that normally tough meat tender. I had learned much when I was my father's squire, but I was still learning.

We were about to turn in when Erik emerged with the wooden bowls. He took them to the loch to wash them with water and sand. He returned and we looked at him expectantly. He shook his head, "If I did not hate Scotsmen before this day then the words I heard while we ate would fill me with murderous intent. They treated Sven as a slave. He was fed gruel and loch water. He was barely able to eat a dozen mouthfuls of the food we cooked for him for his stomach must have shrunk. The ale made him so sleepy that I barely heard half of his story. Sir Petr was taken because of Sir Thomas and yourself, Sir William. He did not know it when he sent Folki off. If he had then he would have instructed his squire to go directly to Stockton and warn Sir Thomas."

"Warn him?"

"Aye, if the king had not come with us then when we arrived or maybe even before we would have been captured, brought to him, tried and executed."

It was even worse than I had thought but at least the high ransom made sense. Not only would he have what he perceived was justice for his brother he would financially ruin my father. Of course, the money was as nothing to us, but Sir Cailean did not know that.

"Then when I leave with King Alexander, I will leave Erik and an archer here to guard the two of them."

"You still intend to help them, lord?"

"Alan, I help King Alexander and that makes our journey home safer. It is now even more imperative that I help him. I know we could handle many times our number in a fight but some of you might die and that is something I cannot contemplate. We smile at them, but we will be vigilant and watch for the knife in the night."

The next morning Lord Dunbar came to speak with me, and we walked along the beach so that we could speak without being overheard. "I have ridden to the siege lines at Oban and I fear that King Alexander has been misled by Sir Cailean. The rebels and their Norse allies hold Dunolie Castle to the north but the bulk of their men have surrounded Oban and are besieging it. I believe we can take them, but it would take more effort than his words suggested." He saw my face and smiled, "As you already knew."

"I have been at sieges recently from both sides and they are never as easy as some leaders make out."

"You have a suggestion?"

"An attack at night will stand more chance of success. It means I cannot use my handful of archers as archers, but they are good knifemen. We need the men coming from the north."

"You do not believe that negotiation will help."

"I know that it will not help. Had King Alexander bestowed his favour on Sir Ewen then aye, but my man Calum has fought on the other side and knows that the two lords and their clans hate each other. You can only have one as an ally! The other must be broken."

"Brutal!"

I shrugged, "It is your system, lord. In many ways, it is easier to understand than the English system where it all depends on a lord's own ambition."

"Just so."

"Who leads the men from the north?"

"Alan Durward the Justiciar of Scotia. He married Marjorie, the daughter of the King." He saw my look, "Not born to a Queen but they seem happy enough."

"I know him and he was of assistance to me once before. King Henry thinks highly of him and I am pleased that it is he who leads this force. I am just grateful it is not Comyn nor the Queen's brother for both are treacherous and hate me even more than Sir Cailean!"

The Mormaer laughed, "You seem to make a habit of making enemies of important Scotsmen!"

I laughed, "I am like my father, a border knight and if I was not hated and feared then I would not be doing my job."

"We leave on the morrow so that we can scout out the enemy lines. I think I agree with you about a night attack but let us look first, eh?"

"Aye, my lord."

His words filled me with confidence. Perhaps I might be home sooner rather than later!

That night we prepared our weapons and our horses. I gave my men an outline of what was expected of us and how I thought we might be used. Sir Petr listened even though he was not coming for he was keen to learn our language.

"We go to support for this is not our fight and I want none of you to earn even as much as a scratch. Sir Cailean's men can bear the brunt for it was they who allowed the siege to begin."

Alan nodded, "If those besieging have any sense then they will flee as soon as we attack for the besieged can sally forth."

I smiled, "They may not have the mettle of those at Elsdon when we were besieged but you are right. When that is done, and Oban is invested once more, King Alexander hopes to take a ship south. Only Thomas and I will be needed. The rest of you can prepare for the ride home. Sir Petr and Sven will both need saddles for their horses, and we will need food."

Calum nodded, "Then when we attack tomorrow, we seek both. There are bound to be horses for their lords."

I could see that my new additions were worth their weight in gold. Any doubts I may have entertained about Calum were long gone.

Chapter 5

Naked Ambition

We ferried the animals and then the men. All of this took time, but it allowed me to see how many men we would take. The largest number of knights were the king's. Sir Cailean had just ten. In total we had forty men at arms, but the only archers were the three I had brought. The other one hundred or so who assembled were clansmen. Had this been in England then they would have been the fyrd or local levy. Clansmen were more than that. They had more allegiance to their chief, Cailean Mór, than to the king. That made them better warriors and truly fanatical fighters but if I was King Alexander, I would have been wary of leading them. His illness meant he would not, and the Mormaer of Dunbar seemed quite happy to be the one to ride before them. We moved at the pace of men on foot which explained the early start. We had nineteen miles to travel and we kept a steady pace as we moved along the River Awe. I rode with the two leaders, much to the obvious annoyance of Sir Cailean. Sir James and Sir Patrick had not liked the way that Sir Cailean had treated his prisoners and more, I knew from something Sir Patrick had said that he was suspicious of the attack near Callander. As we had walked along the beach he had said, "The men who attacked us travelled a long way to get there and the survivors had a long journey back and yet they remained invisible while they did so. This land has few roads, Sir William, why were they not seen?" Whilst not naming Sir Cailean his words suggested that the lord had not been as vigilant as he ought.

I was able to speak with the two of them as we headed to the royal port. We had to slow when we crossed the Bridge of Awe because it was narrow but then we made good progress. Four local men had ridden ahead to ensure that any sentries would be eliminated.

"When I scouted it out their sentries were less than two hundred paces from their ditches but who knows, we may have been seen."

"And this Dunolie Castle?"

"Less than a mile from the harbour. We do not think there is a large garrison there. The Norse and the rebels who besiege it took most of the men from the castle. Ewen MacDougall has better warriors with him at Duntrune Castle."

I was thinking that this was a chance for King Alexander to hurt Ewen MacDougall and make him more reasonable and amenable to his offer. King Alexander was a clever king.

The sun was setting as we neared Oban and I could see, silhouetted against the skyline, the towers of Dunolie Castle. Dusk hid us but Lord Dunbar ordered us to dismount as we neared the enemy. Those at the siege lines had not set sentries. I wondered why they had not tried an assault for the wooden wall was not substantial and the ditch which ran around it could be breached. It was as I walked to view it in the last rays of the sun that the answer came to me. They did not have enough men to risk the assault. I would speak with Lord Dunbar later but was the capture of the port an attempt to draw King Alexander west and then ambush him?

Lord Dunbar had planned on attacking the camp which was closest to the main gate to encourage those within to sortie. That way we would be bound to outnumber them. The Campbells were the largest force by some margin and they were placed in two groups of warriors. They guarded our flanks. We smelled the food cooking and Lord Dunbar nodded. That was when Sir Cailean sounded the Campbell horn, and we ran forward. It was a long time since I had gone into battle with so few of my men, but I was unafraid. Flanked by Calum and Alan Longsword, with Thomas behind me and the rest on their flanks I feared no enemy. I left my shield on my back and used my sword two handed. I would be able to use more power that way and when I hacked through to the spine of the first Norse warrior whose leather byrnie gave him little protection, I knew I had chosen the right weapon. His shorter sword had struck first but my hauberk was well made.

A night attack relies on surprise and speed. I ran with my men as though we were in a foot race. There would be enough clansmen behind us to ensure that any we missed would be slain. The enemy horns and shouts told us we had achieved surprise. The Campbells' war cries rent the air as we chopped and hacked through men who moments earlier had been busily cooking their food. I heard a shout from ahead as the gates were opened and the Vikings and Scots were attacked in their rear by the people and warriors of Oban. Suddenly the enemy before us evaporated and we met the townsfolk, and Lord Dunbar showed that King Alexander had chosen his leader well. He shouted, "Through the town and we take those north of the port!" The orders were repeated, and we formed a long metal column for the knights of King Alexander led and we charged towards the other gate which was already open as we approached.

Those on the north side had already begun to flee and were racing towards the gates of Dunolie Castle where their allies awaited them. We wasted no time in fighting those before us, we just chopped and slashed as we ran. I realised as we did so what an efficient fighter was Calum of the Isles. His blows seemed effortless and yet the wounds he caused were horrific. He seemed to know the perfect place to strike. Lord Dunbar urged us on, and I saw why. Not only were we catching many of those who had been besieging the town but also cutting off those who had been on the eastern side and they were all desperate to get inside the castle walls. The only chance for the castle to hold out was if they managed to close the gates. Shades of Aberffraw filled my head as we had tried to hold the gate to allow more men in and that was when I had been cursed! The memory served to make me run faster and swing my sword as though my life depended upon it. Lord Dunbar and four of his knights were the ones who hurled their bodies at the gates as they began to close. Five mailed men are heavy, and the gates cracked asunder. Once they were inside then we had won but we were fighting Norwegians and rebellious Scots who knew that the punishment for their crimes would be death. For the leaders, it would be a gruesome death. Then I spied the open gate on the west side of the castle, they were heading for the sea. Men were flooding through it.

"Lord Dunbar!" I pointed and then led my men towards it.

"King Alexander's knights, follow Sir William!"

Thomas had never done this, but he showed that he had skills as he parried a blow from a Scottish man at arms, ducked below the flailing sword and rammed his blade into the throat of the warrior. Even my lightly armed archers were showing that they had the skills to deal with part-time swordsmen. The gate was some one hundred paces from us but there was such a press of men that it took some time for us to cut our way through. It was as we burst through that I saw, less than ninety paces from us, a beach and on it were drawn up three dragon ships. Already Scot and Norse were clambering aboard, and archers and slingers began to pelt us. I barely managed to swing my shield around from my back. Tom of Rydal was a little slow to do so and a stone cracked into his helmet. I held up my hand for us to stop. The three ships began to pull out and I watched Norse throw their byrnies from them to jump into the sea and swim out to the ships. King Alexander's knights and my men slew the tardy ones. When the ships disappeared into the darkness then I knew we had lost them.

Alan Longsword was tending to Tom. His head was bleeding, but the helmet and protector had done their job. He would have an aching head and a small scar. Even as he cleansed the wound Alan shouted, "Search the bodies!"

I turned and led Thomas back up the slope to the gate. "Should we not help them, uncle?"

"Do you need the purses of silver the dead might have?" He shook his head. "It is their reward and they do not need us to stand and watch them. They will choose the best blades and pieces of armour. Some of the Norse will have good sealskin boots, they will take those."

He nodded, "I thought to help."

"And the men know that you will be a good lord. You have impressed them."

He looked surprised, "Have I? I thought that I got in their way!"

"My men do not lavish compliments, but I have watched them. They treat you as one of them. They joke with you easily and are comfortable with you. They are the signs. When we forced the gate my archers watched your side to protect you. They need not have done so. I am pleased with you."

He was silent as we passed the Campbell warriors who were stripping the bodies and we headed for the keep where I knew Lord Dunbar would be. My nephew was reflective, "At Redmarshal I always felt a failure." He said nothing and I remained silent. "I was lonely in my own home. That should not be, should it uncle?"

"No, but you have had that rare opportunity afforded to few men. You have the chance for a new start, and I am pleased that you have grasped it in both hands."

Lord Dunbar and Sir James were in the keep and searching through a chest. I turned to Thomas. "There should be a stable close by, find a couple of good horses and saddles." He nodded, "Men may try to stop you."

He smiled, "Thomas of Redmarshal might have been intimidated but the reborn Thomas will deal with them!"

He had changed.

The two leaders looked up as I approached, "The Norse escaped in three of their ships."

Lord Patrick nodded, "We surprised them. When they attacked us at Callander they must have returned here. They thought we were too few in numbers for an attack."

Sir James said, waving a piece of parchment, "Reading this they were expecting reinforcements from Norway and the isles. The Justiciar needs to get here as soon as he can."

Lord Patrick shook his head, "Taking Dunolie Castle has upset their plans. With Innis Chonnell in the south-east and this in the north-west, we can hold out even if King Hákon brings a mighty fleet. If King Alexander is well enough then his plan to visit Lord MacDougall may yet yield results."

By noon the enemy bodies had been burned on the beach. It would be a marker for Norse ships that they had lost this phase of the war. Sir Cailean, who had barely spoken to any of us left a handful of his men in the castle and took the rest back to his island home. I sent Thomas and Alan, along with the archers to fetch our men from the island too. Thomas had secured three good horses. One of them was a courser and even more important were the saddles. We had secured quarters in the castle. Lord Dunbar had also sent for King Alexander. The quarters in the solid castle were healthier than the crowded Innis Chonnell. While we waited, he summoned the leading burghers and the priest from Oban, and we sat around the large table in the Great Hall. While we ate, they told us what they knew. These were Campbells and loyal to Sir Cailean, but they were also aware that the port belonged to the King of Scotland and they were anxious that it did not fall into Norse hands. They had little love for the Norwegian King!

The priest, out of courtesy to me and the other senior lords, spoke in Norman so that I could understand too, "They thought to starve us out, Lord Dunbar, and, in truth, had they chosen to attack the walls then we could not have withstood them for long."

Sir James tapped the parchment he had not relinquished since he had found it, "It was a trap which we have sprung early. Their ships must have been delayed."

One of the Campbells said something in Gaelic, and the priest said, "Sean here said that sailing from Norway is not something which can be predicted accurately. A fleet might take four times longer than expected to reach here if the winds are against them."

Lord Dunbar said, "You are right, and they would need to arrive together. King Hákon may well be to the west of us waiting for his ships to arrive."

"And the three ships I saw leaving the shore would tell him that this part of their plan had failed. We have bought time!"

It was after dark when King Alexander and my men arrived. There were quarters for him, and he looked better than when we had left him. Perhaps his physicians had found the cure. He was full of praise for us all but also mindful that the threat had not gone. "Dunbar, secure a ship and on the morrow, we will sail south and speak with Lord Ewen."

Although looking a little better I thought that this was too soon, "Are you well enough, King Alexander?"

"Thank you for your concern, Sir William, but the sea air may do me good and I might manage a sea voyage where a long ride might reverse all the good which my doctors have done. We need a ship for me and just ten knights. You, Dunbar and Sir William here will be amongst them."

I was not happy about the paltry numbers he planned on taking, "What if he chooses treachery, Your Majesty, and holds you as a hostage?"

King Alexander smiled and I could see that he had thought this through, "I now have a son, Sir William. He cannot kill me for that would turn Scotland against him. He wants the Isles as his domain. At worst he will bargain for them and refuse to turn to our side. I hope to offer inducements to encourage him to return to the side of Scotland."

Lord Dunbar said, "And Sir Cailean?"

"That is a nettle I have yet to grasp. I count on his loyalty to Scotland rather than his hatred of Sir Ewen."

I was weary when I joined my men. The warrior hall we had commandeered was comfortable and although Lord Dunbar had offered me quarters in the keep, I was happier with my men. Sven had begun to recover but he would have a long journey to do so fully. As I entered, I saw that my men had taken to Sven. Folki was already considered a shield brother, even by Calum and it was Sir Petr who was isolated. I was pleased that my nephew had recognised this and was seated talking to the young knight. We had recovered his arms and armour. He and Thomas were cleaning and sharpening as I entered.

All faces looked up at me and Alan said, "And now home, my lord?"

It was clear that all those in the warrior hall, even Thomas were of the same mind. We had done what we had to do and more. We had attacked and recovered the town and the castle, but I would have to disappoint them. "Not yet. Thomas and I will sail tomorrow with King Alexander. We go to speak with the enemy." I smiled, "So that will give you all three days or more to help our Swedish friends to speak our language a little better. I promise that when I return, we shall head home to Hartlepool and Stockton."

Calum shook his head, "Sir William, you go into the nest of vipers. Wise men do not do so."

I nodded, "And I know that, but events are out of my hands. I will trust in God that he does not intend me to end my life here, far from my home."

Alan said as he went to the pot to stir it, "Amen to that, lord."

'Maid of the Isles' was a sturdy and well-made ship. I suspect that she had been left intact as the King of Norway had plans to use her

himself. Her captain was well paid by King Alexander, but he was clearly unhappy about having to sail into such dangerous waters. We left at noon for the short voyage down the coast. The distance was not great, a mere thirty-five miles but as we had to negotiate the islands of Luing and Scab, not to mention the rocks which guarded the Argyllshire coast, we edged our way south rather than racing. It allowed me the opportunity to see how sparsely populated this part of Scotland was and how the Norse had managed to hang on to it. A lord who controlled the seas controlled the land too and the Norse were still the masters of the oceans.

Lord Patrick and I stood close to the King, "Are you sure that you are well enough for this, King Alexander?"

"Aye, Patrick and I believe that the sea air will blow the evil from my chest."

I waved a hand at the rugged coastline, "Is this worth fighting for, King Alexander?"

He gave me a sad look, "Had I not been forced to sign away Scottish claims for Northumberland then no. We cannot have Northumberland, that I accept and so we must cling on to every piece of land that we can. The Norse only began to try to expand on the mainland after the Treaty of York." He held up a hand, "I am not criticising King Henry, I would have done the same had I enjoyed the service of men like you and your father."

The silence which followed told me that although we were still friends King Alexander and the Mormaer of Dunbar still sought the land north of the Tyne. When I returned, I would have to warn my father that we still needed vigilance.

Duntrune Castle enjoyed a fine position and was made of stone. At the northern end of the seawater Loch Crinan, it was a formidable castle, and I would not have relished assaulting it for it had stone walls built on solid rock! There was a small jetty with a couple of fishing boats tied up. The MacDougall standard flew defiantly from the keep and there was no sign of the flag of Scotland. That was ominous. We tied up and a procession of knights headed down to the jetty. We had barely disembarked when they stood facing us. I knew which one was Ewen MacDougall immediately for he spat out his words at us.

King Alexander sighed and said, "You know I do not speak enough Gaelic to understand all that you said, Lord MacDougall. I pray you to speak so that I may understand you."

The Scottish mormaer laughed, "And there you see the problem!"

I was not sure if the words were intended for us or his men who were all grinning. They made a solid wall which prevented us from moving towards the castle but as there were so few of us that was not an option.

"You are not a Scottish king but another Norman. It is time you allowed these lands to be ruled by a true Scot, one descended from the kings of Dal Riata."

"But you are Scottish, and you swore an oath to me on my coronation. Are you an oath breaker?"

The king's words wiped the smile from the Scot's face.

"Do not speak to me of breaking oaths! You never visit this part of your kingdom and the only reason you are here now is to persuade me to cease supporting the Norwegian King!"

I looked at Lord Dunbar. Was there a spy or was the purpose of this visit so obvious?

"Yet you would switch from a Norman king to a Norwegian one. How does this help you?"

I do not know if King Alexander saw it, but I did. MacDougall's face betrayed him. He wanted to be a king. If not of Scotland, then this part at least. I saw it in his eyes. I had learned to read men's faces as it often gave me the edge in combat.

"Let us say that I will enjoy more power and freedom with King Hákon ruling Argyll than with you!" He was now angry, and his next words were heavily laden with threat. "You came here uninvited and I will do the courtesy, for I can see that you are not a well man, of letting you leave alive. Go now and the next time you come then bring an army. You will need it!"

There was a spy!

Lord Dunbar said, "Come, King Alexander, the air here is filled with the foulness of treason." He pointed an accusing finger at MacDougall. "The next time we meet it will be with a sword in hand and on that day your wife becomes a widow!"

We boarded the ship and I saw that not only was King Alexander visibly shaken he was becoming unwell again. As the relieved captain turned his ship to head north once more King Alexander said, "I think I should like to go to the cabin." As Lord Patrick and I helped the king he said, "I am sorry Sir William. I did not get the opportunity to use your family connection. Yours was a wasted journey."

"Not so, King Alexander for I saw another side to being a king. I am pleased that I was here. I should warn you that what I heard and saw lead me to believe that King Hákon's men will be attacking soon and that the MacDougalls will attack at the same time."

King Alexander nodded as we laid him on the narrow bed, "I know and I pray that my hostarius, Lord Durward, hurries with the men of the north or I may lose more than Argyll!"

We sat with the King on the voyage north.

"I would have both of you promise that you will do all that you can to ensure that my son becomes King of Scotland." He nodded to me, "He is to marry into King Henry's family but there are, as I came to realise, many evil and corrupt men at King Henry's court. If you, Sir William, promise to protect my son then I know all will be well."

"King Alexander, this is a fever and although it has struck you down badly, you will recover but I swear that a long time in the future when your son is ready to be king then I will support his claim to the throne."

"And you Dunbar?"

"King Alexander I am hurt that you need to ask but I will so swear!"

"Then I am happy." He relapsed into a fitful sleep.

When we reached Oban it was almost midnight and the sentries had to rouse the physician for the king was clearly worsening. We carried the sick king to his bedchamber. Sir James listened as we told him what we had learned. Sir James said, "Aye, and we have the spy or know his identity, at least. One of the Campbell men at arms was spotted heading out of the castle just as you were leaving. I was suspicious for he did not take the road south, to Innis Chonnell, but rather rode north. I sent men after him and he fled. They almost caught him, but he managed to make the small ship which awaited him. It was a smaller version of their longship but had just four oars on each side. We recovered his horse but that was all. I sent word to Sir Cailean. He has yet to respond."

Lord Patrick said, "From this moment on we are on a war footing." He turned to me, "You and your men are under no obligation to stay, Sir William. If you left, there would be no dishonour."

I smiled and tapped my heart, "In here there would be for I have never fled a fight. We will stay and face this foe with you and then, with the king's permission, we will leave."

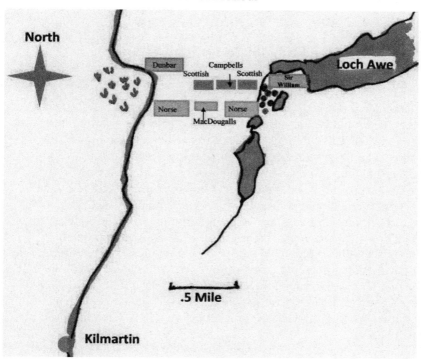

The Battle of Kilmartin

1250

Author's Map Griff 2021

Chapter 6

The Battle Of The Clans

The Justiciar arrived the next day in the late afternoon. King Alexander had not left his bed and from the looks on his physicians' faces, he would be there for a little longer. Alan Durward remembered me and was effusive in his praise of my father and the men of the valley. The flattery, although well-meant, was unnecessary.

Lord Dunbar asked, "And how many men do you bring?"

"Ninety knights and men at arms and over nine hundred others."

That seemed to be a disappointingly low number especially as it would be Norse warriors we were fighting, not to mention the Clan MacDougall who were a major threat. Lord Dunbar kept his face impassive as he explained what we would be facing. "Our strength lies in our mounted horsemen, our knights. We will have to meet them in the open for we damaged the gates to the castle and besides it is too small to defend. Oban would be taken along with every settlement in the area. When King Hákon comes then we will have to face him in open battle."

I waved an arm around, "And from what I have seen the site of the battle would be limited. We need to find where we are likely to fight and use the advantage of that instead of superior numbers."

Lord Dunbar shook his head, "I agree but until we know where the Norse will arrive, we must keep our men here."

Lord Hostarius said, "Keeping them together on the road was not a problem, Mormaer, but these are men who like action. Unless we fight soon then they may well end up fighting amongst each other."

As I heard the debate, I realised why we had enjoyed such success in the border wars. Luckily for us, we discovered where the Norse were the next day. *'Maid of the Isles'* had just left port, but her sails were still in sight when she turned back and made all speed into Oban. Her captain raced to the castle.

"My lord, there is a Norse fleet to the west of us and they are heading south towards Loch Crinan."

"How many ships?" Lord Dunbar knew that was the best way to estimate the size of the army we might face.

"I did not stop to count but there were at least twenty or thirty before me."

"And more to the west?"

"Aye."

"Then that means a minimum of nine hundred men and probably more. If we add the clan MacDougall then they will, in all likelihood, outnumber us."

I smiled, "Yes but we have a better idea of where they will come. From what Calum told me…" Alan Durward frowned. "He is an Irish mercenary who fought for the other side. I sent him scouting when first we arrived."

"Ah."

"He said that the only large, flat area was at the southern end of Loch Awe. There is a ford there and it is just a few miles from the sea. If we took the army there and used scouts, we might be able to hold them. If not, then we could fall back to Innis Chonnell."

All eyes were on Lord Dunbar for he was, despite Alan Durward's title, the leader of King Alexander's men. He nodded, "Had they landed north of here we would have had a dilemma. This way we know where they will begin and we can stop them before they reach us. Lord Hostarius, begin your men to march to the south. Sir James would you ask Sir Cailean Mór to take his men to the southern end of the loch? His hatred for the MacDougalls means that he will take every man that he can, and he should know the land better than most."

I went to tell my men. Sir Petr was keen to join us, but I was reluctant. Sven and Folki had improved their linguistic skills but I was still unsure about the young man and his health. It was Sven who persuaded me. "Give Sir Petr a chance. I cannot go but I can stay here and watch your spare horses as well as the ransom which was not needed." He smiled, "It will give me a purpose again! I beg you to do it for his father."

I nodded, "I will do it for you, Sven, for you have shown that you are the most loyal of men."

We did not travel with the men of Inverness and Lochaber. We rode at our own pace for I was anxious to see the battlefield as soon as possible. Our rapid departure meant that I did not get to speak to King Alexander before the battle. His words on the ship had upset me. It was not that I thought he was dying but because I realised that my father was much closer to death and I had not yet said all to him that I needed to. Our family kept such things hidden and I knew that my father regretted not saying more to my namesake, his own father. I would remedy that.

Folki helped the Swedish knight immeasurably for he had ridden to war with us and knew how we fought. I heard him speaking quietly in Swedish whenever Sir Petr looked as though he would let his old arrogance rise to the surface. It was the informal relationship between my men and me which caused him problems. That made me wonder about the training his father had used with his son. Having spoken to others I knew that Sir Petr had skills, but they did not appear to include social ones. Perhaps the lack of a mother contributed.

Our journey was relatively quick for it was a mere sixteen miles down a road which appeared better than most of the ones we had used. We were met by some of the scouts sent ahead by Lord Dunbar. They pointed to the south-west. "We have left two men on the road from Kilmartin. When the enemy warriors come, we will know."

Leaving most of my men to make a camp before the arrival of the rest of the army I rode with Calum and Thomas to choose the best battleground. The one advantage in arms which we held would be the knights and the mounted men at arms. The clansmen and the army of Alan Durward could use their shields and spears to make a human wall which would hold the enemy, but it would be the one hundred and thirty heavy horsemen who had the best chance of breaking an enemy attack. I had taken long spears from Dunolie Castle in case Lord Dunbar heeded my advice and the plan which was forming in my mind. The further west we went the boggier became the land and beyond it high ground. To the east lay the river and north of that the loch. If we chose this place it meant we would have just half a mile to defend. I took my two companions down to the river. At one point it was less than eight paces wide, however, when we entered it with our horses the river came up to our stirrups.

Calum grinned, "A Viking in a mail shirt would struggle to get through this water, my lord."

"And that was what I was thinking. Come let us cross it and ride east. I have an idea forming."

As we headed east the ground rose and less than forty paces from the river was a wood. The wood was relatively open at the edges. We entered with swords drawn for this was MacDougall land. We climbed for a hundred or so paces and then emerged above a small loch. I turned back and could see the river, our camp, and the hamlet of Kilmartin.

I spoke but I was merely voicing my thoughts. "If we had most of the knights in these woods then they would be hidden from view. We would need to have Lord Dunbar and King Alexander's knights with their banners to maintain the illusion that our mounted arm was still at the fore. Thomas, you could wear armour and have one of the others hold my banner. When the enemy warriors were committed, we could charge. The river is not an obstacle to us and would merely slow us up but as it is so narrow that would not hurt."

It was the mercenary who saw the flaw, "But how would your lordship know when to attack? If you were close enough to see, then you too would be seen, and you might have to charge into a forest of spears!"

"A horn?" We both turned to Thomas. "You use a horn with a unique signal. As soon as the enemy commits to an assault the horn is blown and you fall upon the flanks."

Calum nodded, "And if you had a second signal then the other horsemen could attack once the enemy had begun to turn to face you. That might work, Sir William."

"Indeed but I have to persuade the others first."

As we left the wood, I took out my sword and marked two trees with large crosses. This would be the place we sought for our attack.

In the end, it was easy. The knights and horsemen arrived just as darkness fell and while squires tended to their horses and the three lords who led the army sat and ate the food prepared by my men, I explained my plan. The deer they had killed might have been Campbell or MacDougall but as there was no one yet to ask we ate well. When I had finished outlining my strategy I waited for questions. There was only one and that was from Alan Durward. "And you would lead these men, even though you are not a Scot?"

I smiled for his question carried no offence with it and Lord Patrick had already said it was a sound plan. "I would for of all of us I believe I have the greatest experience in leading such charges."

"Aye, you are right. I would like to be with you. The MacDougalls and the Norse will not know of my presence and it would be easy enough to have another carry my banner."

Sir James counselled, "Remember we had one spy and there may be another. How do we deal with that?"

"We tell no one. We have the men in two blocks and once we know the enemy are heading up the road, we cross the river, further north so that we do not leave clear tracks and then no one else is allowed to leave. Any who try will be the spy."

Lord Dunbar nodded, "I am content. We give the bare bones to Sir Cailean when he arrives. Lord Hostarius you will tell your mounted men that you are the left flank of the army. Now, all depends on when the enemy attacks."

I nodded towards Calum who was laughing with my men, "Calum fought with the enemy before. He says that it takes time for a Viking army to disembark and having seen the size of the quay I can believe it. I believe it will be the day after tomorrow before they will arrive. It is eight miles or so from their castle and they will be on foot. The scouts should give us at least an hour of warning."

We were prepared. Sir Cailean brought the bulk of his men to us just after dark and the rest, marching from Oban, were still arriving at midnight. From the clucks we heard, they had pillaged some farms on the way down. This was not a well-regulated army and I took note.

We told Sir Cailean about our plan. He did not have the wit to question why we would leave our greatest threat idly on the flanks. I think he took it to be a sort of cowardice or reluctance to fight, as he said, contemptuously, "We need no pretty boys in armour to fight for our land and king! Just so long as my boys and I are in the middle so that when that bastard MacDougall comes, he will know where I am. The day we meet in battle will be the day he dies."

I was not so sure. The man I had met at his castle looked to be younger and wore better armour than this most unpleasant of men. I had neither seen nor heard anything that suggested Cailean Mór was a great warrior.

It was just after the sun had reached its zenith the next day when the scouts rode in. "The enemy comes and there are more than fifteen hundreds of them."

Lord Dunbar nodded and his lieutenants began to give out their orders. The men were camped at their battle lines and all that was needed was for them to move back ten or so paces so that the enemy would have to pass through the ground upon which they had defecated and made water. Already water and urine were being used to douse the fires making them a blackened and muddy morass. "You know your places. We do this for King Alexander and Scotland!"

I went to my horse which was held by Thomas. In his hand, he held the horn which would signal the attack, "Today you will come of age, Thomas. Trust to my men for they will defend you and my standard to the death!" They all nodded as they heard my words. Unusually our four archers would stand behind Thomas, Folki and my four men at arms. When the battle became too close for arrows then they would draw their swords and fight as Thomas' defenders. We exchanged no words for they were my men.

I mounted Destiny and, with Sir Petr on one side and Sir Alan on the other, Folki handed me my spear and gave a lance to Sir Petr. He nodded and headed back to Thomas. When all were mounted, we rode north. There we crossed a shallow ford close to the end of the river and then headed northeast to the woods. Once we entered them then we disappeared as did the battlefield. All now depended upon Thomas and his judgement. I found the marked trees and took the line of men into the woods. We dismounted and took off our helmets. I knew that the enemy would not be in position for a while and when they were, we would hear them. Even so, it was hard to wait and the noise of men making water was a clear sign that others were nervous. The horses grazed and we waited in silence.

The Viking horn was the sound which told us that the enemy approached, and we mounted. We could hear a noise, but the trees and the undergrowth hid both sides from us. When we heard the clash of steel I wondered if something had happened to Thomas. I began to walk Destiny down the slope and the others moved too. Then we heard the five strident notes, and I knew that Thomas had not let me down. I spurred Destiny, not to make her charge, but to get her moving. When we emerged it was like going from the dark into bright sunshine. The two battle lines ahead of us were interlocked, and we were just behind their main lines. I spurred Destiny who opened his legs and we galloped towards the Norse who occupied the right flank. It was as we splashed into the river that we were spotted, and men shouted the alarm. As we clambered up the bank, I pulled up my shield and couched my spear. More than half of the men I led would be behind the Norse and MacDougall line. The enemy lines were less than eighty paces from us. We would not hit them at full speed, but we would be together. I could feel Petr's boot on one side and Sir Alan's on the other.

The Norse were trying to turn but they would not be able to form a solid line in time and I pulled back my arm when we were ten paces away and then slammed it forward so that the Norse warrior who I struck had no chance to defend himself. Even had I hit his shield he would have been knocked from his feet and crushed by my horse's hooves. God guided my hand for I hit him in the mouth. He was dead before his body pulled the spear from his skull. The next Norse to die wore mail for he was in the second rank, but his back was to me and the metal head drove through his mail and into his back.

I saw a Viking chief with a good helmet and a large war axe. He was exhorting his men to go forward. They were attempting to form a wedge and I knew, from experience, that such a formation could hurt us. I knew that they were less than forty paces from Thomas and my standard. We needed to stop them before they could form it. The Norse were so busy trying to get into their allotted position that the first three were slain by us before they even knew of our presence. The chief, whose shield had a red skull upon it, did not know that we were there but something made him turn and he saw us. Luckily for me, he turned to his right and I was able to lean from Destiny's back and lunge with my sword. His axe was swinging around but my blade entered his throat

73

and the speed of my horse drove it into the back of his head and the axe fell from his lifeless hand before it even came close to my chaussee. I wheeled Destiny to the left and clattered my sword, as I passed, into the back of another Norse helmet. We had broken the wedge and even if they reformed, their most potent weapons, the chief and his hearth weru lay dead. We had to get through as many of the enemy as we could.

Sir Petr appeared to be a good rider for he had not enjoyed many opportunities to learn the ways of the courser we had taken from Dunolie, yet he rode well. His lance was shattered, and so he laid about him with his sword. My spear lasted just one more warrior and this was a MacDougall. As my spearhead entered his side the huge warrior turned and hacked into the wooden shaft. It cost him his life for a Campbell took his head. I hurled the stump into the lines of men ahead of me and drew my sword. We had driven deep into the enemy flank and I saw my standard fluttering to my right. The arrows of my archers soared above the lines to plunge into men who did not see their death approaching. Ahead of me, I saw the standards of Galloway and Dunbar as the rest of our horsemen sliced deeply into the Vikings on the two flanks. The two Scottish standards, the MacDougalls and the Campbells were engaged in the centre and there, I knew that it would be the bloodiest.

Then I spied a livery I recognised. It was a blue shield with three white harts for I had seen the knight fleeing at Callander. I rode towards him and he, spying me, responded by spurring his horse. We were now in a loose line and, ideally, we needed to reform so that we could ride towards Lord Dunbar and close the mouth of this metal net. The knight was an obstacle and I charged him. He rode at my sword side. He too had a sword. Our speeding horses meant that one mistake could be fatal. I would rely on all the experience gathered over the years I had been fighting. I held my sword behind me and invited the first blow. I held my shield horizontally above the cantle. He saw the way I approached, and he raised his sword so that he could swing it across me and my chest. It is hard to understand the skill involved in riding a courser at full tilt towards an enemy. The ground was not perfectly flat, and Destiny rose and fell. The knight was also jinking his reins from left to right as he sought to confuse me. I focussed my attention on his face for he wore an open sallet. We were ten paces apart as our two horses neared each other. I used my reins to pull Destiny further to the left and that also brought my shield closer to my right. As he swung his sword down, I started to bring up mine. I had my shield to protect me from his sword, but my sword would, I hoped, strike his arm. I flocked up my arm and his sword struck my shield, slid down and embedded itself in the wooden cantle. My sword swept up and into his arm, just above the elbow. The blade was still sharp, and it tore through the mail and tunic before grating off the bone. He screamed as he passed. The sword remained in my cantle and he slid from his saddle, blood pumping from the wound. I did not see but I heard the crack and crunch as he was trampled by one of the knights who was following me.

The fight had taken us across the battlefield. We needed to join Lord Dunbar and so, raising my sword, I shouted, "Wheel!" I was helped in that I was leading and when I turned Destiny both Petr and Alan Durward were able to mirror my actions. Now we were charging the right of the MacDougall clansmen. They had long spears which, had we been attacking from their fore, would have held us at bay, but they were not and as they tried to turn their clumsily long weapons our swords, lances and spears found flesh, for none of these wore mail of any description. Very few even possessed a helmet and my sword first found wood and then flesh. As the brave clansmen fell they were trampled by our warhorses. They did not break as I would have expected. These were men fighting for their chief and their clan. Hitherto the Scots I had fought were intent of rampaging through my homeland and pillaging. That day north of Kilmartin, I saw how real Scots fought and died. Our progress to join up our two bands of horsemen was slower than I had hoped. After slaying five men my blade was becoming blunted and sheathing it I took the sword embedded in my cantle. It was not as well balanced as mine and one side was blunter than the other but I used the sharp side to hack through the neck of a clansman. We achieved much but not without paying a price. My legs, side and arms were all struck by spears and swords. Had any used an axe then the injuries they caused might have been serious but when this was over I would only need cuts and bruises healing rather than flesh stitched.

The ones who did break were the Vikings. They had borne the brunt of the attack of our horses and now the men from the north who had been on our flanks hacked into them and they turned and fled. I had just slain another MacDougall and was just forty paces from Lord Dunbar when he raised his sword and pointed south, "Drive the Vikings into the sea!" It was a command which made sense but not one I would have given. The threat of the MacDougalls might have been ended had we butchered them on that bloody field but I suppose eliminating the threat from the west was as good a result. I wheeled Destiny and the two lines of horsemen joined to make one and we began the chase to the sea.

I know that there had been a time when the Norse warriors were seen as a mighty threat but they had outlived their time. One of my ancestors had been at Stamford Bridge when Hardrada had died. That had been the moment when they ceased to be feared. The men who had defeated them there had moved on and now rode horses and used better weapons. The Vikings who wore mail still wore the same byrnies and used the same swords as they had almost two hundred years earlier. As I sliced down to rip open the back of a leather-clad Viking, I reflected that the sword I used was lighter, stronger, and longer than the ones used by the Norse. The fuller down the blade made it so. It was Petr who was enjoying his moment. He had been betrayed by his employers and his squire abused. This was his chance for vengeance and to show us what he could do. The young Swede showed no mercy. While I took no pleasure in slaying men who could not defend themselves Sir Petr cared not, and he used his young body to lean first from the right and then from the left as his sword smashed into backs and heads breaking bone and metal.

It soon became clear to me that some Norse warriors had left the battle before we began the pursuit for, as we reached Duntrune Castle, we saw some longships heading along the coast. These seafarers must have realised that they could not take their whole army off from the single quay and were using the coastline's full extent to extricate their men. To respond we had to spread out. I led some of Alan Durward's men at arms further east. We were no longer a long line. Instead, we were split into small conroi. I led Sir Petr and fourteen men at arms. We passed helmets, shields, and spears which had been discarded for speed. The Norse were like mountain goats as they used every trick that they could to avoid us. They could clamber up rocks and between shrubs and trees. A warhorse is valuable and the warriors we chased were not worth the damage. We struck fewer Norse but everyone we killed was one less to return and raid this land. I wondered, as one unlucky Viking turned the wrong way and my sword hacked into his shoulder, if the Norwegian King would give up on his ambitions to take even more of this land for his Kingdom of the Isles.

Destiny, like the other horses, was wearying and the pursuit became a fast walk. Some of the men at arms I led had been forced to pull up and there were just eight of us who reached the rocky shelf on the northern shore of Loch Crinan. One of their longships was just twenty paces from the rocks which might have torn out her hull. The Norse discarded their byrnies and hurled themselves into the sea. We were impotent to stop them and when archers on the ships sent their arrows to shore, I ordered the handful of men I led out of range. The war arrows they used could do little harm to us, but our horses were another matter. We made a line of horsemen and prevented other Norse from escaping this way. We slew but one or two more for those who were still fleeing saw us on our horses and chose another route. Had we had twice the number of horsemen then barely eight or nine crews would have escaped. When the men of Inverness drew close to us then I knew we had won the battle. The brief rest and the grazing they had enjoyed, not to mention the water from the small stream which emptied into Loch Crinan meant our horses could ride the short way to Duntrune Castle. To my dismay, I saw the standard of the MacDougall's still flying. The gates were barred, and the walls were manned. Sir Cailean and his clansmen were gathered before the gate but beyond crossbow range.

I dismounted, took off my helmet and walked towards him. He had been wounded and it looked to me as though he needed a healer. For once he was smiling and his hatred of the MacDougalls had made him forget, for the moment, his hatred of me. "We almost had the bastard, but the coward made his way back here to hide in his nest of vipers!"

"Sir Cailean, you need a healer!"

"Aye, well first we make sure his bolt holes are barred and then we surround him!" He pointed with his sword which showed the effects of the battle, it was bloody and notched, "I have men burning his quay! They will not use that again!"

Just then Lord Dunbar rode up. He too had taken off his helmet and, like me, lowered his coif, "Your plan worked, Sir William."

I nodded, "Aye, and now what?"

"You and I are done here. Sir Alan and Sir Cailean can accept the surrender of MacDougall. We are the knights of King Alexander and must return to his side to give him news of his great victory. You, Sir William, have fulfilled your promise and more. You and your men can take your share of the spoils of war and head home."

I nodded, "The animals will need a day of rest, but I thank you." I turned to Sir Petr, "Come, sir, we will see if our men fared as well as we." To be honest I was fearful for I had asked much of Thomas and although I trusted my men the press of Norsemen had been so great that I feared some would have suffered an injury.

Sir Petr and I passed dead warriors, but we did not stop to strip them of their treasure. I almost shouted with joy when I saw my men searching the mountain of bodies which lay on the battlefield. As most of the clansmen had followed Sir Cailean and the men of Inverness had pursued the enemy there were just my men and those of Lochaber who enjoyed the bounty of war. Thomas and Folki looked up as our horses approached. Their surcoats were bloody, and they looked more like men who work at an abattoir than squires but their smiles suggested that they were whole.

"Are any of our men hurt, Thomas?"

"Tom and Alan needed the healer, and they will struggle to walk for a while, lord, but they are whole. Is it over?"

"It is for us. We will camp here and on the morrow return to Oban. Lord Dunbar will be heading there directly. It was a great victory. Thomas, take your horse and you and Folki can find the body of the knight with the blue shield and three white harts. I slew him. He had mail!" They both ran for their horses, eager to see what else they could take from the battlefield. Leaving our men to harvest the dead we walked our horses back to the camp. We would not be the ones, but someone would have to burn the dead. If they did not, then there would soon be a plague of rats upon the land. The land would be scarred not only with the black of bone fires but also with the blood which lay pooled, a testament to the ferocity of clan warfare. We washed in the river and took off our surcoats to let the water soak away the worst of the blood. When they eventually returned Thomas and Folki took our mail and theirs. Placing them in hessian sacks with loch sand they cleaned them. It was a relief to be without the weight and the stink of blood. I revived the fires and put on a pot of water. My men returned and they were laden. Even Alan Longsword was pleased with the loot they had taken. Had any of my men died it might have been a different story, but the victory, weapons, mail and the purses made it one to savour. We still had venison and so we ate as the rest of the army slowly returned to our camp.

As we ate my men told me their stories. It became clear that Thomas had not panicked and judged the moment for the horn to perfection. Alan said, "Lord, it is as though Master Thomas was born to it. You can see that the blood of the Warlord is in his veins."

Calum nodded, "Sure and the Norse were brave but your archers, Sir William, were a wonder. The four of them disrupted the enemy so that by the time they reached us they were easy to defeat."

Alan said, "But now we go home, eh Sir William?"

I nodded, "We go home!"

Chapter 7

King Alexander's Last Battle

We had to pick up our spare horses and Sven before we could leave for home and it took some time to make the journey to Dunolie Castle. The roads were filled with the men Alan Durward had brought from the north. Their work was done and they, like my men, were laden with the booty they had taken.

"We will stay the night for we will need to pack the horses well."

However, as we approached the town and the castle, we could see that something was amiss. The guards at the gate were vigilant. They allowed my men and me through, but the men of Lochaber were barred.

"What is wrong, sentry?"

"I know not Sir William, but the Mormaer of Dunbar said only you and your men were allowed in."

We went to the warrior hall and I was pleased to see that Sven had improved even more in the short time we had been away. I left the rest of my men to tell Sven all and hurried up to the Great Hall where I met Sir James Galloway, "What is the matter, my lord? We have won a great victory but the faces I see suggest a defeat."

"King Alexander is dying. The priests have heard his last confession. I go to seek Sir Alan for we need the Justiciar of Scotia now!"

This was a disaster. We had been on the cusp of ending the threat from the Norse and now the Scots had the unenviable prospect of a king in his minority. All those with a vague claim to the throne, like the Balliol family and the Comyn's, not to mention the de Brus' would now begin to plot and plan. They would seek a weakness which might bring them the Scottish crown. I wondered if Sir Alain de Balliol had heard the news. He had not struck me as a plotter but I did not know the man well.

I hurried, after Sir James had left me, to the chamber of King Alexander. The guard admitted me, and I saw Lord Dunbar kneeling by the bed with the priests and praying. I knelt and joined them in silent prayer. King Alexander had been good to me and I doubt that I would have been able to save Sir Petr without his help. It was as I prayed that I remembered there was now another debt of honour to be paid. I had promised the king that I would do all that I could to protect his son, the next King of Scotland.

When Lord Dunbar stood, so did I. He shook his head, "Perhaps Scotland is cursed. Young Alexander is just seven years old and we are beset by enemies." He lowered his voice, "Your father is close to King Henry. Your king would not seek to take advantage, would he?"

I shrugged, "You know kings, my lord, but as King Henry's daughter Margaret is engaged to be married to Alexander then I would hope not." I did not know but I knew that I now had an impossible task ahead of me. One oath bound me to the next King of Scotland, but I owed fealty to King Henry. I was getting ahead of myself for the king was not yet dead.

It was afternoon when Sir Alan and Sir James returned. The king had yet to recover consciousness, but he was alive and while he lived there was hope. It was just before midnight when he breathed his last and the doctor pronounced him dead. He died not knowing that we had won. His death rendered the victory almost meaningless for it gave the Norwegian king time to build up his army once more and Ewen MacDougall still lived. While the body was prepared for a journey east, I went with the Scottish leaders. There was food prepared in the Great Hall, but none felt like eating.

Lord Hostarius was now the effective commander of the Scottish army until a regency could be established and he spoke, "I will take my household knights and ride to Jedburgh where I will apprise the future King and his mother, the Queen, of the situation. I shall take them to Melrose Abbey."

Lord Dunbar nodded, "And we will escort the body to Melrose."

Sir James looked at me, "This is not a command, Sir William, but it might be for the best if you came with us to Melrose and thence back to England. Your journey would be slower but also safer."

"Safer?"

"You have made enemies here. The Campbells, the MacDougalls, not to mention the Norse. Not all took a ship and there are bands of them will need to be scoured."

Sir Patrick said, "And I believe King Alexander would have wanted it."

"It would be an honour to escort his body home." I looked around. We were alone in the dimly lit hall and the guards on the doors ensured privacy. "My lords, whence lies the danger to the new king? I swore an oath to the king that I would do all that I could to ensure his son was crowned king, yet I live in England."

Sir Alan smiled, "And a good choice was made by the king. The Comyn family is close to the Queen and seek to control the course of Scottish politics but Walter still aspires for power and of course, Lord

John Balliol, who lives in England has a claim to the throne on the female side. The de Brus faction also has a claim through the female line. Had we taken King Hákon or killed him then things might have been different, but we will need to keep warriors in the west and there will be many who seek to gain power from this tragedy. I will take young Alexander under my wing. It is my appointed duty, but I will need you two to support me."

Sir James said, "Scotland cannot afford a civil war."

"Then the way to avoid it is to be strong. Sir William, you will need to tell King Henry how the king died. There will be rumour and gossip. Better that he hears the truth from you. I know this keeps you from your family…"

I waved a hand, "My family, better than most, understand their responsibilities. I will deliver the news although he will, no doubt, have heard it already."

Sir Alan managed just an hour of sleep before he hurried, with his knights, east. We followed the following day. It was a sombre procession, and his coffin was laid, each night in the church of the town we passed through. Armed knights surrounded it and three days later we arrived at Melrose Abbey. My men and I would not be staying but I was summoned to the presence of the new king. I knelt before him. I could feel his mother's eyes glowering at me. She did not like my family.

"Sir William, I understand, from the Lord Hostarius that we are indebted to you for your courage and tactics at the Battle of Kilmartin. Know that I am grateful and had my father lived to hear of it then you would have been rewarded. When time allows, I will reward you."

"Your father asked me to ensure that you were safe until you attained your majority. Know that I am ready to do so and protect you from enemies, foreign and domestic. If ever you need me, King Alexander, then send a message to me. I shall keep my word."

The Queen said, her voice icy, "There are enough loyal Scotsmen for that!"

King Alexander was a boy, but he had been brought up to be a king and, in his voice, I heard steel. This was not a piece of clay to be moulded by others, "Mother, a wise king spurns no offer of help. Thank you, Sir William, I shall bear that in mind, and I would have you present at my wedding in two years' time."

"I would be honoured."

My men and I headed south and although we were vigilant, we encountered no danger. I think we had left our enemies in the west. We reached Hartlepool safely. Mary was understandably upset when she heard the news. The two people who had made possible our marriage were now dead. That night, as she lay in my arms she wept. I had seen no tears from Queen Marie, now the Queen Mother, but my wife mourned the death. I suppose that was always the way it was, '*The King is dead! Long live the King!*' Almost as soon as he died a king was consigned to posterity regardless of how he had lived. In some cases, King John came to mind, when a king died then his death was greeted with celebration. There would be those who would mourn the passing of Alexander but far too many would be looking at how they could benefit from his death. We spent one night in my hall, but it would be a brief halt for I had to get to my father and then King Henry. This was the valley and so I left my men at my hall and went with Sir Petr, Thomas, and the men who I had taken from my father. Sir Geoffrey also came with me. Of the men I had taken to Scotland only Calum came with us. On the way home, he had told me that he felt he had not done that for which he was hired, "You never needed my tongue, my lord. If you wish to let me go then I would understand."

I told him that he had shown that he was the type of warrior I wanted and if he wished to serve me then I was happy. It was reassuring to have him riding behind Thomas. Whatever happened on the road, my nephew would have a protector.

I needed an escort to Stockton if only because I had four hundred marks to return to my father. I had not asked where it had been kept but I suspected in some religious house or perhaps in York. My family had close connections with that city. We reached the castle before noon and a rider sent the previous night warned my father and particularly my mother that guests were coming. Sir Petr was a connection to the place my mother and father had met when he had rescued her from barbarians. The debt of honour had been paid and now the old connections could be renewed. We dismounted in the outer bailey. Thomas showed Folki where to stable the horses. Sven looked a little lost. What was his place in this new world?

"Erik, see to Sven. Take him and Calum to the warrior hall and see that they are made welcome."

"Aye, lord, and the others will wish to hear the tale." He hesitated, "Will you be travelling on?"

I nodded, "But you have done your part. I will take others with me."

"I am happy to serve, Sir William."

"I know but Sven and Folki will be staying here. Your familiar face and voice will help them become part of the castle."

When he saw me my father clasped my arm and said, "I am pleased you all returned whole and saddened by the news you bring. I fear it

82

may not bode well for us." I noticed that he looked grey and even thinner than he had when I had left.

I nodded and waved my arm, "Sir Petr Birgersson."

My father held his arm out and then began to speak in Swedish. He gestured to my mother who also spoke to Sir Petr. The Swede took my mother's hand and kissed it. It was the right thing to do and she beamed. "Come," she said, "I have rooms for you, and we shall feast this night although it will just be a small affair." As my father led Sir Petr into the hall, I hugged my mother and kissed her cheek, "And welcome to you, my son. My prayers were answered, and you returned to us in one piece. Your story will be an interesting one." She took my arm and led me in, "I have asked Henry Samuel and Eirwen to join us for your father wishes to make an announcement."

I nodded, "He plans on giving Elton to my nephew!" Since Sir Geoffrey FitzUrse and my cousin Rebekah had been given the manor of Thornaby by King Henry there had been no lord there. It was a small manor but, along with Hartburn, the closest to Stockton.

She laughed, "Are you a witch?"

"The manor has no lord and Henry Samuel is ready. My father will miss him around the castle, but he always thinks of others and besides, he will have Sir Petr to mould and shape."

My mother was astute, "And he needs such work?"

"I will not speak ill of the dead, but I fear his father did not do as good a job on him as my father did with us. He has changed in the time we have been with him, but he needs to learn a little more humility and to learn to respect those who fight with him. He is redeemable!"

I had my usual room which was high in the north tower. It was not a large chamber, but it suited me, and I had enjoyed it since my brother Alfred had been alive. I never wanted another room for I feared that it would bring bad luck! There was a chest with clean clothes and a large jug of water. I dressed and headed down to the Great Hall where I found Sir Petr with my father and Henry Samuel.

"Well Sir Henry, how is married life?"

He blushed and then laughed, "I am still learning. Women were a mystery to me!"

My father lowered his voice and said, "That will not change with age but do not let you grandmother hear that!"

I was aware that although Sir Petr had improved his language skills there were still many words he did not understand.

My nephew said, "Did I hear that you are to visit with King Henry?" I nodded, "The last I heard he had returned from Wales and was at Windsor."

"Where do you get all your information, nephew? Here you are out of the main current and yet you know such things."

He smiled, "I write to Sir Gerard for he is able to watch Eirwen's family. He mentioned in passing that King Henry had left Wales for his son, Edward, was ill once more."

"He is a sickly child."

My father said, "And yet when I have seen him, he appeared in robust health! It may be a thing of childhood. Wait until he is a man grown before you judge his health, William."

I was aware that Sir Petr was excluded from this talk and I said, "My father drops pearls of wisdom like that all the time!"

The serious Swede said, "I am just grateful that he has offered me a home."

My father nodded, "I have told him, William, that he shall be one of my household knights. It may well be that he chooses to wander and hire out his sword, but I said that he will not want for action here and now that King Alexander is dead then I fear the border will once more ignite with unrest. Your visit to King Henry is important to us. I know that his eyes are on Ireland and Gascony but we do not want a Scottish ulcer again! The last time it was you and Henry Samuel who held the breach. I would like others to shoulder the burden this time."

Folki and Thomas waited with the wine, ready to serve us. Folki, like his master, was being given an education. It was good that Henry Samuel was there for he was able to tell the Swede about our life in the valley. My father and I just chipped in as and when it was relevant. My mother came in during the afternoon and flapped her arms at us as though we were a flock of geese, "Go hence! We need to set the table. Walk outside or go to your solar! I care not!"

My father smiled, patiently, "Come, Sir Petr, we shall give you a tour of the castle and then the town."

I believe that the time he was disinherited were the saddest days of my father's life and he was proud of what he had achieved in the town since then. He had made it important and he planned on seeking a market charter from King Henry. After we had walked the walls, we left the castle by the town gate and entered the cobbled streets of the small walled town. Scottish raids had ensured that we built good walls and had deep ditches. The townsfolk all made a fuss of my father and it was like a royal procession as, despite his protestations, all bowed and doffed their caps as he passed. Many lords demanded it but not Sir Thomas of Stockton.

"We had better get back and prepare for this feast, Lady Margaret will want all done just so."

Sir Petr had said little as we had wandered through the small town but, as we approached the gates he said, "Sir Thomas when you left my father, what did you have?"

"Little hope of peace but a small manor in France. My aunt left me a house here and all that you see we have built since then."

We walked through the gate. The walls were nine feet thick and would take siege engines to reduce them. "My father had more and yet, when he died, he was almost a pauper. The manor house was made of wood and was falling down and the land had to be sold to pay off his debts. You began with less but now you have so much that you could afford to pay a small fortune for my ransom. How can that be?"

It took him until we were approaching our chambers to say all that he wanted to say. He stumbled over words and my father had to give him the right one. Had he spoken in Swedish it would not have taken long but Sir Petr was anxious to be part of this family and I liked that.

My father nodded, "I cannot give you an answer which would make sense. Better to say that some things are determined by a higher power and leave it at that. You live your life as best that you can and hope to leave a mark on this world so that people remember you." He smiled, "And now, prepare for the meal! You and my son will provide the entertainment this night. Neither jester nor troubadour will detract from your tales!" My father said it with a twinkle in his eye. Petr would not be made to suffer.

Mary would have been more than interested in my tale for it involved her homeland, but she was in Hartlepool and I was glad to spare her the description of the slaughter. I tried to lessen the numbers and the deaths for the sake of Eirwen. My mother knew such things already. For my father, it was a reminder of the world he had known. I prayed that his last days would be peaceful. I could not help but speak, at some length, of the enmity which Sir Cailean bore us.

Henry Samuel had been at Elsdon and he shook his head, "A man makes his own decisions uncle. This lord's brother chose to come east and attack Elsdon! A man lives with the decisions he makes. They attacked you, Uncle!"

My father shook his head, "And that is why, grandson, even though we are at peace, we are still vigilant when strangers come. Who knows what malice lies behind smiles? Until we know a man then we are wary."

I saw Sir Geoffrey looking a little uncomfortable for he had just hired strangers. My wife had said that the men appeared to be what they said but as with Calum, until Sir Geoffrey had fought alongside them, he would not know their true character.

When I had finished and Sir Petr had ended his tale my father asked, "And when do you leave for Windsor?"

"I must leave on the morrow. I will travel light with just Calum and Thomas. As Sir Alan said, there will be rumour surrounding the death of King Alexander and coming after such a battle then conjecture may conjure plots which are not there."

My mother asked, "Will that be enough?"

I nodded, "My enemies lie in the north and I think that the plots and intrigues of the Scottish crown will outweigh any thoughts of murder. I have brought Lion and he is fresh and eager as well as four spare horses. Calum and Thomas have shown themselves to be more than capable and I shall stay on the main roads. We will ride hard: York, Nottingham, Northampton and then Windsor. It means riding sixty miles a day but with the changes of horses it should be possible, and speed will outrun any malicious attempt to stop us."

"I could come with you."

I smiled, "Henry Samuel, that is kind, but I would not take you away from your bride." I looked at my father.

"Your uncle is right, Henry Samuel, and besides, you will have much to occupy you for you are to be the new lord of Elton." He looked stunned although he must have expected something like it. "It is a small manor but, as your uncle discovered at Elsdon, a small one is often the best way to learn how to be the lord of the manor."

Out of the corner of my eye, I spied Thomas who suddenly saw his own future. He would become a knight one day and would either be lord of Redmarshal or somewhere else. He was now following the same path as Henry Samuel. The conversation buzzed and I begged leave to retire for I needed an early start. "Thomas, I have done with you for the night if you wish to remain."

"Thank, you, my lord." He looked eager to talk to his cousin and Sir Petr.

My father rose and put his arm through mine, "I will walk you to the stairs." He wished to speak. Once we were in the sconce lit corridor he said, "There will still be a danger for our family has made many enemies. I will write letters before I retire this night. Give one to the Sherriff. He will give you an escort from York and I will have some of my men ride with you to York." He held up his hand for he saw that I was going to object. "They will be archers and will not hinder you. You are right in that you should outrun the carrion crows from the north, but you did not make a swift journey home. There is a chance that some may be south of the river. When you reach Lincoln then you should be safe. I will also have a letter to King Henry. I was of some use to him in the past and he may well heed my advice. We shall see."

"Very well but I think it unnecessary."

He nodded, "And there will be a chest of marks for you. I did not need the ransom and it was you who saved it. Take a hundred marks. I am sure that Mary can use it."

"We have money enough."

He laughed, "I thought that until I went to the crusades and Prince John and the Bishop of Durham took it. There is no such thing as enough money for you never know what the future holds. I may be up to see you off, but I will say God speed now." He hugged me and I was aware that he was old. Each time he said farewell he did not know if he would see me again. I hugged him back and I could feel the bones beneath his tunic.

Chapter 8

The Blood Oath

It was Gruffyd son of Tomas and Mordaf son of Tomas who led the dozen archers my father had sent to accompany us. They were as experienced a pair as could be found anywhere and were happy to ride with me. I felt almost redundant as, once we had crossed the ferry to the south side of the river, they took charge, and four archers were sent two hundred paces ahead of us while four more were given the spare horses and placed at the rear. Calum, Thomas, and I were safely secured in the centre. Calum was a little bemused, as we headed towards the road south. It would not be until we were more than thirty miles south of the river that we would pick up the road which went from Piercebridge to Northallerton, York and the south.

"An archer commands a lord?"

I smiled, "Welcome to the land of Cleveland, Calum, for we do things our way here. I have known these brothers since I was a squire like Thomas here. They have senses which I do not understand, and we are safe in their hands. If they wish to organise this column, then I am happy to accept their advice."

Mordaf, who rode just before us, said, without turning his head, "You see, Irishman, that our ferry acts as a defence for us. None pass across it without we know but the Great North Road is another matter. If there were enemies who wish to cause Sir William harm, then they would come down the Great North Road. They could be ahead of us and until we reach York's mighty walls then we will be like dogs which guard a farm. If we bark, then you will obey."

His brother said, "Aye, heed our commands and you will live longer!"

I felt Calum bristle, "I have done well enough thus far, Welshman!"

Calum had spent time in the warrior hall, and all knew his story. Gruffyd said, quietly, "But not so your shield brothers eh, Calum? You are the last of them." It was not meant cruelly, and it was true. Calum was silent.

The road led us down the edge of the escarpment of hills. We broke the journey just thirteen miles from the river at the Priory to the east of East Harlsey. We changed horses and enjoyed the hospitality of the brothers there. We did not waste time and would be able to make faster time with horses which had been watered. It was an hour after the sun had reached its zenith when we approached Easingwold. We had done the harder part of the journey, but the horses needed a brief rest. There was an inn there for we were thirteen miles from York, and it was convenient for merchants to make a halt there before heading north to Thirsk. The archers saw to the horses and we entered the inn to order ale for us all. The time of day meant that there were few people in the inn. Those who had stopped there we had already passed heading north and the ones heading south had yet to arrive for we had travelled quickly.

When Mordaf entered the inn his face showed concern. "Is there a problem Mordaf?" I wondered if one of the horses was hurt.

He sat next to me. "We spoke with the stable boy. He is a good fellow, and we know him well. He said that two days since some strangers passed through. They sounded foreign. He was not sure if they were Norse or Dane, but they had that look about them and they were heading south."

"They wore byrnies?"

"He could not tell. They rode ponies and there was baggage with them which may or may not have held mail. They had swords but that is not unusual. He took them for merchants but..."

"But?"

"From his description these were warriors. They dressed as merchants, but he said they had battle bands on their arms. That sounds like warriors to me."

"He volunteered this information?"

He looked at Calum, "No, Sir William, we were just doing our job and ensuring that there is no danger ahead."

My squire asked, "But if this was two days ago, they could be in York. If they were Danes or Norse would they not blend in there for there are many there with Norse blood?"

Mordaf nodded and smiled, "That is good thinking Master Thomas, but the Sherriff is a friend of Sir William's and when we reach the city, we will be safe and any who wished harm would stand little chance of evading capture."

"You are forgetting, Mordaf, that there are fifteen of us. Do you think any would risk taking on Sir Thomas' men unless they outnumbered us?"

"Sir William, if these men are innocent then they will have been in York for more than a day and the next thirteen miles will be easy. If, however, they met confederates then within the next seven miles or so there will be an attack."

"You know where?"

"South of Sudtune, lord. The Nevill family hunt there. Your father took us there once when Sir Ralph invited him. The road passes through the forest."

"I remember the place."

"We will be close to it in the late afternoon. This may be nothing and I may be behaving like an old woman." He smiled at Calum, "If that is so then I will pay for the ale in York. Your father asked me to take care of you and I will do so even at the risk of looking foolish. Joseph and James are the two best noses we have and they are already heading south. If there is a trap or an ambush then they will sniff it out and if not they will be at the Bootham Bar Gate before dark. When we have drunk this beaker of ale, my lord, we should leave!"

This time we donned our coifs and helmets. The archers strung their bows and hung them from their cantles. Calum, Thomas, and I eased our swords in and out of our scabbards so that they would come out easily if we needed them. Finally, we hung our shields so that they protected our left side. Of course, any potential ambusher would try to take us from our right but Gruffyd had thought of that and two archers rode to our right each with a nocked arrow.

Mordaf knew precisely where the forest began but I only had a dim memory. I had passed along this road on my way back from Wales, but I had been so anxious to get home that I had barely noticed anything. I saw the forest ahead and the road grew darker as it passed between trees with burgeoning new growth. As soon as we were enveloped, I looked around for the flash of flesh or metal in the trees. It was when I saw Joseph and John tending to their horses that I knew Mordaf was right. They were pretending that they had problems with their horses. They had cleverly placed themselves between the horses. I knew that they would be bantering as though they had not seen the ambushers. As much as those ambushing would wish to kill the two archers, they dared not for fear of alerting us. As we headed towards them they would hear our hooves on the cobbles of the Roman Road.

Gruffyd whistled. I did not turn but I knew that the two archers with the spare animals had dropped the reins and they would head from the road and race through the trees to outflank the ambushers. I said, "Thomas, be ready. The secret is to close with an attacker. Our horses are a weapon." I was not sure if Calum had ever fought from the back of a horse, but he struck me as a capable warrior who would adapt quickly. I rode with my left hand on the reins and my right hand on my cantle but touching the hilt of my sword. I did not know about the other two, but I could have my sword out in a flash.

We were just a hundred paces from them when Joseph cupped his hands and shouted, "My lord, my horse is lame, can you fetch one of the spares!"

My father's archers were all clever men. I raised my right hand to my mouth and shouted, "Aye, Joseph!" When I lowered it, I dug my heels into Destiny and reached for my sword. At the same time, all but the two archers riding at our right peeled off into the wood. Joseph and James raised their bows and as their horses galloped down the road the two archers loosed arrows at targets which we could not yet see. I saw James drop to one knee as an arrow struck his leg and arrows came towards us but by then I could see the Norse warriors who were racing from concealment. There looked to be at least fifteen men in sight and that meant we were outnumbered for there would be men we could not see.

The spear which was rammed at me came from my left and although I did not have my arm through my shield's brases the guige strap kept it to my left. The spear hit my shield a mighty blow and then Calum leaned from his saddle to strike a backhand blow into the neck of the Viking. I swung at the helmet of the second Norseman who held his shield close to his chest. My blade hacked into the nasal and drove it into his skull. The Norse attackers had to step from behind the trees to fight us and when they did, we had the advantage for the three of us each had a horse to barrel into them. Mordaf, Gruffyd and their archers were also using their bows to great effect. It was clear that these ambushers wanted the three of us for they ran at us as though their lives depended upon it. Lion was a true warhorse and he snapped and bit at anything which came close to his teeth. The Vikings were brave, but I doubted that they had met a warhorse as big as Lion before.

Four men hurled themselves at me with a flurry of spearheads, swords, and an axe. Thomas managed to bring his sword into the side of one Viking head and as the man had an axe then he had eliminated a real threat to me. Lion's snapping teeth sank into a spearman and my sword drove into the mouth of another. The last swordsman hacked at my right leg. Thomas' horse veered towards me and although the sword bit through the chaussee he was crushed between two huge horses. And then there was no one before me.

I reined in and shouted, "Stockton!"

I heard my men call the same battle cry one by one to show me they were still above ground. There were twelve responses. Then I heard another cry and Mordaf shouted, "That is the last of them, my lord!"

I looked around and saw that none of my men were hurt. "Gruffyd, find their ponies!" It was not that I wanted the ponies but that would tell me if any had escaped.

Thomas said, "Sir William, you are hurt!"

I nodded and dismounted, "Aye but thanks to your horse it is not as bad as it might have been. Help me to take off the chaussee and you can tend to it."

Calum dismounted and walked over to me with a shield. "I know whence they came, lord." He held up the shield. "I recognise this design." It was a shield with four small red skulls upon it. Thomas had taken off my metal legging and was washing the wound as Calum continued. "The battle, do you remember, lord, you slew their hersir when they were forming the wedge."

Thomas said, "Hersir?"

"Aye, Master Thomas, a chief. You might call them a lord. There are other markings like this one."

Just then my archers returned with ten ponies and a wounded warrior whose hands were bound behind his back, "Four others fled, my lord. Should we chase them?"

I shook my head, "This one will do, and we will tell the Sherriff when we reach York." I turned to Calum, "Question him and confirm that they were at Kilmartin."

Calum began to question the Viking who remained silent at first. Calum knelt next to him and whispered in his ear. The man answered. Calum stood, "These are the last of the clan whose hersir you slew, Sir William. That one," he pointed to the warrior who had been crushed by our horses, "was his brother. They swore an oath to follow the vengeance trail. The ones who escaped will come after you, Sir William. They are oathsworn." He bent down to lift the right hand of the man who had been crushed. He turned it over and there was a long, scabbed scar running down the palm.

I nodded, "Then when we reach York, we will ask Sir Ralph to send out hunters to apprehend them."

Calum nodded, "And this one?"

"We will take him with us."

Calum took out a seax, "Lord, let me give him a warrior's death. I promised him as much and that was why he spoke."

The Norseman's eyes pleaded with me and I nodded.

Calum put his sword into the Viking's hand. He would be able to hold the sword but not use it. Calum then said something in Norse as he slit his throat. He took the sword and put it back in its scabbard, "Thank you, lord."

Thomas had applied honey and bandaged my leg.

"Come we ride to York. Leave the bodies here but fetch the ponies and their weapons." The helmets were not the best and none, save the one who had been crushed, wore mail.

Mordaf said, "Gruffyd and Joseph will pick up their trail, Sir William. When we have safely delivered you, we will return and hunt them."

"The Sherriff can do that."

Mordaf shook his head, "Sir William, you were hurt, and it was our fault. We will redeem ourselves and when we return to your father, we will hold our heads high."

I knew that no matter what I said they would do this. It was their way.

Thomas and Calum flanked me. I was silent but Thomas was curious, "A blood oath?"

Calum said, "Just as your father sent Sir William because of a debt of honour so the Norse and Danes for that matter, will happily swear an oath using blood. They slice their palms and mix their blood over a bare piece of earth and then they cover the earth with turf. When they were not Christians then a witch would weave a spell and bury that too. These men have not fallen far from the pagan tree."

I smiled, "I wonder at you Calum for you seem to have some of the pagan in you!"

He grinned back, "We do not follow the Roman church, my lord. We are Irish and have a flexible attitude to such things."

We managed to reach York before dark and when Sir Ralph heard what had happened, he sent ten men at arms back with my archers. I nodded my thanks to my archers, "I thank you all and I will reward you on my return."

Mordaf grinned, "There is no need, my lord, for we serve Sir Thomas of Stockton. We need no blood oath to protect his family for they are ours too! May God watch over you." Taking the captured ponies they headed north, even James who had a wounded leg. My father's men were special, and I was lucky that they had escorted me.

Even if Sir Ralph had not received the letter from my father, he would have sent an escort with me. His healers sewed the wound to my leg, and it was bandaged. They gave Thomas a salve to quicken the healing.

When we ate, I told him of the death of the Scottish King. He nodded, "We heard rumours that the Clan MacDougall had him murdered. It is good to hear the truth but I fear that this will make the northern border unstable."

93

"And that is why I must get to King Henry as soon as possible. He needs to show King Alexander that he has the support of his future father-in-law."

"Just so."

"Do you have many Norse in York?"

"Yes, Sir William, for this was their capital before the Conqueror came. They dress as we do now, but their words and their customs mark them as different. The ones who escaped you might try to make it here and blend in. We will be vigilant. If they swore a blood oath then the only end to that is death, either yours or theirs. Do not worry, my men will catch them and when you return north you will see their heads and those others who ambushed you on the gates of the city. It is what you do with carrion. You warn others of the penalty for such actions."

He gave us a strong escort when we headed south. It was not needed. South of Nottingham, despite the Forest of Sherwood, we enjoyed a peaceful journey and Northampton was a royal town. For both Thomas and Calum, the experience and the places were new to them and, knowing that the danger lay to the north of us made the journey enjoyable. In contrast, my mind was in turmoil. My enemies seemed to have increased. We had ended one threat but how many more remained? Cailean Mór was still an enemy and I had little doubt that Ewen MacDougall would blame me for his defeat. As our journey from the west had shown me, an enemy could be at our door in less than four days! I was pleased that I had left Sir Geoffrey watching my home.

I had been to Windsor before but it impressed me every time I saw it and Calum and Thomas were rendered speechless as we approached one of the greatest castles in Christendom. I was aware that Calum in particular was intimidated. He was used to the wild lands of Scotland and Ireland. Much of his natural confidence and bluster disappeared as we entered the outer bailey. My service in Wales meant I was welcomed, and we were given reasonably decent quarters. Calum and Thomas would have to sleep on the floor of my chamber, but we would be together.

As we changed from riding clothes and mail into more comfortable and finer ones I said to Thomas. "This may be a trial for you, Thomas, but try to make it enjoyable. You will be serving at table with the squires of lords even greater than your grandfather. Better to listen more than you speak. Do not rise to insults but just take them. Not all squires are the same and some are just bullies. We will not be here long, in fact, I hope to return north on the morrow but all of that depends upon King Henry."

We had barely changed when a pursuivant came for me, "King Henry would speak with you before the feast this night, Sir William."

"Of course."

King Henry was in a small chamber with just a scribe and his eldest son Edward. When I entered King Henry said, "And this, Edward, is one of my guardians of the north, Sir William of Hartlepool. You will learn that such border knights are vital to our safety. Indeed, not only has Sir William helped us in the north he was instrumental in securing Wales for us."

"I am honoured, Sir William."

I nodded, "And when you are the king, Prince Edward, then I will do the same for you."

The king waved a hand, "Sit. You bring news?"

"Lord Dunbar sent me to apprise you of the truth of the death of King Alexander."

He nodded, "We heard the rumour, of course, and I was saddened by his death. Was it, as they say, treachery?"

"No, Your Majesty, he died of a fever."

"Ah. And Scotland, how stands it?" There was a hint of relief upon his face. Treachery and murder were always a fear for a king.

"King Alexander has good advisers, at the moment. Sir Alan Durward, Lord Galloway and Lord Dunbar are strong men but there are others who will try to control the young king."

Silence filled the chamber. "And do you advise me to visit the young King of Scotland?"

I nodded, "I spoke with him and he seems to have an old head on his young shoulders but his mother, as you know, is French. Walter Comyn has his eyes upon the crown too or, at least, has his eyes on controlling the new king."

"Then we will travel north. When do you return home?"

"With your permission, King Henry, on the morrow."

"No, Sir William, I need you here for at least three days. I need to pick your brains. You and your family know how the heart of the north beats. I have had little to do with it. Since de Montfort lost Poitou for me I have begun to look less towards France and more towards my own borders and lands. Tonight we feast and tomorrow we will ride and hunt in the park where we can talk and sport at the same time."

"Yes, Your Majesty." We would be staying, and my hopes of a quick return were dashed!

I enjoyed the hunting for I had Thomas and Calum with me. Calum was a natural hunter who had an easy grace when moving through the parkland. Other lords were present that morning but I was close to the royal pair so that they could talk with me. King Henry was a clever man and he used me as a model for his son. Edward was never placed in danger but was close enough to see my skills and, as the morning progressed, Calum's. While the animals we slew, a handful only, were gutted and taken off then he questioned me about the north. I began to realise that he had ambitions there. Although the dead King Alexander had paid homage to King Henry it had only been for his lands in England. King Henry hoped he could persuade the new king to pay homage for Scotland as Wales now did. He was a young king, but I did not think that Alexander would accede to that request and I told King Henry so.

He turned to his son Edward and smiled, "See, my son, if you do not surround yourself with those flatterers who will agree to anything, you will hear the truth." He turned back to me, "Nonetheless, Sir William, we will try for there is nothing to lose and such fealty would keep the north safe."

We returned to the castle in the late afternoon and then retired to our rooms to prepare for the evening meal. This time there would be more than the previous night for the castle had filled up during the hunt and it was clear that King Henry had plans. I stayed in the chamber until we were summoned. The lords who had arrived and were milling around the Great Hall were not the ones I knew. Those knights were either on the borders or in Wales with Sir Gerard and the other lords who had helped to defeat Llewellyn. I did not want to put on a false face and feign interest in their politicking. I had done what I was asked and now I wanted to return home. The attack by the Norse had made me anxious about the valley. Calum was happy to be in the castle. He was a gambler, and he was good at it. He had made money in the warrior hall. Thomas, too, was enjoying rubbing shoulders with great lords, princes and, of course, the king. That evening I took the advice I had given Thomas and listened more than I spoke. I learned much.

King Henry now made a great deal of money from Ireland. He had replaced lords whose loyalty was in doubt and rewarded his supporters. As a result, the land was at peace and that meant he was taking in almost two thousand pounds a year from the land. His judiciar in Wales was also helping the coffers of the exchequer to grow. The loss of lands in France had hurt England and King Henry was gradually recouping some of the losses from Ireland. The fact that King Louis had gone on crusade meant that France could not afford a war in Gascony and so those lands were more profitable than they had been. When I retired, I knew more than when I had sat down but it did not compensate for the time spent in a company I did not choose.

The next morning I resolved to ask for permission to return home. King Henry smiled, "You may leave on the morrow, Sir William, but there are two visitors who will arrive this afternoon and I would like you to meet them."

"Of course, Your Majesty." At least I now knew why I had been kept here and Calum and Thomas would be able to prepare for an early start. I would be home in four days.

I was walking in the park when the guests arrived. I recognised one of them and knew why I had been asked to stay. I saw Alain de Balliol, the young knight who had accompanied King Alexander and from the banners, I took the other man to be his father, John de Balliol. What did King Henry plan?

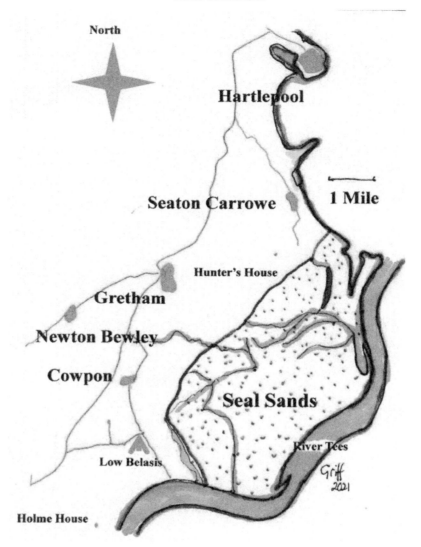

Hartlepool 1250

Author's Map

Griff 2021

Chapter 9

The Vanishing Men

"Do you know each other?" King Henry's question was innocent enough for Barnard Castle, the de Balliol home, and Stockton were less than a day's ride apart.

I smiled, "Sir Alain and I fought together at Kilmartin."

The young knight smiled, broadly, "Would that I had as much honour as you, Sir William, for it was you and Lord Hostarius who led the charge which won the day, and it was you who forced the gates of Dunolie Castle." As he spoke I realised that I could not remember seeing the knight when we charged the Norse.

King Henry looked thoughtfully at me, "Your account was more modest Sir William. It merely confirms that the north with your father and our Scottish ally, John de Balliol, is in safe hands."

The hairs on the back of my neck began to prickle. It told me that the de Balliol family were Scottish, and their hearts were in Scotland. Barnard Castle had once been part of the Warlord's domain but while my father was on crusade it had been lost to the de Balliol family. I would learn as much as I could and then tell my father. Barnard Castle guarded the road from east to west and the headwaters of the Tees. Whoever held the castle could hold the north to ransom.

That evening I was elevated to King Henry's side while John de Balliol occupied the other. Ladies were absent as was Prince Edward. Having spoken to him on the hunt I knew he would be unhappy at that. It was clear to me, in the conversations over the food, that Alain de Balliol had been sent with King Alexander to ensure that his family had their foot in the royal door. Sir Hugh, the eldest son, was now at Jedburgh and he was close to the young king. The family was ensuring that with a change in ruler they would be a party to it and if they could, somehow, manage to control the young king then they would do that also. De Balliol's claim was not for him but his sons. His wife was descended from the brother of King Malcolm of Scotland. Devorguilla was a rich and powerful woman and her family connections also reached into England. I confess that by the end of the evening I was dizzy from the family trees which were discussed. King Henry and John de Balliol seemed as familiar with them as the folk tales about King Arthur. I retired more confused than when I had sat down but equally, I feared for King Alexander. I had promised I would see that he attained the throne and I was honour bound to do so.

King Henry rewarded me, for my services, with a fine Spanish sword and a richly decorated scabbard. It was too fine to use and, to be honest, I felt more comfortable with my old one, but it was a fine gift and a measure of the esteem in which I was held. I thanked King Henry who said he would be visiting my father soon. That would put my mother in a spin!

When we neared York, we saw the heads adorning the spikes on the gates of the city. Sir Ralph had been as good as his word. Sir Ralph was a friend and so I told him what I had learned. He too was a guardian of the north and needed to know all. He promised to keep us informed of any news he gleaned from those using the road to the north.

As I had expected the imminent arrival of King Henry made my mother a whirlwind. My father merely smiled and we went to his solar so that he could be told about the really important news. He had been shocked by the attack, but it had been a week since the archers had returned and he had been able to put it into perspective. There was no immediate threat but those from the Baltic who passed through our valley would be scrutinised and having our Swedish guest made that much easier. He agreed with my assessment of the situation and, like me, regretted my oath.

"Of course you could not refuse the request, but it puts you in a difficult position, William, tread carefully."

I left the same day for home. I had travelled enough, and I would fulfil my duties closer to home.

For all his apparent concern King Henry did not arrive in Stockton for six months. With Sir Geoffrey in the hall too we bustled! My wife loved it as did Matthew, who, whilst still a toddler, now had two knights to try to emulate. When Thomas had first come he had wondered what enlivened our lives for there appeared to be little for a knight to do. Two months after our return he discovered that there could be danger even on the stretch of coast to the south of us which had more seals than people!

At the mouth of the river was a huge area of mud which appeared at low tide. The seals would bask there in such numbers that the mouth of the river was named Seal Sands. North of there were sand dunes and little else until the village of Seaton Carrowe. It was the area to the south and north of the village that was used by smugglers and those who sought to cause mischief. Two jagged scars poked out from the dunes, to limit the area smugglers could land. The Bishop of Durham charged taxes for the use of his port and there were men who did not wish to pay the taxes. If it was just an occasional boat landing some goods for private use then the Bishop's officials turned a blind eye. My father knew that some boats landed goods in the Tees itself but the twisting nature of the river made the beach the landing site of choice.

Brother Martin who had recently been appointed as master of the port by the Bishop came to speak to me one evening. "My lord, if I might have a word?"

"Of course." It was a pleasant evening for the days were lengthening and so, with Thomas behind us, we walked around the herb garden. It was pleasantly aromatic and peaceful.

"We have had fewer ships landing their cargo at the port. This has been happening for a month or more. I thought it was just a natural occurrence and that trade must be bad all over. Then one of my clerks overheard a mumbled grumble from one of the captains which suggested that cargo was being landed further south. More than that, Sir William, men were being landed."

Cargo and the evasion of taxes was one thing, but a band of men was more sinister. "Men?"

He nodded and held up a tally sheet, "When I took over my post, I read all the tally sheets and documents from my predecessor." He smiled, "I like to be efficient. I have discovered that the ships which used to frequent the port but no longer do so are Norse. In fact, fewer than one a week now lands cargo and that is mainly Baltic Pine. They take away the salt from Seaton Carrowe."

I wondered if the Norwegian King had instructed his captains to do this out of spite for my involvement in his defeat. Speculation was not going to give me the answers. "Ask the captains who still land their cargo where they think the smugglers are coming ashore. Tomorrow I will take some men south and see if we can find traces of them."

"Will not the tide have eradicated them?"

"Perhaps and if they use the dunes then the wind will wipe away their tracks but if they use horses then there will be traces of them and if there are men then they, too, will leave evidence of their passing. Remember, Brother Martin, that south and north of Seaton Carrowe there is little farming for the land is salt marsh, samphire beds and bog. We will look for the signs and then I will try to end this trade. I do not like the idea of men being landed." A sudden thought struck me, "Last year a boat landed with men from Norway, so the landing of men was normal. Look in your tally sheets, when did that cease?"

He nodded, "My predecessor told me about that ship. Was there not a man who wished to speak with your father?"

"That is the ship."

His fingers ran along the lines of squiggles and ticks like an ant seeking its home. He tapped one sheet triumphantly, "That was the last ship to bring men to this land and from the numbers only two of those who landed were Scandinavian. They were cargo ships and did not bring numbers of men."

"Well done, Brother. We learn little from that other than men were coming from the east and landing at Hartlepool. Why no longer? Go and question the captains and I will organise my hunt."

My son and Sir Geoffrey were also intrigued and, to be honest, I was excited for this would be an interesting distraction and a good opportunity for Thomas to learn new skills. Calum was even more excited. He craved action and, if truth be told, I had expected him to ask to leave my service after a couple of months of idleness. Carl the Betts was one of my best archers and a local man who was the best tracker I knew. He knew the sands better than any. I consulted him.

"There are many places men could land a ship, but a man would have to know the waters well. It is a good beach but there are rocky scars."

"And the people of Seaton Carrowe, would they help smugglers?"

"Like everywhere, my lord, in the main they are good people and would not wish to incur your wrath but there are those who would seize a chance to make coin and others who could be threatened. What you could not do, my lord, is to involve the whole village. Wherever they are landing will be far enough from houses so that the ships cannot be identified. The ships themselves must be small enough not to attract attention."

"Good, then on the morrow we will seek their landing site. Choose ten good men and I will bring my knights. We will dress for hunting and not for war."

That evening, as we ate, my son, squire and Geoffrey were keen to debate the hunt, "But father, why here and why now?"

"A good question and one we can use our minds to answer."

Sir Geoffrey said, "Here is north of the river."

Dick became animated, "And that is important. If they landed south of the river then they would have to cross the Tees either at the ferry or Piercebridge."

I nodded, "And both are watched. Numbers of men would attract attention."

"Sir William, you are making an assumption that it is a large number of men. What if it is just a few?"

"A good point, Geoffrey, but as Dick says, if it was just one or two then they could easily slip across on a ferry."

Thomas had been listening and he could contain himself no longer, "No my lord for if they were from Norway or Denmark then they would be scrutinised. After the ambush, your father initiated searches."

"You are right, Thomas. Now we are getting somewhere. North of here there are many beaches which are as good, if not better than Seaton Carrowe. Let us assume that they are not being used or, if they are, they are not our concern. Thomas, fetch a wax tablet." We had many of them for they were used to help the children to read as well as being a useful tool for my steward.

Mary laughed, "You boys like your games do you not? I have never seen grown men so excited! I shall put Matthew to bed."

My youngest complained, "No, mother, let me stay and listen, it is interesting."

"Matthew, if you go with your mother now then we shall take you tomorrow on your pony. How would that suit?"

He happily went and Thomas said, "You have made him content, lord."

"Aye, well, Thomas, tomorrow he is the responsibility of you and Dick!"

The wax tablet was smooth and so I drew a line along it, "This is the river." I marked a couple of crosses, "Here is Stockton and here is Piercebridge." I put two more circles on it. "This is Hartlepool, and this is Durham." Lastly, I put an S. "Here is Seaton. What does this tell us?"

It was Thomas who made the connection. He took the scribe and drew two parallel lines from the coast, "This strip of land is twenty miles wide, uncle. The only place of any size is Seggesfield. You can get all the way to the west coast."

I nodded, "Except that you would have to pass Barnard Castle. You are right, Dick. If someone wished to recruit men, then they would land them at Seaton Carrowe and then they could disappear without a trace. This is more serious than I thought."

"Should we leave Matthew behind then, lord, and travel as though to war?"

"Not tomorrow, Geoffrey. They land at night. We need to find out where and then use our minds to discover when! As soon as I can predict their arrival, I shall take just my archers and Calum of the Isles, but you and your squire can come with me. It may well be that I need you to help me hunt these unwelcome visitors."

We were more serious when we rode forth than we had been the previous afternoon. The first place we looked at was the least likely landing site. Between the Long Scar and the Little Scar, there were less than four hundred paces, and it was also close to the north end of Seaton Carrowe. It did not take long for us to establish that it was not the place. There was neither human dung nor traces of animals. If this was the smuggling of goods, then it would require horses to haul it away. We rode to the village where the fishing boats were drawn up on the beach. Seawater was being boiled to make the salt they used to preserve the fish they caught. The village produced sea salt all year round.

John Tom's Son was the headman. His four sons each had a fishing boat and so I questioned them but I looked at the headman when I did so, "Have you seen ships landing men or cargo at night?"

His eyes gave him away as did the shoulders of his sons. They were like naughty boys caught doing something they should not have. I wondered if we had managed to find the smugglers and then I put the thought from my head. I knew John and he was a good man. "Not here, my lord! We would have told you."

"John, the truth, do not be evasive. I want the truth."

He sighed, "We want no trouble, my lord, and we keep our doors closed at night, it is safer that way." I waited, "We have heard, on quiet nights, sounds coming from further south."

Carl the Betts said, "Hunter's House?"

John nodded, "That part of the beach, aye, Carl."

Carl turned to me, "There used to be a family of seal hunters lived there, my lord, long before you came, in fact before Sir Thomas improved the castle. The story goes that some raiders came from the east in ships. The family was never seen again. The house lies empty."

John Tom's Son said, "Aye, lord, it is haunted. None would go there at night."

I nodded for the picture was becoming clearer, "We will investigate but the next time you hear noises at night, John, then send to me!"

I could see that they were all contrite, "Aye, Sir William. We will."

I turned to Thomas, "Keep Matthew and Dick at the rear."

"Aye, Sir William."

Sir Geoffrey said, "If they are using the house they will not be there now, Sir William."

I smiled, "You can now see far into the distance. Good, that will save us having to search." He dropped his head. "Until we discover the truth then Matthew will have his own bodyguards!"

I could not remember ever seeing the dwelling and, as Carl led us to it, I could see why. It was in a dell behind the dunes and, being single-storey was hard to see. I saw that it was the upturned hull of an old ship and the reason it had survived so long was that it was covered in turf and the rain had made it continue to grow. It looked like an oasis of green hidden in the sandy dunes. We dismounted and I left two men with the horses while Carl led us carefully down the dunes to the dwelling. It mattered not where we stood on the shifting sands; there would be no footprints, but Carl was looking for other signs. He saw none. When we reached the end of the dunes my archers nocked an arrow and the rest of us drew a sword. Carl dropped to all fours and began to examine, seemingly, the very blades of grass. He moved closer to the house and when he reached the door, which hung from rotting leather hinges, he raised his arm and waved us forward. No one had yet spoken. I looked at the door and Carl nodded. He pulled the door open and I stepped inside. There was movement but it was not large and must have been some sort of creature, a rat, mouse, or shrew.

"There is no one, Carl."

He entered and looked around. It did not need a skilled tracker like Carl to see that there were the remains of a fire and whilst not warm it was recent. Men had used it. It took Carl to find the bones of the fish they had eaten and discarded. That explained the rodents.

"Check around outside and see if you can find tracks."

I went outside too and spoke to Geoffrey and Thomas, "This has been used and recently. The answer may be a simple and innocent one but until Carl eliminates the presence of horses and warriors then we will view this as the place the smugglers use."

It seemed to take an age, but I knew that he was a thorough man. He returned and nodded, "It is the place they have used. There is horse dung and human dung. They tried to hide them, but I found it. Some of it is less than a week old. Tracks of men and horses lead off to the west and head to the road which passes through Gretham."

"Can you tell if they were warriors?"

He paused, "They wore sealskin boots for I found the prints in the mud. As it rained ten days ago then they are recent."

Calum said, "Sealskin boots mean Norse or Danes."

Something in the way he said it made me turn, "Do you know something, Calum? If so, then speak."

He nodded, "When I was waiting for a boat to take me back to the isles and before I took the berth on the Hartlepool bound ship, I was approached by a warrior who said he was recruiting men who did not care for whom they fought. It was good money and would be in the west. I did not take him up on the offer, but it had to be somewhere on this east coast for there is nowhere else which is further west and can be reached by ship."

I said, quietly, "And why did you not take him up on his offer?"

"I did not like his look and he wore no mail. He had just two battle bands, and his sword was a poor one. I do not mind fighting for anyone, it is in my blood, but I want to fight for a man I can, at least, respect. This one was untrustworthy."

"Did he have a name?"

"Guthrum the Dane."

"Then he was not Norse? I thought this might be King Hákon's work."

"No, but he wanted Norse or Danes, Irishmen and even Englishmen however, he made himself scarce when there were men who served the king approaching."

I knew that Calum was telling the truth and that Carl had found the evidence we needed but none of it made sense. "Carl, how many men are we talking about?"

He shrugged, "Hard to tell. There were at least four ponies or small horses and two men who wore boots but other than…"

My squire shook his head, "This is a puzzle and no mistake!"

We mounted and followed the tracks to the road. There we could not tell in which direction they had gone but it made sense to assume they continued the way they had set off. The road passed through Gretham and there we found evidence of men crossing a field of oats. Again, the number could not be ascertained and when we picked them up again, we lost them in the North Burn. Someone had local knowledge and the warriors were heading west or perhaps south-west. I sent Sir Geoffrey and two men to Elwick and I went to Gretham. Later, back in my hall, we shared what we had discovered. Both settlements had experienced thefts over the past six months. None of it worried the villagers; some fowl were taken while cooling bread was also stolen and other minor crimes which they put down to vagabonds who were starving. It was only when you compared them that you realised these were warriors making their way west and feeding themselves.

"We could camp by the house and catch them."

"We would have to use a number of men and we might warn them off. I need to find out the purpose of this band of warriors. It is obviously intended for somewhere other than here for we would have noticed such a large number. This cannot be good for our country."

"They could be on their way to join MacDougall's rebels against King Alexander in the isles."

I nodded. What Calum said made sense, but it would be easier to sail the ships from Norway to the islands. "We will wait until John sends us word that they have heard these ghosts. At least we have laid that lie to rest. Ghosts do not eat fish and cover up their own dung!"

Chapter 10

King Henry and the Scottish boy

Before we could act on any information which the folk of Seaton could give us, I was summoned, along with Sir Geoffrey to attend on King Henry at Stockton Castle. He was still at York when the rider reached me. I left Alan Longsword in command of my men. We would not need either archers or men at arms for King Henry would have enough of his own men and there were few castles in the north which could accommodate such a royal progress. My little tower room would be the best my son, Richard and I, along with Thomas could expect. We reached Stockton the day before King Henry and that allowed me to discuss with my father this apparent invasion of Viking warriors.

"Like you, William, I cannot see what they would hope to gain and they have not passed through Stockton. Since the men ambushed you we have closely questioned every Scandinavian whether warrior or merchant."

Henry Samuel had arrived for King Henry had specifically asked for him. He gave the most ominous explanation, "Is someone gathering a hidden army ready to wreak havoc on the north?"

"Let us hope not. Do not say anything to King Henry until we have more solid evidence. From what you say William, you do not know numbers. It could just be thirty or so Vikings trying to get to the isles. I do not believe that to be the case, but it is the only explanation which fits the facts."

King Henry, his son and his lords used our ferry to cross the river. It suited my mother as she was able to greet each party and have them shown to their chambers before the next ones arrived. There had been enough notice to arrange plenty of food and to have the chambers not only cleaned but filled with fragrant flowers. The shutters on the wind holes had been kept open to blow away any unpleasant odours. My mother was a real lady. It was she who had arranged the seating and, of course, she and my father flanked King Henry. I sat next to Prince Edward and the Archbishop of York, Walter de Gray. The Archbishop was an important man and had ruled England when King Henry had travelled to France. I was curious as to why he was with the party, but it soon became clear that he wished to extend his power into Scotland. He had tried before and perhaps thought that a king who was a minor could be persuaded to make the bishops in Scotland accept his authority.

107

I noticed that Prince Edward was rapt by the conversations around him. I doubted that he had much time for playing but as he would be a future king that was not a bad thing. He was older now than his father had been when he became King of England. "What do you think of the North of your future realm, Prince Edward?"

"I have seen little of it yet, Sir William but it seems to me that it has fewer people than there are further south. Is that because of the threat of the Scots?"

The Archbishop laughed, "The Scots are not a threat any longer and that is largely down to Sir William who, when a younger knight, held Elsdon and Otterburn against raiders. It was he and Sir Thomas, along with the Sherriff of Newcastle who ended King William's ambitions. King Alexander's ancestor had been the last one to try to retake Northumberland. No, Prince Edward, while this castle and this family stand firm then the Scots are no threat. The real reason is that the winters are harsh and the land which is fertile lies between greater areas of rough and wild land!"

I warned, "Just so long as King Alexander rules then that is true but there may be others who seek the throne. The de Balliol family along with the Comyns and the de Brus each has a claim to the throne. A distant one, it is true but that matters little in Scotland. King Alexander had but one son."

Edward nodded. I almost smiled except it would have caused offence for his serious look made him look like a little old man.

The king turned to speak with me, "Sir William, you and your father will escort us to Durham where we shall meet with King Alexander and his lords. I would like Sir Henry to accompany us too. He did great service in Wales."

"Of course, Your Majesty. And Sir John de Balliol?" I made the question sound innocent but their presence in Windsor had intrigued me.

King Henry kept his face impassive as he said, "Sir John and his family may yet be useful to us, but I do not need him for this meeting. We go to discuss the wedding arrangements for next year shall see my daughter, Margaret, wed to King Alexander and the two kingdoms will be joined, once more."

I did not think that the King of Scotland, even though a minor would see it that way.

Along with the rest of the knights of the valley Sir Petr was not invited to join the king and he was not happy to be left out. My father gave him tasks to keep him occupied and, I think, would have taken him with us had King Henry allowed it. I could see that my father still had a long way to go to make a good knight out of Sir Petr. Sir Robert and the others accepted that they had not been invited and saw no slur or insult. Sir Petr did. I was not happy that my father was asked to come for he still looked, to me, a little frailer than the last time we had ridden north.

We left the next morning for Durham. I had forgotten how slow the royal progress could be. The journey of a couple of hours took all day and I was grateful that we were not travelling to Jedburgh which would have been interminable. We reached the city the day before the Scottish Royal party and that was, as I later learned, deliberate. King Henry, the Archbishop of York and the Bishop of Durham were in close conference and the rest of the party dined without them. My father was the senior baron and he sat at the head of the table. It was at that meal that we learned, from the household knights, of the unrest amongst the barons further south. King Henry was not popular. Whilst not reviled in the same manor as his father the barons had become used to opposing him and demanding more power and fewer taxes. I could now see why King Henry had ensured that we won in Wales and why he had arranged this marriage to Scotland.

"It is Simon de Montfort who raises bad feelings against King Henry," Thomas de Multon, Baron de Lucy, was a baron who was younger than I was and had only recently inherited the title from his father. His manor was in Cumbria and he was obviously a loyal supporter of King Henry. When he told me he had just been given a manor in Ireland, I saw King Henry's strategy. "We need the north to be strong and to be behind King Henry. I hope that this peace with Scotland will continue."

"As do we all, Sir Thomas."

"Tell me, Earl Cleveland, what do you feel about having a claimant to the Scottish throne so close to both of us? Barnard Castle is as strong as any castle in the north and yet the family is Scottish!"

My father frowned for he hated politics, "De Balliol is loyal is he not or have you heard other?"

"There is traffic between his lands and Argyll. He did not support MacDougall in the recent rising, but he did not accompany King Alexander did he, Sir William?"

I dislike being used and felt honour bound to defend the Balliols even though I had my suspicions. "Alain de Balliol accompanied us, and he fought against the rebels."

De Lucy smiled and it did not endear him to me for it was an oily smile, "But did you see him at the Battle of Kilmartin? We have all heard of your courage when you and Sir Alan led the charge. I have spoken to others who were there, including the Swedish knight, Sir Petr, whom I met in Stockton. None of them remembers seeing Sir Alain at the forefront of the battle."

I leaned over to him, "I would not insult Sir Alain with that kind of talk. There were perilously few of us at the battle and all fought bravely. If you ever have to fight a Viking army, Sir Thomas, then you will realise that."

My father smiled, "Come, here we are all friends and there is no need to insult anyone. I have fought in more battles than any other who is here, and I know that a knight only sees the battle which is before him."

The Baron de Lucy said, "Sir Thomas, I would dearly love to hear of the Battle of Arsuf from the hero of that day."

I knew that my father did not enjoy the retelling of it, but he did so if only to create a more harmonious mood. Later that night as Henry Samuel and I escorted him to his chamber he said, "I do not like this, William. This was the sort of mood we had when King John ruled. Barons plotted against others and took sides. It seems to me that it is happening again. We must keep the family out of politics and be as neutral as we can without being disloyal."

Henry Samuel gave a wry chuckle, "And that is some trick, grandfather. My uncle will tell you that when we were in Wales it was hard to tell friend from foe and that was amongst those fighting the Welsh!"

I nodded, "And remember, father, I swore an oath to see that King Alexander attains the throne. I know that King Henry supports the Scottish King but that can change. I would not put the rest of the family in danger."

"And if you continue to behave honourably then you will not."

The next day we dressed in our finest and the Scottish Royal party arrived. Lord Hostarius was there along with Lord Dunbar and Lord Galloway. That pleased me for those with a claim to the throne were absent. So long as the triumvirate of my friends were there then King Alexander was safe. Most of the day was spent on legal matters. Lawyers were present so that the contracts could be scrutinised. The wedding would take place on Christmas Day in York. The couple would be too young to consummate the marriage and, as such, it was a political act. Margaret was not even present but remained with her mother in Windsor. Once the documents had been signed then the politicking began. King Henry tried to assert his authority and to make King Alexander accept that King Henry was King Alexander's liege lord. It was interesting that it was Dunbar and Galloway who opposed such a move and my friend, Alan Durward held his tongue. It was then I remembered that he and King Henry had got on well after the last war and he had been given many estates in England. I liked Durward but he was motivated by his ambitions. Then Walter Gray tried to gain religious power but the Scottish bishops and abbots who were part of the royal party fought against such a move. I wondered if what had begun as a meeting to plan a happy event might disintegrate into a rift between the two kingdoms. The Bishop of Durham, however, was a clever man and he broke up the arguments by saying that it was almost time for the feast he had planned. We all returned to our chambers.

My father was happier than I expected him to be, "Do not worry William, King Henry has tried and failed to gain power here in Scotland. He is a clever man, and he will use other means. He is not a warrior king and he finds men to use as tools rather than lead armies and use force of arms."

"Like Durward?"

"Just so and he has de Balliol too. De Lucy was right. De Balliol is a Scottish lord with a claim to the throne and lives in England. That is a double-edged sword for he owes fealty to King Henry. I think that young Alexander, if he lives long enough, will make a good king. You will have to ensure that he does so!"

At the feast, we were not relegated, as I had expected us to be, to the bottom end of the hall. Instead, whilst not on the same tables as the two kings, their bishops and the three advisers to King Alexander, we were close enough that I could speak to Lord Dunbar.

"It is good to meet you, Sir Thomas. You have raised a most noble knight in your son, and I am pleased that I did not have to cross swords with you in your prime!"

"Thank you, Lord Dunbar, but my prime was so long ago that I can barely remember it."

"I doubt that, sir, and you, Sir William, are you now enjoying a more peaceful life?"

"Yes, my lord, back to the life as a lord of the manor who has all sorts of problems to deal with." Both Sir James and Sir Patrick smiled. "Tell me, Sir Patrick, your manor is on the coast, do you have any problems with smuggling, either of goods or men?"

"Goods, aye." He frowned, "Men? Why would people be smuggled for we do not stop those who wish to visit our land or even to live from coming?"

"Even Vikings?"

Lord Dunbar shook his head, "You have me intrigued, Sir William, I pray you to elaborate." He lowered his voice a little. "The conversation might be more interesting than the debate to my right about the collection of tithes!"

"It may be nothing but there seem to have been small groups of men from Norway and Denmark, possibly even Sweden and Frisia too, landed at a lonely spot at the mouth of our river. They move west and, seemingly, disappear."

My father and Sir Henry were also interested. I had mentioned the problem to my father, but he had been preoccupied with the imminent arrival of the king and his party. Now he began to see the ramifications. My father said, "None have come through Stockton, son, for we would have noticed them if they were warriors."

"We think that they were but they may, from what Calum has told us, be mercenaries rather than Norse or Danish."

Henry Samuel spoke, "And since they have not taken the ferry south, they must have continued west."

Lord Dunbar sipped the wine his squire had just poured, "Then could this be another of the King of Norway's tricks? Is he reinforcing Lord MacDougall from the south?"

Sir James shook his head, "We damaged his men, Sir Patrick, not his ability to bring them by ship. Why send them in small numbers when he could deliver them by the boatload?"

Thomas had just poured my wine and I drank deeply for I felt amongst friends here, "And that is why I am puzzled, Sir James, for I came to the same conclusion. I suppose, Lord Dunbar, that I hoped you would say you had the same problem and that my beach had not been selected purposefully. When I return home I will get, if I can, to the bottom of the matter!"

Just then King Alexander stood. He was just a boy, but he was unafraid to speak in such distinguished company. My father had said that when King Henry had been a boy and elevated to kingship, he had been afraid of his own shadow. What had made Alexander the way he was?

The young Scottish King turned to King Henry, "King Henry, I thank you for the fine gift that you have given to me. Your daughter, Margaret, is a rich addition to our royal crown. I hope that the marriage will tie our two kingdoms closer together. Since the Treaty of York thirteen years ago our two nations have not had to fight each other. Long may that continue for it is in peaceful times that we all prosper."

There was a murmur of approval. The churchmen and King Henry nodded theirs. Some of the Scottish barons nodded too but others remained impassive. Those who did not own lands in England sought the riches that such manors brought.

When silence reigned once more King Alexander turned to look in my direction, "Lord Hostarius has brought to my attention the role played in the recent defeat of the Norwegians by an English knight." All eyes swivelled in my direction. "Sir William of Hartlepool was a friend of my father's and was held in great esteem despite the many hurts he has caused Scotland. That speaks well of his nobility and his honour. I would like to mark the moment by making him a knight of the chamber. He has shown that he is a defender of kings and, when he visits Scotland, he shall have all the rights accorded my closest knights and advisers."

The gesture was a magnanimous one for knights of the chamber often slept, like chamberlains, behind the king's door, or, if he was on campaign, in the tent opening. I did not think for one moment that I would be asked to do that, and I saw Alan Durward's hand in all of this. Even as I stood to give my thanks, I was looking around the room. Not all the Scots were happy with the announcement. The Comyn faction had dark and glowering faces. As I had expected Durward, Dunbar and Galloway were smiling. It was then that I saw that there were none of the de Balliol family present. I had expected to see the eldest, Sir Hugh, but he was absent. Then the thought disappeared, and I spoke, "I thank you, King Alexander, for this mighty honour. I am humbled."

He nodded, "And of course, you shall be at York next Christmas for my wedding." I nodded, "And now, all be seated and enjoy the feast."

I smiled as I sat for I saw that the king was relieved that his ordeal was over. It had been a political act and that meant his acting regents, whom I knew liked and trusted me were making a connection with me. That it was a device to make communications easier was made clear when Lord Dunbar leaned over and said, "And now you may visit Scotland as often and freely as you wish, Sir William, for you are now a friend of Scotland."

We did not speak of the honour on our table. There would be time enough for that on the way home. We chatted about the food, the wine and those who were not present. Of those with pretensions to the crown, only the Comyn's were there and I wondered if that was significant. The de Brus and de Balliol factions had greater claims. Had they been invited and declined or was this the work of the regents? I confess that my mind was only half on the feast for I was still dwelling on my Scandinavian visitors. Calum had given me an insight but Folki might know even more. I realised that I had yet to question the others who had landed at Hartlepool legitimately. John son of Walter and Carl the Dane might also have been offered the chance to come to England by that route.

113

King Alexander left the next day to return north, as did the lords who had accompanied him. I watched them leave and saw that King Alexander and his mother were surrounded by the three lords who would shape Scotland's future and their household knights. The Comyn's were at the rear and well away from King Alexander. If this rival was regarded as a threat, then why had he been invited? I saw then a reason for the honour I had received, for Comyn hated me as I had been instrumental in his defeat north of Newcastle all those years ago. I was being used as a threat. It was like a game of chess and someone, probably Alan Durward, was putting me in play on the board. He was warning Comyn that the king had English allies and a warrior who had his measure.

When the Scots had returned north my father and I met with the Bishop of Durham and King Henry. King Henry wanted us to know his strategy. "I had hoped that young Alexander would acquiesce to my demands, but the boy appears to be made of sterner stuff. No matter for we have friends there and, Sir William, I am pleased that this boy and his advisers seem to favour you. It means that you can keep me informed of developments here in the north." I nodded but I was not happy. "Now to other matters." I was almost dismissed for King Henry then spoke directly to my father and the Bishop of Durham. "Know you that there are barons in the north who are unhappy with both my rule and what they perceive as rights lost since my father was forced to sign that charter. I need all of you to keep your ears to the ground and let me know of any who wish to cause mischief here in the north. It is far from London and while I do not fear the Scots any more some Scottish lords might choose to join rebellious barons and seek to gain more power in England."

I saw my father's shoulders slump. He had lived through this sort of turmoil before and he was too old for it. When we returned home, I would see if I could lift some of the weight from his shoulders. We left with the king and that meant I could not speak to my father as I had wished. It was only when the royal party left to return south that I was able to sit with my father in his solar.

"You know that you need not worry about rebellious barons, father."

"I know that you will do all that you can but even when I served in the Holy Land and Estonia, this valley was always on my mind. Your news of these Vikings has made me worry. You cannot take the worry away, that will always be there but know that I trust you. My ancient body will stop me from going to war, but my mind still works. I would have you keep me informed about events which might hurt the valley. Do not spare my feelings."

I nodded and an idea came to me, "What if I were to send Dick to you? He has come on well but you as a mentor and your clever mind as well as the experience of your men, will all make him a better warrior."

"Of course, but how does this help the other matter?"

"We know not if there are spies in this land. I visit but when I do it is normally for some event like the visit of the king or a major feast. If my son is here, then regular visits from me would seem to be normal. Besides, I do think he will learn more from you than from me. I have many other pressing matters and I do not like to neglect my son."

"Then I am happy, and your mother will be delighted to have a grandson in the house! Sir Mark is training his squire and he can take Dick under his wing. Your former squire and Sir John will be kind but firm with him and I will see to all other matters. Does he play chess?"

"He does."

"Then by the time I return him to you, he will beat you three times out of four!"

Chapter 11

The Ghosts of Hunter's House

When I reached Hartlepool Sir Geoffrey told me that John Tom's Son had not yet sent word. There had been no landings. I had noticed in the north that there had been stormy skies to the east. Although the weather had been clement one never knew what it was like out to sea and that was the most likely explanation. I wasted no time in telling Dick of his new opportunity and he was delighted. Sir Geoffrey, his squire and Thomas rode with my son to Stockton. When they had gone, I sent for Carl the Dane and Will the Sword. They both looked nervous for I had spoken but little with them.

"How long were the two of you stranded in Norway and seeking a boat to England?"

They looked relieved and Carl said, "A month. The captains all charged too high a price."

"Two months, my lord. I had to work loading ships with timber before I raised enough to make the passage."

"Did anyone offer to take you for free?"

This time they looked down and Carl said, "Aye, lord." I said nothing and he added, "We spoke with Calum of the Isles and he told us about the hut and the tracks."

"And why did you say nothing?"

"We both thought we might lose our places here."

"This has had the opposite effect. I expect honesty from the men in my hall. You are Sir Geoffrey's men, but you live in my home. Speak now, tell me all and I will bear that in mind when I speak with Sir Geoffrey."

It was as though I had burst a dam and their words poured forth in a torrent. That they were speaking the truth was obvious. They both confirmed the name of the one hiring men, Guthrum the Dane. I looked carefully at Carl when he told me that. "Aye, lord, we are both Danes, but he is not a man one would want to fight alongside." Again that confirmed what Calum had said. It seemed that the Dane was not choosy and was not recruiting a Viking warband; he wanted hired swords of any nationality. Will the Sword confessed that, until he took the job loading ships, he had been tempted and he knew of other Englishmen, Welsh and Scots who had taken the offer. One of John's friends had been desperate enough to take up the opportunity and I think that was the factor which had held his tongue. He did not wish to lose this position. From what I gathered there were many who had joined the crusade and now wished to return home. Neither knew the ultimate employer. That had been the deciding factor in Will's case, he did not want to fight against King Henry. By the end, I was satisfied with their stories and their reasons for silence.

"From now on you tell me all, do you understand?"

"Aye, my lord!"

"One more thing, how many times did this Guthrum the Dane sail?"

"As soon as he filled his knarr. Sometimes it was with fifteen men and once or twice he came overloaded and had twenty. Sometimes it was once every ten days but occasionally once a month. The winds and the seas had an effect."

When Geoffrey returned, I told him what I had learned and my judgement. John son of Walter also looked shamefaced and Sir Geoffrey said, "When we were at the Hunter's House why did you not speak?"

"Calum of the Isles said all that I knew and more. I only knew that the man who tried to hire me was a Dane."

Sir Geoffrey shook his head, "I have much to learn about choosing men wisely, lord!"

"No harm was done. We must be ready to ride as soon as we receive word from John Tom's Son. I will have Alan Longsword and Idraf of Towyn keep the men ready to ride at a moment's notice. I am anxious to snuff out this candle!"

It was two nights later that John's youngest, Michael, banged on our door. It was dark but the sun had only recently set and we were not yet abed. We were using candles. Mary and I had been apart enough to wish more time to talk and to sit, sometimes, in pleasant silence.

At that time of night, I was the first to reach the door. Michael was out of breath and I took him in, knowing his news before he spoke, "Get your breath. Thomas, Geoffrey, rouse the men!"

I heard their feet and knew that they would be dressing already.

"My father sent me. We were returning with a catch when we saw a ship out to sea. We have watched each night since you asked us, lord. As we headed inshore, he saw that its sails were set to take it west and that meant either the estuary or to land on the sands. He sent me as soon as he saw that it was heading for the sands." He coughed for he had spoken in a gabble. "He said if the ship was innocent and just chancing the sands at night, he would take any punishment you had to offer."

"There will be no punishment and merely rewards for doing as I asked. Can you ride?" His face, before the shake of his head, told me

117

that he could not, "Then you shall sit on Thomas' saddle. Go to the stables and await me."

Mary nodded, "Be careful, husband."

"I will."

I hurried to my chamber and dressed. Normally Thomas or, had he been at home, Dick would have helped me, but time was of the essence. I did not bother with my chausses and I would not need my helmet. By the time I ran to the stables then Destiny was saddled, and my men were ready.

"To the house. Carl, lead!"

"Aye, lord!"

We galloped out of the cobbled yard and the folk of Hartlepool must have wondered what was amiss for none left my walled port at night. The night watch saw us as we approached and knew better than to delay us. The gates were opened, and I shouted, as I passed, "Keep them barred until I return!" Had Michael not been recognised he would have been denied entry. At night we were vigilant.

"Aye, lord!"

We reached Seaton and I saw that John had armed the men in the village, "I will not need you, John, and I thank you for this warning."

"It may be nothing, my lord."

"Aye, but if it is then we might end this threat this night." I turned to Sir Geoffrey, "Take half of my archers and ride to the Gretham Road. Fan out and approach the house from the west. I wish to trap as many rats as we can but take no chances. I want none with so much as a scratch. These vermin are not worth it."

Even as we rode along the beach towards the dunes, I was planning how to use a ship to catch this Norse knarr. There was little point in capturing men if there was still a watery road for them to use. The sand muffled our hooves a little, but I was unconcerned that they might hear us for I was barring their escape with Geoffrey. When we had investigated the house, we saw that they lit a fire and ate. It was my guess that they spent the day there and then travelled west at night time. It would explain why these ghosts could disappear so easily. We were strung out in line with Carl at the fore and the rest of my archers close behind. They wore no armour and would reach our prey before we did. I saw the ship edging away from the shore. It was in the distance and it was only the lightness of the sail which enabled me to see her. They would not see us and so I hoped that Guthrum the Dane would be blissfully unaware that we had the measure of him. We would set a trap for the ship the next time it came.

Carl was a hunter and he slowed to a walk as soon as he saw the trail of footprints in the wet sand. The tide was on the ebb. The dunes were less than forty paces from us. He dropped his reins and strung his bow. My other archers did the same. Two would stand with the horses. We dismounted and I drew my sword. I was not wearing a helmet for my coif would suffice. My archers spread out in a long hunting line and we followed. The sound of the surf would have masked the sound of our hooves but even had the men heard it and fled they would find themselves running into the rest of my men. It was as I climbed the dunes that I cursed myself. There had been no hoof tracks on the beach, yet we had seen horse dung at the house. We should have been watching the house for men had to have brought ponies or horses for the men to use. We reached the top of the dunes and I saw glowing embers rising with the smoke from the fire. The enemy were complacent. They had got away with this so many times that they thought they were, truly, ghosts who could pass through the land unseen. Alan Longsword marked one end of the line and Erik Red Hair, now fully recovered, the other.

They were, however, not that complacent for they had a sentry, and he shouted the alarm. We were seen.

I shouted, "I am Sir William of Hartlepool! Lay down your weapons and identify yourselves." My words were greeted by silence as the men tried to silently scatter through the dunes and marram grass.

A night battle is never easy, but my archers knew that anyone before them had made themselves an enemy by their refusal to answer me. My men at arms kept behind the shadowy screen of the men who were deadly with the bow. There was a glow ahead as the door of the former ship was opened and whoever had been inside fled. For three men that was fatal as a shower of arrows struck them. I saw a shadow move to my left and, leaving the archers to continue to pick the enemy off I hurried through the dunes to follow what I knew to be a man. He was heading for the estuary and had the advantage that he did not appear to be wearing mail. My boots sank into the dunes as I struggled to catch the man. In daylight, there were paths which could be followed but I could not see them. I took a chance and began to edge further west. I would try to cut him off. Behind the dunes and the marram grass, there was a sandy grassy area which had been flattened. It would give firmer footing and the alternative was to continue following the man and watch him increase the distance from me. I made my way through the dunes. As I glanced behind, I saw a shadow following me. Either that was Thomas, or I was in trouble! I could hear cries as men were slain. I hoped they were the enemy and not my men. I had asked for prisoners but only if possible. Until we discovered the identity of the man who sought a warband and their purpose then we could kill all that we liked but we would not stop the flow.

As I crested one dune I saw in the distance light reflecting from water, it was the river. A chilling thought struck me, did they have a boat moored there? If so, then my prey might evade me. I saw, a hundred or so paces from me, the shadow move, and it was heading for the river. There were rocks there and they would hide his tracks whereas the damp sand would show me where he had gone. The man knew the area and that meant he was not one who had just landed. I headed to my right for the dunes there were lower, and I might be able to cut him off. As soon as I reached sand which no longer slid from beneath my feet, I turned to run parallel with the dunes. I had not heard the man behind me for some time. Perhaps I had lost him. I saw the water ahead. There were pools of it, and I knew they would soon disappear. The shiny rocks showed me where the shadow would be heading. Had he passed me? I had my answer when I stepped from behind the last large dune. I saw not ten paces from me, a man at arms. He was not Scandinavian. He drew his sword and his dagger.

I still wished a prisoner and I said, "Give yourself up. I have men in the dunes, and you will be taken!"

He answered me which told me he knew our language and when I heard his accent then I knew who the enemy was. He was Scottish! "Give myself up? I will kill you, take your fine sword and purse and disappear. I have yet to meet a Norman I could not beat!" He ran at me and I knew, in the first flurry of blows that he was a skilled swordsman. I just had my sword, but I wore leather gauntlets. I had to use my hand to fend off the dagger which arched towards my throat.

From the dunes I heard Thomas' voice, "Sir William, where are you?"

The Scotsman laughed, "So I can earn an extra reward from my lord when I take your head in a sack. He wishes to have Sir William of Hartlepool as a trophy. Prepare to die!"

Although he wore just a leather brigandine studded with metal he had an advantage for he could move more quickly, and until I drew my own dagger then he had the edge. He also had a helmet. A blow to the head would be unlikely to hurt him. He lunged with his sword and I was forced to use my sword to bat away the strike. It tore through my surcoat and his dagger came for my head. The coif would barely stop it. I did the only thing I could do; I whipped up my left hand as I stepped into the blow. I was lucky for the dagger caught on the mail links at the side of the coif and although it drove through them it struck air and not my flesh. He was a veteran, and he pulled his head back to butt me. If he had connected, then I would be a dead man. I hooked my left leg around his right and leaned my shoulder into him. He began to overbalance. That was when the weight of my mail came to my aid and neither of us could keep our balance. We fell to the ground and the sloping stone there added to the weight of my mail made my body roll on the wet sand. As I rolled, I reached around for my dagger.

The Scotsman was fast, and he was on his feet in an instant. His own dagger had been torn from his grip for it was entangled in my mail, but he had a small hatchet in his belt, and he pulled that. He swung his sword at my prostrate body and I rolled away, the blade hitting the damp sand. Even as I began to rise, he chopped at me with his hatchet and I was barely able to block it with my sword. I saw, on the top of the tall dune a shadow and I assumed it was Thomas. That gave me hope for it meant that even if I was wounded Thomas' help might enable us to take him. First, I had to survive this encounter with a chillingly skilful warrior.

"You have had luck up to now, but luck can only last so long." He gestured with the axe, "And when you are dead, I will have your man too! You should have left well alone, Sir William, and not bothered yourself with matters which were not your concern!" He thought he had distracted me enough with his words and he brought his sword around from behind his back in an attempt to slice through the mail on my left side. He must not have seen me draw the dagger and thought I was undefended on my left side. The blades screeched together, and my dagger slowed down the sword but it was a powerful blow. The sword sliced through mail and my gambeson to draw blood and it encouraged the Scot who ripped his sword backwards to enlarge the wound.

I tried his own tactics on him, "You mean I should not be concerned that war bands of Vikings are loose in the heartland of England? All I now need to do is to establish your identity and I shall know your lord!"

I did not think it would work but he lost concentration, albeit briefly. I wondered if he thought he had something on him to identify his master. Whatever the reason I swung my sword, backhand at his left side. He had quick and natural reactions. The hatchet came down, but it had a wooden handle and my sword hacked through it and ripped open his brigandine. He swung his sword and I blocked it with my sword and my dagger. As he pulled back his head to butt me Thomas' sword came up through his back and out close to his neck.

Even as he died, he cursed us, "Treacherous English bastards! Have you no..." He got no further and fell in a pool of blood on the damp sand.

121

A figure stood on the tall dune, "Sir William! Are you hurt?" It was Calum.

"Nothing but my pride. We are coming!"

"Thank you, Thomas, but I hoped I could take him prisoner."

"Sorry my lord, I had to be sure."

Sheathing my weapons I said, "Let us search him… We can leave his body here for the tide, but I want everything he wears from his brigandine to his boots. We seek a clue to the leader of these ghosts."

We took a purse and a ring, as well as his weapons and we headed back to the house. When we reached it, I saw that Sir Geoffrey had lit brands and my archers were spread out searching for any who had survived. We deposited the Scotsman's goods and I asked, "Anyone hurt?"

Sir Geoffrey shook his head, "Just scratches. There were fourteen of them, including the one you pursued, and we overwhelmed them before they knew what we were about. We are searching just to make sure. There were twelve ponies and one horse." He glanced at Calum. "Your man here recognised one of them."

I looked at the Irishman. He nodded, "Fergal. He was a shield brother, but I thought him dead. I had not seen him since we fought and lost against Sir Cailean." For the first time since I had known him, Calum looked less than confident. He shook his head, "If I had thought any were left alive then I would have waited in Norway. He must have arrived there and taken up Guthrum's offer. I knew in my heart that he was not dead."

I nodded, "And the others?"

Carl the Dane said, "I recognise some from Norway. I could not tell you their names. Perhaps they tired of being without work."

Sir Geoffrey asked, "Something I do not understand. Surely their King would employ them? He is desperate for warriors."

Carl shook his head, "Their king demands total loyalty. You fight for him. These men wished to fight for themselves."

I nodded as things fell into place, "Then these men were not destined for service with King Hákon but some Scottish lord. That much we have learned." Sir Geoffrey nodded his agreement. "Take everything from them and then make a funeral pyre below the high-water line. We burn them and the sea will take their ashes away. Their Scottish master may know something has happened when his men do not arrive but Guthrum may not and I want no sign that we have discovered their nefarious plot. Take everything back to the hall where we can examine it at our leisure." I put my mind to what this all meant. There was a great deal of planning here and there had to be someone who was a local. They could predict within a week or so when the next men would land but they could not have strangers coming regularly from the west. Someone who lived in our land had to be aiding them and fetching horses and ponies for them.

By the time we reached my hall, it was almost dawn and I sent Thomas to tell the cooks we would need to be fed. The horses were stabled, and we assembled our finds in the inner courtyard. Many lords like to keep that a private area for themselves and their ladies. I was not precious for my men knew when to give us our privacy. As might be expected neither the weapons nor the helmets were particularly special, and most would be discarded and reused by our smith. The exceptions were the sword and dagger of Fergal. Calum begged those and the necklet with the wolf amulet he wore around his throat. The death of his shield brother had badly affected Calum. The other exceptions were the belongings of the Scotsman. His tunic had once borne a livery, but the colours were so faded that the best we could say was that it was some sort of rampant lion but as that was a sign of their king and many other lords it did not help us. His sword was a good one but was old. There was no fuller and it was shorter than the ones we used. The purse contained a variety of coins and while some were Scottish, many others were English. The only clue we had came from the dagger. Alan Longsword recognised it as belonging to the Atholl clan. That suggested the Comyn family for they had used a member of the Atholl family to cause dissension before.

Alan Longsword tended to my wound with vinegar and honey while my men spoke. Erik Red Hair said, "I know two of these. I have not seen them since I left my home, but they were brothers and were not bad men. They must have fallen on hard times to be seduced by the offer of Guthrum the Dane. Men will fight for a captain who has a good longship or a hersir who leads warriors but from what others have told me Guthrum is nothing more than a minor warlord. He is gathering those without hope and that suggests that the war band, wherever it is to be found, will be desperate men." He looked at Calum, "These could have surrendered with honour, but they did not."

It was a sobering thought.

Food was fetched out to us for it was a pleasant morning and while the wind was a chilly one the sun shone. We had slices of fried ham on freshly baked bread smothered in butter. It was a feast. It lightened the mood a little, but we knew that we had failed for we were no closer to discovering our enemy. That and the death of Fergal, which Calum blamed on no one except the three sisters, conspired to take away from what had been a victory.

"We have one glimmer of hope." All eyes turned to look at me. "The ponies. Someone must know when men are coming for there are ponies brought. Even if they are brought at night, the reverse of the journey the men would have taken, they still need to be brought. From this day, Carl, I want two riders to ride the road to Gretham and looked for signs that ponies have crossed it. They can disguise and hide the dung but when they leave the road, they will flatten the grass."

Carl's red head nodded, "I will make it myself, Sir William and one other. That way we can ride the same route and not miss anything."

Alan asked, "And when we find the animals?"

"That is simple, we take the man or men with them and question them until we find when the next ship is due. I want to take Guthrum and his ship. We stop this trade at the source and that way we can discover where the warriors are bound!"

It was a plan!

Chapter 12

The Deadly Marshes

Five days later Calum came to see me, "Lord, I am troubled." I nodded. Everyone had commented that this normally cheerful warrior had been anything but since his shield brother had died. "Fergal was more than a shield brother. He was my cousin and when I thought him dead that was when I went with the others who had survived and went a-Viking to Roskilde. I know, for my part, I wanted a warrior's death, but I can now see that I was meant to stay alive. I owe it to Fergal to find out what happened to him and to discover if any others survived. Something I cannot explain tells me that this is so. I would like to be released from your service lord. Perhaps this was meant to be and when I have found the truth then I will return, and if you will have me, become your warrior once more."

I nodded, "I told you once, Calum, that I would release you when you asked, and I will let you go and give you a horse and a pony as well as gold but what is it you hope to do?"

"I will go back to Argyll for it was there we were captured, and I was told that Fergal was dead. We lost many friends in that battle and I did not question Fergal's death. I will find out the truth for there are men there who will know."

"You have fought for both sides and made enemies on both sides. You will be friendless."

"That does not worry me, Sir William." Looking at him I knew that to be true. He was the most confident warrior I had ever known.

He left two days later. I gave him one of the captured ponies and a good horse we had found at the house in the dunes as well as gold I thought he had earned in my service. My wife also provided him with food and a skin of mead for he had seemed fond of that. He was a popular warrior, and all were sad to see him go. He promised to visit Stockton and speak with my father on his way west. I had only been to visit my father once, and I did not wish to leave in case Carl found horse or pony tracks. Calum left and Matthew wept. My youngest child enjoyed being around the warriors and Calum had always found time for him. It was like my father's debt of honour to Birger Persson. Calum's was to a dead kinsman. He would honour that debt.

Calum had not been with us long, certainly not as long as most but his absence was noticed. Life, however, went on. It was five months from the royal wedding and my wife was determined that both of us would dress as finely as any. Thanks to my father's generosity, money was no object and she sent to Flanders for the finest of cloths. We had women who worked for us and they would sew the tunic and dress for the wedding. Each day, of course, Carl would ride to the road and check for a disturbance.

Sir Geoffrey doubted that they would return, "When that Scotsman, ponies and warriors fail to turn up then they will know that we have caught their men."

I nodded, for I agreed with him, "But Geoffrey, if you were this unknown Scottish lord would you not wish to know for certain? I know that the unknown would eat at me. He may send someone, or he may, simply, shift his attention elsewhere and find another deserted beach."

Carl did not mind the seemingly endless task. He and whichever other archer accompanied him would stop in Seaton. There they would enjoy salted fish and they would talk to the villagers. The folk of Seaton Carrowe were grateful that they had not been punished. Many other lords would have done so. They became even more loyal and it was they who, six weeks after we had slain the Scot, told me that they had seen a Norse knarr heading for the mouth of the river. They sailed one of their fishing boats into the harbour so that we might know immediately.

'The Maid of Hwitebi' was in port and had just unloaded. I knew her captain and I approached him, "There is a suspicious vessel in the river. I would like you to take my men and me out to question her captain." He looked worried. "I will make good any damage which you incur and if it proves to be an enemy, I will give you first refusal on any equipment on the ship."

He nodded, "Under those terms, I will take you, Sir William. I pray you to hurry for the tide is on the turn and the river can be treacherous although the recent rain has risen the level a little."

It took less than half an hour to load my men and head south. What was unusual about this visit, if it was Guthrum, was that he normally came at dusk so that he could slip away in the dark. It was early afternoon when John had spied him and the men of Seaton Carrowe had still been out fishing. I mentioned my fears to the Captain, and he shook his head, "He may have wanted to land in the dark but if he has sense then he would want to get as far upstream in daylight. Do you know which side he will land?"

"If it is the one I think it is, then the north shore."

He nodded, "Then he will sail just half a mile upstream. Beyond that the only place to land is Stockton and he would not wish that."

I regretted not sending half of my men by road to cut off any who landed. It was a mistake and an understandable one, but a lord of the manor could not afford to make such mistakes.

The ship seemed to be very slow and yet I knew that the captain was making good time. It was just that I was used to travelling at the speed of a horse. Captain Alf had a good lookout and he shouted down from the top of the mast and crosstree, "Sail ahead, Captain, just entering the estuary."

I looked to the right and saw the dunes. There was nothing to mark the cottage and dunes were constantly changing but I had the impression that we had just passed it. That meant we would soon be close to the place Thomas had slain the Scotsman. I turned to Idraf, "As soon as we can I want her showering with arrows. They cannot have archers and from the men we have already seen, few will have mail. I would have them surrender sooner rather than later."

"Aye, lord, but the wind is from the north-west."

I nodded, "And that aids us for their progress will be slower, but I appreciate it will lessen your range, Do your best."

He went around the archers and arranged them along the gunwale. He knew better than any the range of the men he led.

Sir Geoffrey approached, "I should have led men by horse, lord, as I did last time, to cut them off."

I laughed, "You read my mind! It is too late now. We will try to land and then pursue them afoot."

Captain Alf heard me, "It will mean a muddy dousing for you, Sir William. Your boots will be ruined!"

"Better new boots than we allow this treachery to continue!"

Nodding he shouted, "Prepare to come about! Keep a good watch on the mud banks!"

It was as we turned that the knarr, now much closer, saw us. The ship had been forced to reef her sails as she entered the muddy estuary. I could see her now that we had turned for what she was. She was a knarr, a ship which had not changed for more than two hundred years. Shallow bottomed and wide they were a perfect vessel for navigating the shallowest of rivers. This one, however, must have had a weed-infested hull for we were gaining inexorably on her. I saw, in the late afternoon light, metal on the decks. That and her flight confirmed that this was our enemy.

I saw that we still had full sail for the captain knew this part of the river as he had often sailed to Stockton. It was as though we had a rope on the knarr, and we were drawing her back to us, "Captain, can you get to her larboard side and stop her leaving?"

127

"Perhaps, why?"

"If we can drive her on to the mud, we can take her and her crew. That way you should still have enough water beneath your hull."

"I can try but how will you force her over?"

"I will conjure a shower."

He looked up at the sky which just had a few scudding clouds, "There will be no rain, Sir William!"

I smiled, "A shower of arrows and that will be far more deadly."

"Aye, then we can close with her. Nob, break out the grappling hooks. We will secure the ship to us if we are able!" I saw from the busy way they went about their business that the crew were enjoying this. They would be in no danger as their ship was filled with my warriors. It would make a change from their normal work.

The knarr captain, I assumed it was Guthrum, decided to cut his losses. He headed towards the shore. The tide had still to turn and there was an inlet which he turned towards. He did not slow but headed up the narrow patch water.

Captain Alf said, "Clever! It is as though he read your mind, Sir William. We cannot grapple him. The best I can do is to land you on the muddy grass."

"Then do so and when we have gone secure the knarr. Will you be able to take it back to Hartlepool?"

"Aye."

"Then land us."

"That is Snook Point, Sir William, and it looks like he is heading for Cowpon Marshes."

I turned to Alan Longsword, "I will go with the archers and Sir Geoffrey and his men. I want you to take half of the men at arms and return to Hartlepool. Mount horses and cut these off. It will not be the Gretham Road this time but the road to Cowpon. The wind will be with you and you should do the journey back to our home quicker than the one here."

"They may be long gone by then," he pointed to the ship whose passengers and crew were disgorging from the knarr which was now grounded.

"I doubt that their horses will be close. We forced them to land here. This was not their choice." I shrugged, "We can do little else."

"Aye lord." He turned and began to divide the men. It meant I would have twelve archers and, with Sir Geoffrey and our squires, eight men at arms. It would be enough.

Captain Alf had reefed the sails and I looked at the sky, we had just three hours of daylight left. Ahead of us was marshland dotted with scrub and the occasional hardy but stunted tree. We would have to negotiate small creeks and mudbanks, but the enemy would too, and we had, at least, ended the threat of more men coming over. We had their knarr. Captain Alf did not want to damage his ship and he went in gently. Idraf and my archers waited for no command and leapt ashore when the side of the cog was still ten feet from the bank. A couple splashed into the water, but more than half landed on the bank. They took off like greyhounds after their prey. I could see heads appearing and disappearing as they ran through the mudbanks. I waited until we were close enough for me to guarantee dry feet.

"Sir Geoffrey, take Tom of Rydal and make sure there is no one left aboard the knarr. Fetch any papers with you. Alan Longsword and the men at arms can assist you. Then have Tom follow us."

"Aye, Sir William."

As I turned to follow my archers and the other men at arms, I saw arrows rising and falling as targets were seen. There were cries as those fleeing were hit. As much as I wanted prisoners, I wanted none of my men hurt. If there were any wounded, then they would be made to talk. We found the first body just two hundred paces into the grass and scrub. Thomas and I stopped by the corpse for there were rings upon his fingers and the tunic he wore was made of good material. He was dead. An arrow had struck something vital and the wide pool of blood told me he had bled out quickly. Erik Red Hair knelt next to me and tapped the warrior bands. There were just two of them, "He is a Dane and has a full purse."

I nodded, "I fear that this is Guthrum for Calum said he bore two battle bands. We will not learn anything from him." Thomas took the purse and put it in his leather satchel. Erik took the sword and seax and put them in his belt.

We stood and ran after the archers and the other men at arms. Idraf and Carl were almost out of sight as we passed another body. This one was not well dressed and was young. He was another sword for hire. This was a footrace and the deeper into the marshlands we got the wider the enemy spread out. We were spread out in a long line more than half a mile long and we were no longer running. That was not because we were unfit, but the enemy could be hiding and so Thomas and I worked as a pair. One moved forward while the other watched for a blade darting from the grass. The sun was setting but there was at least an hour to go. There was an occasional shout and cry from ahead of us, but I had no way of knowing if it was my men or the enemy.

Our caution was rewarded. The sun had slipped a little more and we were approaching from the eastern shadows. The shrubs and weeds had taken over from the mud. Thomas was ahead with his dagger in one hand and his sword in the other. Two men rose from either side of him and it was clear that they had not seen me. Thomas had quick reactions but not quick enough and I saw one sword glance off his dagger and cut his leg. I brought my sword over and my sword chopped through the arm of one of them while Thomas' dagger drove up under the chin of the other and into his brain. The warrior whose sword-arm I had chopped through dropped to his knees as he attempted to stem the flow of blood, but it would be in vain. However, I had to try, and I ripped the bottom from the dead man's tunic and tied it above the wound.

I turned his face to me, as I tightened the bandage, "Where were you bound?"

His eyes widened and he tore himself from my grasp and ran. He was bleeding too heavily to get far. I was aware that Thomas was bleeding and I let him go. I tore another length of tunic and fastened it. The cut was not deep, but it would need attention.

"Can you walk?"

He nodded, "Aye. It was just a shock."

We wanted to hurry on, but I was aware that dusk had descended and there were even more shadows now. I went ahead of Thomas expecting a blade to lunge at me any moment. I still heard cries from ahead of us, but I was confident that my archers and men at arms would get the better of these mercenaries. I smelled smoke before I saw the embers from the fires of the houses of Cowpon. As I neared the hamlet, I heard hooves in the distance and wondered if that was my men or survivors riding away.

When I reached the village, I saw that all my archers and men at arms were intact but there was no sign of horses. Sir Geoffrey and John appeared from the north end of the hamlet. The villagers had emerged from their houses and the headman, Edgar, approached me, "We heard noises and cries, my lord. It is late. We armed ourselves and then saw your men. What is going on?"

"Were there any strangers hanging around for the last few days?"

"Not that I saw. What about you others?"

Most of them shook their heads but old Tom who lived at the southern end of the village said, "Not a stranger but I did see Oswald, you know, my lord, the son of Alec the Scot. He lives Norton way; on the Billingham side." He pointed to the south.

I had heard the name but did not know him. I nodded.

"I saw him down at the deserted house at Low Belasis."

"Why do you mention that, Tom?"

"Why, he was riding a pony and I saw him light a fire in the house. It has been deserted these last ten years since Annie and Ned One Leg died of the pestilence. The house is falling down."

Just then Alan rode in with my men at arms. Their horses were lathered, and they had been riding hard. "Alan, did you meet anyone?"

"No my lord. Peter and Harry are bringing horses for you to ride. They had to go slower than us. I thought you might need a ride."

"I know your horses are tired but ride to Low Belasis." It was just a mile down a narrow greenway. "Look for signs of horses. It may be that they were kept there but I suspect that the noise on the marsh will have carried there and the prey will have fled."

"Who am I looking for?"

"Someone called Oswald."

They rode off and Edgar and the other villagers fetched us ale. "What was the trouble, Sir William?"

"Men have been landing on the river. I did not realise that it was so close from Cowpon to the river."

"Aye, but it can be treacherous for them as don't know it."

I nodded, "And that is why they needed Oswald." I looked at Idraf. "Were all the men from the knarr accounted for?"

"I know not my lord. Tomorrow, when it is daylight I will return, and we will scour the marshes for their bodies."

"Edgar, keep a good watch from now on and if you spy anyone then send a rider to me!"

"Aye, my lord!"

Harry and Peter arrived with horses for us. I took a decision then, "When Alan returns, if it is empty handed, then Thomas and I will ride to my father's castle in Stockton. I fear we may be too late, but I would have liked to speak with Oswald from Norton way."

Alan and the men at arms returned. They were walking their horses. On the backs of their horses, they carried sacks. "Whoever was there has left but he left in a hurry. I am no Carl the Betts but even I can read tracks. There was one man and he had two ponies or small horses. We found food in the sacks and there had been a fire. Someone had doused it. I think they were going to hide out in the deserted house. Perhaps they were waiting for horses."

I nodded, "Give the food to Edgar and when you are ready, head home. Come, Thomas, we need to see my father and have your leg tended by his doctor."

Thomas' leg was stiffening up when we reached Stockton and both the gates to the town and the castle were barred. As soon as I was identified we were admitted and my mother and father, dressed in nightclothes, rushed down when they heard the commotion. Dick, Sir Mark, Sir Petr and Folki also arrived a few minutes late. I guessed Dick had been given my room in the tower. My mother, of course, was naturally upset when she saw Thomas' bloody leg and she and the doctor took him off. Wine was brought and I told my father all.

"I do not know this Oswald, father, although I have heard the name; who is he?"

"His father was a warrior who was in the garrison at Carlisle. He came here just after the Scottish wars when King Henry was just twenty. Being Scottish he was viewed with suspicion, but he farmed Holme House between Norton and Billingham. He never bothered anyone and kept to himself. He married a Danish woman and they had one son Oswald. To be honest, son, I had not heard of Oswald for some time and I thought he might be dead. Tomorrow I will have men seek him out and ask Edward what he knows." Edward ran the largest tavern in Stockton, '*The Blue Gryphon*' and he knew all the gossip.

My mother returned and I asked, "How is Thomas?"

"He says it is a scratch, but the doctor has stitched it!" There was veiled criticism in my mother's voice.

My father shook his head, "He has a wound and it will not harm him. He is a squire, and such things are to be expected."

My mother frowned and then said, "And you, young man, should be in bed!" Poor Richard bore the brunt of my mother's irritation.

When she had gone my father said, "You have learned no more then?"

"Other than a Scottish lord is involved, no. It could be any of half a dozen men, but I am not sure that the treachery is intended to England. I cannot give you a reason, but it is just a feeling."

"I think I agree with you. If England was the target, then they would not use the valley as a thoroughfare. Tomorrow we shall see Edward and ride to Norton. I do not like to think of traitors dwelling here. Perhaps I should use Sir John and Sir Mark here to make my presence known." John and Mark had been knighted some years earlier. As John and Henry Samuel got on so well, he lived at Elton for he was unmarried.

"Aye, that would be a good idea. Sir Fótr can identify danger in the village but there are many outlying farms. Sir Mark could take some of your men at arms and archers. He is an affable young man and well-liked in the valley. None would see him as a threat." My father knew what I meant. There were other knights, who had married into the family, who were slightly more aggressive. Perhaps that was the issue with Thomas' father, Sir Robert.

I saw Mark beam at the compliment and he nodded, "I will do so at first light, my lord."

I turned to Folki, "When you were waiting for a ship were you offered a free passage?"

He nodded, "But as it involved working for another lord, I would not even consider it."

"Were you told what it would involve?"

"Yes, Sir William, we would be taken to England and make our way in secret to join other warriors. That was another reason I chose not to take passage. It was all vague. When Sir Petr and I had been seeking work there were some offers but they did not sound right for a knight. Was that not so, my lord?"

Petr nodded, "When the king's man came to ask if we would serve him it sounded like the work for a knight. He made it sound as though we were freeing oppressed people from the Scots."

My father nodded, "I was lucky, Petr, like your father I found crusades and they were willing to pay for my sword. I think we can see now that this trade has been going on for some time. There may be almost two hundred mercenaries somewhere in England or, perhaps Scotland! That is a large number of men to hide."

"And that helps us, father, for there are few such castles and the one we seek must be out of the way. We are closer and getting closer each day. I just pray that we are not too late for whatever it is that they have planned."

Like Hartlepool, my father's manor rose early, and my father and I went with Richard to speak to Edward. My mother forbade Thomas to stir. Sir Petr went to fetch Henry Samuel and Sir John. Edward was a friendly man and he loved having two such famous knights in his tavern. I knew that he would make much of it and the whole town would know our business by the end of the day. That was no bad thing and would warn others of the dangers of bad behaviour. I had to tell him of the incursion else the questions I asked would make no sense.

He shook his head, "That is bad, my lord. Well, we have had neither Dane nor Norse through here in many a month. Now, Oswald, it is a funny thing, lord, but I had not seen him here for more than a year until he came in one day and sat at that table." He pointed to a small table in the corner. "He nursed a couple of ales all morning and then a Scottish chap came in to speak to him. The Scot paid for food for them and I took him to be a relative. Oswald's dad being Scottish, like. They ate and left. I guessed they went to Oswald's farm. I never saw them more."

"What about Oswald, Edward?" My father knew how to get more information for he knew Edward, "You say you had not seen him for a couple of years, but you must have heard rumours."

"I do not like to gossip, my lord."

We both kept a straight face, "Just this once, Edward, indulge me."

The landlord leaned forward conspiratorially, "His farm, so I hear, has not been doing too well. He keeps but a few animals and his land is all tares and weeds, yet he rides a good horse and when he came into town he was dressed well in good boots. Jack the cordwainer did not make them that is for sure." We waited for there was obviously more. "The word was that he worked with smugglers. His farm is only half a mile from the river and is close to Samphire Batts. There used to be a family lived by the river, but they could not make a go of the fishing. The house fell down but the wooden jetty they built is still there." He leaned back, "I am not saying that is all true, but you asked me, my lord."

My father slipped him a shilling, "Well that is for your trouble, Edward, and if any other strangers, especially Scottish ones, come to town then I would know, immediately. Do you understand?" There was steel in my father's voice and Edward looked suitably chastened.

My father had sent for Henry Samuel and Sir John before we left and when we returned the two of them were talking to Dick and Thomas. My squire was retelling the recent events. We had spoken on the way back to the castle and my father said, "Thomas, are you fit to ride?"

"Aye, Grandfather."

Dick looked eagerly at my father and he said, "And you, too, Dick. The ride will do you good. You have been stuck inside Stockton too long. Henry Samuel and John, I shall need you two and a couple of archers and men at arms."

"Aye, Grandfather."

Thomas said, "But Grandmother said…"

My father put his finger to his lips, "And if we slip out quietly then she will never know." He was like a naughty boy and he grinned.

We headed first to Holme House. As Edward had said, it looked ill tended but when we entered we saw that it was comfortably furnished and more, there was an armoury. When Henry Samuel investigated the stables, they found that they would hold a dozen horses and there was both tack and feed. My father sent two men back for a wagon. We would empty the house for the hole in the floor of the kitchen told us that Oswald had taken his money with him. He had fled. We then headed to Low Belasis. We spied two other dwellings, but all were far enough away from each other so that any goings on were hidden. They were High Belasis and Middle Belasis. John questioned the farmers while we went to the ramshackle and rundown house. Sir Mark would be further afield seeking answers and looking for signs of the invaders.

My men had already searched the farm but that had been in the dark. Now we saw that there were straw mattresses and that there was cookware to make food. When we headed to the river, we found that Edward was quite right. It was close enough to the river to be able to land goods but it had not been goods which Oswald had smuggled but people. We dismounted and looked at the jetty. It had been recently repaired and there were enough footprints in the mud to show that someone had used the track regularly.

Thomas sat on the jetty and rested his injured leg on a post, "Uncle, this is the way I see it. This is too far from the coast to be able to land successfully at night. I think that when we assumed that after they had gone around Gretham they took the Newton Bewley road, we were wrong. They took the road to Cowpon which also leads to Low Belasis. We have just come from Holme Farm and seen how close they are. I think our attack on Hunter's House made them change their plans. This Guthrum had to risk the river but he was not confident about using it at night. Low Belasis was a halfway house. They intended to land at the jetty, spend the night at the deserted farm and then make their way to Holme House. After that, the plan would be the same."

It made sense. Henry Samuel said, "Then if you are correct, when we find Oswald then we find the identity of this rogue lord."

Thomas nodded. My father said, "And Oswald could be anywhere!"

Henry Samuel shook his head, "Not so, grandfather. This lord must have money and be west of here. It stands to reason that he needs to have a very large castle! I have an idea. Why do we not make a progress along the valley? We could use the excuse that we are showing Sir Petr the land."

I shook my head, "It is a good idea, but we do not involve my father. I saw my father about to object and I held up my hand, "We cannot take a large number of men and so this will be dangerous. We need knights, men at arms and archers who are fast and quick thinking. It also needs planning. I have to be at the royal wedding in six weeks. This will take at least four days to plan. Let us say that we meet at Stockton castle in five days. Sir John, Sir Petr, Sir Mark, Sir Henry Samuel and Sir Geoffrey should be enough. We take ten archers and ten men at arms."

I saw no objections on any faces and my father eventually nodded, "Very well, the old warhorse will stay at home!"

Chapter 13

A Royal Wedding

Sir Mark returned before we headed home. He found no evidence but enough hearsay to confirm that men were using the route which Thomas had suggested. We still maintained our patrols along the dune road and the two farms at Low Belasis and Holme House were watched. It was a deterrent more than anything else. Ships were also more closely scrutinised. Captain Alf had done well out of the knarr and all the local captains saw the benefit of being watchful. Even though all of this was in place I was unhappy. Each night when Thomas and I played chess we discussed what we knew. I felt that our enemy was two steps ahead of us. It was almost as though they could read our minds. We had thwarted them twice, but they appeared to have contingency plans in place. I assumed that they were bringing warriors in but using a different route. Unless, of course, they had enough. Most frustratingly of all we still did not know the target.

My wife was not happy that we were off again so soon, but she understood the need. This time I took just six of my men at arms and six archers. The rest would come from Stockton. We headed along the Tees and used the road which was familiar to us. We had discussed a possible threat to Durham and, indeed, Sir Fótr had visited with the Bishop to inform him of our suspicions. We first visited Walworth Castle which was the home of the Hansard family. They were not a family of knights although when needed they obeyed my father's summons for men. It was clear that they knew nothing, neither was the castle big enough to house the mercenary warband. Indeed, on our progress half of our men had to sleep in the barn and stables. Sir Robert Hansard was bemused by our progress, but Sir Petr's story entertained him and his family.

It was while we were with Sir Robert that he mentioned Richmond and Middleham castles. Although both were south of the Tees both qualified due to their size. Richmond intrigued me for it had been given to the Duke of Brittany and there was no lord of the manor, just a castellan. It struck me that it was the perfect place to hide a large number of soldiers and was close enough to both the Tees and York to be a threat. As Henry Samuel said, when we rode south, the problem was that it was too far from Scotland and the only man we had spoken to had been Scottish. As it turned out the visit was a productive one as

Alan Durban was a gracious host who enjoyed the visit of so many young knights with tales to tell. We stayed for three days and he was able to put our minds at rest about Middleham. Henry Samuel and I had dismissed it already for the distances were too great.

We then headed to Raby and the Nevill family. Sir Geoffrey was a good warrior, and he was astute enough to ask the right questions. He did not live at Raby but was visiting for there was good hunting nearby. I had to give him a version of the truth and said we were hunting men who had been engaged in banditry. He promised to keep an eye open for strangers. That left us with Barnard Castle. We were stopped from visiting the castle, not by treachery but the weather. Snow and ice usually arrived in late December, early January but that year it came at the very end of November. We were forced to change our plans when we reached Greta Bridge and we headed back to Stockton. The journey took three days rather than the one. We were all disappointed, but Henry Samuel promised that when the weather improved, he would lead men out again. I would be unable to help my father's knights for I had an appointment in York and a royal wedding to attend.

Mary, of course, was relieved, for it meant that not only had I not suffered any harm but also that we could get to York early. I was not senior enough to warrant accommodation in either the castle or the Archbishop's palace and Sir Ralph would be hard put to find chambers for us. Getting there early meant that we could find rooms in one of the inns. My family's name was well known, and I hoped to find rooms for not only me but also my eight men. Sir Geoffrey would guard my home and my family. Dick would be coming with us as my page. As we were going to York, I took Erik Red Beard, Alan Longsword, Tom of Rydal and Ralph of Middleham. I was confident that we would be protected both on the road and in York. Idraf and Carl chose two archers with York connections, Harry Longbow and Andrew the Walker.

We had one night in Stockton where we found that the icy freeze was thawing a little and Henry Samuel hoped to travel to Barnard Castle in the first week of January. We broke our journey at East Harlsey, Sir Richard had died, and it was his son Sir Roger who was lord of that small manor. We rode hard and reached York the next day. We found an inn close to the Bootham Bar and the Minster. My men were not as happy as they might have been as the better alehouses were closer to the river. As the other royal guests had yet to arrive, we were able to dine with Sir Ralph.

Sir Ralph had aged in the last couple of years and the royal wedding had not helped. He was aware of the threats to both King Henry and King Alexander. He was, therefore, very interested in my story of the

Vikings and other mercenaries. "We have many Norse and Danish families within these walls but I can see why they did not try to smuggle them in here. Our Scandinavian families are very loyal, and strangers would have been noticed. As we knew we had a royal wedding here, for the last two months, every visitor with a sword has been questioned at the gates. Any who behaved suspiciously were either barred or confined. I think I agree with you, Sir William, this threat is to Scotland and King Alexander. I know that our king is unpopular but I cannot see him being a target for killers; those barons who oppose his policies are either further west or further north."

I nodded, "I swore to protect the young king and I have a duty to my king too. If you need me or my men, then call upon me."

He nodded, "You know that I would have you stay with me if I could but…"

"I understand. Where will King Alexander reside while he is here?"

"With Archbishop Gray at the palace. Princess Margaret and her family, along with the King and Queen, will be here. We have a large castle, but I know that noses will have been put out at some of the accommodation."

I knew the problem. When King Henry had stayed at Stockton even though it had been for just one night the disruption seemed to last for weeks. "At least they will wish to return south as soon as possible." Although the early cold weather had gone both Ralph and I knew that the worst northern weather usually waited for January.

"They will but none of us knows what the Scots will do."

My wife and I also visited with Walter Gray, the Archbishop of York. He was more philosophical about the arrival of the Scottish delegation. "It is my understanding that it will be a modest group which arrives." He smiled at me, "Perhaps King Alexander invited you for he views you as a friendly face. Anyway, the Queen will be accompanied by the Lords Durward, Dunbar and Galloway. I am able to accommodate just a few of their knights. The rest will be housed in the servant's quarters. I am afraid that the servants will have to make do with storerooms and outbuildings. We have many of those but December is not the month to be sleeping in unheated buildings."

We nodded. "And what of those with pretensions to the Scottish crown?" My wife flashed me an irritated look for she did not like what she called meddling in the politics of Scotland.

"You mean de Brus, de Balliol and the Comyns?" I nodded. "As far as I am aware none will be attending but I am not sure if that is because they were not invited or chose not to come. For my part, I am just pleased for I would have been hard-pressed to find a suitable chamber for any of them. And you are comfortable at the ***Golden Fleece***?"

My wife nodded, "It is just an honour to be at the wedding of one who was, until I married, my liege lord. The inn is comfortable, and we have virtually taken it over. The landlord is keen to do all that he can to make us comfortable."

The Archbishop smiled, "And he knows better than to displease me for I am his closest neighbour."

We chatted about inconsequential matters until my wife asked if she might pray in the cathedral and light candles for her parents. The Archbishop was delighted to oblige and the Dean himself accompanied her. That afforded the Archbishop and me the opportunity to speak openly and I told him of the threat which was still present. After I had presented him with the facts and my actions he said, "So, Sir William, there are a large number of mercenary warriors loose in the north of this land." I nodded. "Then they are being gathered for a purpose. Is it a threat to Scotland or England?"

"Or both?"

"Quite so. And does King Henry know of the danger?"

"Not yet but I shall tell him when he arrives. I know that the king likes facts and all we have is conjecture. I could not, in all honesty, say that any Norsemen or Danes have landed. The evidence is a little thin."

"From what you say, however, it may be more than just Scandinavians. Irish, Islanders, Welshmen and Englishmen may all be involved. I will see what I can discover. There will be bishops and priests attending the wedding and most come from the north. One of those may have information which is of use to us." Now that the Dean had left us, we were alone and the Archbishop of York waved away the servants. Leaning his head in he said, "The king has angered some of his barons by taking the cross but doing nothing about it beyond gathering taxes for the crusade."

He had surprised me, "I did not know he was going on a crusade."

"He is not but King Louis did and so he feels honour bound to say he is going on one. We both know, Sir William, that he is no warrior. The earl marshal is dead. Who would lead his armies? The ones who might, yourself included, were sent to secure Wales. His other leaders hold Scotland for him. Who is left? De Montfort? It will be interesting who is brought by King Henry for this wedding!"

The weather was wet and cold rather than icy when the two royal parties arrived. It was not long past the winter solstice and the days were so short that if you rose a little late you saw no light in the sky at all. I thought it a little strange to choose such a date for a wedding. I think when the date was arranged there were other considerations and they were political ones. King Henry arrived first and I spoke with him on the first evening of his arrival. The Archbishop had been prescient. None of the great dukes and lords attended him except for his younger brother Richard of Cornwall and his son Henry of Almain. Prince Edward was there too and he had grown, now twelve years old he was a tall gangly youth but he took a keen interest in all matters both military and political. When I spoke of the incursions, he leaned forward with the fingers of his hands pressed together almost as though he was praying. I later learned this helped him to think and stopped him flapping his hands around.

His father, the king, said, "Then we know not where this unknown number of warriors may be hiding or, indeed, if any have actually arrived. It could be that someone is just bringing warriors back from the east."

"It could be, King Henry, but the evidence I have is of a trade which goes back months. You met Sir Petr at my father's castle and his squire was invited to take ship and that was long ago."

The king waved a hand over the table, "But where are they and what is their purpose?"

Richard of Cornwall said, "There are many rich lords in the north, brother. They could afford to fit out and maintain an army of killers. This is not the south where castles and manors almost overlook each other. The land is so poor for crops up here that the manors are huge and still unprofitable."

King Henry stroked his beard, "Keep us informed, Sir William. Do you think there is a danger to us here, in York?" I heard the fear in his voice for he knew that there were enemies who wished him harm.

"York has strong walls, my lord, and the Sherriff knows his business. When the weather allows, my knights and I will ride west to look for signs of them."

"Before I leave, I will give you the authority to question all my lords. You and your father have shown yourselves to be as loyal as any." He turned to his sons, for the six-year-old Edmund was also there, "When you are older be wise and surround yourselves with such loyal lords. The crown is a perilous prize, and many will wish to take it, and your head from your shoulders. My father had to endure enemies from all sides."

I said nothing for his father had been a bad king.

When King Alexander arrived, not long after King Henry and just two days before the wedding, I was summoned to the Archbishop's Palace. It was not to meet with the king but Alan Durward and Patrick

Dunbar. I thought they might have heard of the problems I had encountered on the sands, but they were blissfully unaware of them. They were more concerned with any information I had about the western side of Scotland and they saw this new threat as more of the MacDougall mischief.

We went out of the palace and, wrapped in our cloaks, walked the cloisters. We would have looked like three monks were it not for the spurs. I told them of the men landing on my beach and the incident on the road. "Is King Alexander safe here? Many Norsemen live here, and they may have loyalties to the Norwegian king."

"Sir Alan, in this part of the world that could be true in every town with more than five hundred residents. This side of the country was called the Danelaw! Even in small places like Elsdon, many men could trace their ancestry back to a Norseman. If someone wishes the king harm then it does not matter how many guards surround him, they will still try."

"Can we call upon you and your men, Sir William?"

"Of course, Lord Patrick, but I only brought a handful. There is but one gate into the palace and the Archbishop has his men there but if you ask him, he may well allow you to double the guard with your men." I took a deep breath, "My brother was murdered in this city and my father's life came within a heartbeat of being ended. All that you can do is keep a good watch. King Henry has the same problem. Have men sleep behind King Alexander's doors at night." I pointed to the walls which surrounded the palace. They were there for privacy rather than as a defence. "Have men watch the corridors too. Those walls could be scaled easily."

They both nodded and Sir Alan said, "We will be his chamberlains while he is here."

"Good idea!"

"You are staying at the inn?" I nodded, "Then we will send a man if we need you."

I almost laughed, "And how will I know he is from you, my lord? If you go racing off after wild geese every time a message comes from someone purporting to be a friend, then the king is doomed. I am known in the palace. While you are here, I will have my men make an informal and irregular patrol. I will also walk the perimeter. It is all that we can do." I had a sudden thought, "Tell me, have you had a specific warning about an attempt on his life?"

They looked at each other and Sir Patrick spoke, "There was a rumour that someone was hiring killers. We thought until you spoke with us that it was the men who landed on your beach, but those men do

141

not sound like hired killers. They sound like warriors down on their luck."

"Aye but what better place to hide a killer than in such an assembly of men?"

With that unpleasant thought in their minds, they returned to the palace and I joined my men. We would eat in the inn and I would set up the patrols. We managed to do it before my wife and her servant joined us for the meal. Dick sat next to me and while Mary chatted to Alice he said, quietly, "Can I join you on these patrols, father?" I was about to say no when he went on, "I have ridden to war with you and grandfather told me how you acted as a squire when you were younger than I."

He was right and I nodded, "But not a word to your mother and you will stay close to me the whole time!"

"Aye, father!"

Although in the days leading up to the wedding we saw no one behaving suspiciously, it was a useful thing to do as we came to know the area immediately around the palace and cathedral. It was Tom of Rydal who noticed that we could use the city walls for they overlooked all the places an enemy could hide. It meant that, at night time, when we watched we did from the wall and as we did not have to move we were as good as invisible. The one time the couple, as well as King Henry, would be guaranteed to be safe was during the ceremony. All who entered were scrutinised by two sets of royal guards and, as it was Christmas Day, I gave my men the day off and they went to drink in their favourite alehouses. None would drink to excess for it was not their way.

King Alexander had invited me to the ceremony, but I was the lowest ranking knight who was present and Dick, my wife and myself found ourselves well to the back of the mighty cathedral. We were with the senior northern knights. These were the barons who supported King Henry and that explained why they were present. The prestige of being invited to a royal wedding would strengthen their ties to the king. Robert de Nevill held Brancepath castle which was close to Durham. Henry de Percy had a manor at Topcliffe and Robert FitzMaldren held the castle at Raby, a key castle! Sir Geoffrey Nevill was also there. I vaguely knew the others but the three barons all made the effort to be close to me in the cathedral. I did not see myself as important but the fact that my father was Earl of Cleveland meant that the family was. The knights with whom I sat were not powerful yet but I knew, from speaking to them as we waited for the arrival of the two kings, that they would be. They were ambitious.

The ceremony was as long as I had expected and as tedious. This was not an ordinary marriage but a joining of houses. Senior clerics from both countries each had part of the service which was their responsibility. And then it was over. It was late in the day and already dark when the couple emerged from the church to a flurry of snow. Until I had delivered my wife to the inn, I could do nothing to protect King Alexander. I had to rely on his three advisers. When they entered the palace, I breathed a sigh of relief. There would be no feast for all the guests. King Henry held a feast at the castle to which I was invited, and King Alexander held a smaller feast for his people.

My wife rarely attended such feasts. Stockton Castle was the grandest place she dined. This was a wonderful novelty for her and she loved seeing all the ladies in their finery. Queen Eleanor was a lovely lady, and she was gracious to all. I had little to do with her and knew her husband better but that evening, she was the hostess and my wife fell under her spell. From that moment on, she would hear not a word spoken against the Queen, and by association, her husband. Even when King Henry did not behave as well as he might she supported him and championed his actions.

Prince Edward sought me out while my wife was speaking with Isabel de Nevill and Queen Eleanor, Other young men were busy downing as much wine as they could manage but not the heir to the throne. Henry Almain was almost drunk before the third course was served. "Sir William, you have recently fought the Welsh and, so I hear, the Norse and rebel Scots. Tell me, sir, which of them is the more dangerous enemy?"

I smiled, "A good question and I mean no disrespect when I say that each of them is as dangerous as the other but in their own ways."

He frowned, "What do you mean, my lord?"

"You travelled from Windsor, did you not, Prince Edward, on the Great North Road?" He nodded. "What was the land like?"

He shrugged, confused I think by the question, "Fields, farms, towns. Why?"

"But all of it was flat, was it not? Right up to York."

"What of it?"

"Scotland and Wales are mountainous countries with valleys and peaks. The land is poor for farming and in both countries, animals outnumber people. It means that any lord who wishes to control either country has to find a way to contain them with castles and use knights and men at arms to impose their will. If the two countries were like England, then your father would rule them both now. But remember

Prince Edward, castles are expensive and as your father has found Parliament does not like to give the king money!"

He spoke to me throughout the evening and I confess that I found his questions stimulating for he was a thoughtful prince. Perhaps his many illnesses had given him the time to think.

It was late when the feast ended and the three of us hurried through the streets back to the tavern. Erik and Alan were waiting for us by one of the smaller churches, Saint Saviour, and they escorted us home. "A quiet night?"

Alan knew what I meant. I was asking had they seen anything which constituted a danger. He shook his head, "It will be livelier in Hartlepool, my lord."

"Good!"

King Henry and his party did not stay long. In fact, most of his lords had departed soon after dawn the next day. King Henry only delayed as he would be staying with some of the lords who had left, and this would give them the opportunity to prepare their homes. He had told me that he wished to see me early on St Stephen's Day and I was there as the barons who were from the south began to leave.

"I have given thought to your warnings, Sir William. I fear you may be right, but I would have you be cautious. It is possible that England can benefit from this."

I did not like the implication of his words, "King Henry, I am honour bound to protect King Alexander!"

He gave me a patronising smile, "And I would not have you do other but if and when you do honour your promise it would be useful if you could remind King Alexander of the debt he owes England. That is all that I ask. Remember, Sir William, you are an English knight. This is where you owe your fealty!" There was a thinly veiled threat in his words.

I decided to bite back my response and merely nod. I had not been commanded to do anything which went against my oath.

Prince Edward also sought me out, "Sir William, you strike me as an honourable knight. When I am old enough, I would have you serve me. You are a warrior, and I would learn from warriors." The glance he gave his father told me that he realised his father was not a warrior. He was an astute prince!

Once the castle had emptied the streets of York became quieter. It was not just the lords and their ladies, it was their men at arms, servants and priests who had filled up York. The burghers of the city would have reaped the reward. Prices would have been raised and men would toast the two kings for the bounty they had brought.

I had expected King Alexander to leave too. The couple were little more than children and it was doubtful that they would even share a room until they were much older, but King Alexander was keen to stay in York and that meant I had to. My wife proved to be a boon for Queen Eleanor had asked her to keep an eye on Queen Margaret. My wife was delighted and that meant that she was accommodated in the castle. There was no room for me and so Dick and I stayed in the inn. For us, there was no relaxation and we kept up the watches. King Alexander seemed happy to speak to his new wife and his senior lords. His mother kept apart, and I found that significant.

We enjoyed a quiet two nights, and I was with Dick, Erik and Carl the Betts on the walls anticipating a journey home soon. We were well wrapped up in our cloaks for although there was no snow there was a biting wind. As Carl said, it was a lazy wind for it went through you and not around you. The four of us were used to watching in silence. For three of us, it was just good practice and Dick wanted to be like us. Carl was the archer and had eyes and senses which were different from ours. I felt him stiffen. Erik had sensed it too and we watched as he pointed. At first, we saw nothing and then we saw that someone was climbing over the wall from the Dean's herb garden. Even as we slowly stood, we saw another four men slip over and that decided us. I pointed to the inn and Dick nodded. He knew he had to fetch the rest of my men. He ran silently and we went to the stairs which led from the city walls. As we reached the bottom, we drew our swords and went through the gate to the Dean's herb garden.

We had stood watch enough times to know the layout of the Archbishop's grounds. The Dean's herb garden backed onto a pleasant green area around the cathedral. If they were going to the palace, they had two routes that they could follow. They either went along the north side of the church or risked the front and then head down the south side. The northern side was in shadows and as we clambered over the wall, we saw the shadows disappear along the north wall. There were at least four men but there could have been more. There were just three of us but there would be help within the palace. The trouble was that the guards would be more relaxed now. It was in the nature of such matters. I was grateful that the icy wind had stopped ice forming. It would have made the ground not only slippery but there would have been the risk of the noise of cracking ice.

There was another wall at the eastern end of the cathedral. They would have to climb the obstacle and the other side was guarded. We ran and Erik cupped his hands to boost Carl up the wall. The lithe and supple archer had little trouble and then I ran, planted my foot in his hands and Erik tossed me in the air. As I put my hand down to help Erik up, I saw two dead Scottish sentries. It was dark but sentries do not lie in puddles. I guessed that the puddles were their blood. The three of us slipped down and ran for the foxes were now in the henhouse. We could have shouted an alarm, but I wanted to get to the bottom of this conspiracy, and we were still in the dark. We knew not who the head of this snake was.

It was as we entered the small door and stepped over the bodies of the Scottish guard and the two servants that the shouts rent the air. I knew where the royal couple were housed; it was close to the Archbishop. Walter Gray was brave, and I hoped he would remember that he was a churchman and did not have the reactions of a warrior for these were deadly killers. I had not heard a sound. My hope lay in the presence of the three men sworn to watch over Alexander. Dunbar, Durward and Galloway could handle themselves. I knew the way and Carl and Erik followed me. Ahead of me, I heard the clash of steel and heard the shouts of battle. The palace was lit by brands in sconces and they threw odd shadows. I found the first of the attackers who had been killed by a Scottish sentry. Both lay entwined in death.

I heard an English voice shout, "Death to King Alexander!"

I turned the corner of the corridor and saw seven men dressed in tunics I vaguely recognised. The three Scottish lords had their backs to the door of King Alexander's chamber. Two more guards and an attacker lay dead, the pool of blood widening as they bled out. I did not hesitate, and I rammed my sword into the back of one man who started to turn even as my sword entered his body. Erik's shorter sword had a wide blade and when he brought it down on a second attacker it drove through a mail hauberk, gambeson and almost split the man in two. Carl's sword was augmented by his bodkin blade and he slew his man by slicing through his throat. The men who remained were now outnumbered by the six of us and I shouted, "Yield!"

The man who must have been the leader punched at Lord Durward with his dagger and whirled to try to slice through my neck with his sword, "Never!"

I blocked the strike and pulled my hand back to punch the man in the head and eliminate him. Erik was a killer and the thought of taking a prisoner was not in his nature. His sword hacked through the neck of one of the other men as Lord Dunbar slew his opponent. Alan Durward just reacted, and his sword came through the leader's back and out of the front. The last man saw his chance and pushed through between Lord Dunbar and Sir James. They fell backwards as the door was burst open. King Alexander was in the room and I leapt over the bodies, both living and dead to get to his side. The dagger which killed the last assassin came from the side of the door and took the man completely by surprise. It drove under his right arm into the armpit and thence, as it was a long dagger, into the neck of the warrior. I turned and saw that young King Alexander had waited behind the door and the dead man's blood was on his hand. The king was alone, and I saw that his bloody hand was shaking.

I smiled, "Well done, Your Majesty. It is over!" His eyes were wide, and it was a mixture of fear and excitement. I gently took the dagger from his hand. I put my arm around his shoulders and knew even as I did it that it was unseemly for this was a king. I also knew that he was just a boy. He shook as he sobbed on my shoulder. I said nothing. King Alexander's father was dead, and I was just taking his place for a brief moment.

Alan Durward entered and saw the bloody hand of the king, "Is he?"

King Alexander pulled away from me and nodded, "Thank you, Sir William."

I nodded to the last dead killer, "King Alexander showed he has warrior's blood in him, and he killed the killer."

Sir Patrick said, "They were English, and I recognise the tunics. They are from the Nevill family!"

I shook my head as I sheathed my weapons, "There is something not right about this. One was English, we heard his voice but the others?" I pointed to the one who had been killed by the king for I had been studying his body as I had held the king, "Sealskin boots!" I rolled up the sleeve of the tunic. "Battle rings!"

Erik was in the corridor examining the other bodies and he shouted triumphantly, "Tattoos!" He had lifted the hair on one dead warrior and found the tattoo.

I knelt to examine the dead man closer and opened the palm of the man the king had killed. There was a long fresh scar down the palm, "A blood oath! These men swore a blood oath and that confirms who they are!"

Sir James looked confused, "Surely they could still be from the Nevill family?"

I shook my head, "These are Vikings. The tunics are to create suspicion that the killers were sent by an English lord. My lords, Your Majesty, I believe these are some of the men who were landed close to my land. I think that they are part of an army being gathered, somewhere in England, to seize the Scottish Crown." They looked dubious. "Think about it, my lords, if Geoffrey de Nevill wished to kill

King Alexander do you really think he would send men wearing his livery?" The argument convinced them.

An examination of the bodies confirmed our suspicions. All had sworn a blood oath. Only one of the men who had entered the palace was English and the rest were all either Norse or Danes in disguise. We sealed off the palace and the Archbishop joined us. He shook his head, "This is a sorry sight and I apologise, King Alexander, that your life was placed in such danger."

Lord Dunbar shook his head, "You have no reason to reproach yourself, my lord, for this is not a fortress. We should have left for home when King Henry did."

The King was in shock but Lord Hostarius, Alan Durward, recovered quickly, "Sir William, send your men to block both ends of this corridor and bar anyone from entering."

"Erik, Carl!"

"Aye, lord!" The two men disappeared so that we were alone.

He turned to King Alexander, "We leave today, Your Majesty, and we dispose of all these bodies. We tell no one what went on!" King Alexander nodded. He had recovered his wits.

The Archbishop said, "How can you hope to hide this bloodbath!"

"We spread the story that some of our men became drunk and fought with each other. That is why we are leaving in such unseemly haste."

Walter Gray was a churchman who understood politics, but I could see that this was beyond him, "But why?"

"To gain us time. If it is announced that killers entered the palace and tried to kill King Alexander, then it might encourage others to view the young king as weak. This way the men who sent the killers will not know if they have succeeded or not. We burn their bodies, and it is as though they never existed. The only ones who know the truth are here in this corridor and chamber. We keep silent and none will ever know that an attempt was made on the life of King Alexander. That buys us time to find out who is behind this plot. I will find men to guard the king and queen until we have succeeded. Agreed?"

We all nodded our agreement, but I could see that it did not sit well with the Archbishop.

"Sir William, would you and your men accompany us to Stockton? Your father will be able to provide an escort to Durham and there we will be safe for the Bishop of Durham is our friend. It is the land between here and the River Tees where lies the danger." We nodded. "And remember we tell no one, not the Queen Mother, the Queen nor any guards. All of us are sworn to secrecy." He gave a rueful smile,

"This will be our own blood oath but without the need to resort to bloodletting!"

Chapter 14

A Warrior's Death

Dick brought my men, and it was they who took the bodies, every single one and burned them. They asked no questions, but I saw them in Dick's eyes. I just said to them, after they had piled the last body on the pyre and we headed back to the inn, "No questions and no speculation. What was done was done and here is an end to it. We do not speak of this again but we will have to be on our guard until we are safely in Stockton. Only then can we relax our vigilance." They all nodded for these were my men and as close to me as brothers. Dick's eyes pleaded with me for the truth, but I shook my head, "This is a lesson about life, Dick. Erik, Carl and I made a promise and that was a promise of silence. I do not like to do this but I must and you have to obey my commands and put this from your mind."

"I will but I do not understand."

I smiled, "As I said, a lesson in life! There are many things you will not understand. It is how you deal with them which marks you as a man."

I hated lying to my wife, but it was necessary. I smiled to her, "You have made a real impression on King Alexander, my love. He has asked us to escort him to Stockton for he says you are good company for his English wife."

She was suitably flattered and so did not question our hasty departure. Alan Durward was like a whirlwind and we left by the Bootham Bar less than an hour after dawn. The innkeeper was paid for an extra two days and I am sure that he would speculate on our sudden departure. Many others would too for the smoke which rose from our funeral pyre might raise questions. The blood had been washed from the corridors and the story of feuding, drunken guards was thin but all the ones they might question were so elevated that they would not dare to ask such senior lords not to mention a king and archbishop.

We intended to ride hard and to stay at the Priory of Mount Grace. If we did not have the Queen Mother and the other ladies, we might have made Stockton in one day but a day with less than six hours of daylight was too great an invitation for more treachery and we had the chance to reach Mount Grace before darkness fell. I rode at the van with my men. We knew the road well. Idraf and Carl rode a mile ahead of us and would be our watchdogs in case of danger. We were not helped by the

day which was both cold and misty. It was the most nervous ride of my
life for not only was I guarding the king and queen but my wife and
son. As we neared the priory nestling at the foot of the escarpment, I
breathed a sigh of relief. While Alan and my men went ahead to warn
the prior of our imminent arrival, I waited for the others to join us. We
were a smaller number now, thanks to the battle, and every warrior's
eyes showed the same trepidation as mine.

Alan Durward forced a weak smile, "Well that is half of the most
dangerous part of the journey over with."

I nodded, "Except that we do not know they were alone. We found
no horses."

Sir Patrick shook his head, "They may have been stabled in York.
We left too rapidly for a thorough search."

"That is the one thing we could not have done, my lord, had we
searched then men would know of the killers. This way a mystery
concerning horses which languish in a York stable will be a nine-day
wonder." As we dismounted at the priory gates I said, "I confess that
until we step from the ferry I will not be at ease."

Sir James said, "Should we send one of your men to warn your
father of our arrival? He could send men to meet with us."

"Had I brought more men then I would say aye, but if I send two
then that puts those two in danger of ambush and diminishes our ability
to defend ourselves by two good men. No, the die is cast, and we live
with this plan for good or ill."

Mount Grace was a small priory, but they had enough chambers for
the great and the good. My men and some of the Scots had to make do
with barns, outbuildings, and stables but that was no bad thing. We had
a perimeter of guards in addition to the ones who stood armed.

We left early to cover the last miles to the ferry. As we neared
Yarum I contemplated riding there and hiring boatmen to ferry us
across, but I dismissed it for the sake of speed. The road, once we had
crossed the Leven, was relatively flat but the woods at Red Hall and the
ford at Mount Leven were a tricky part of our route. The ford was not
deep but, to ensure our safety I rode with my men and we had all ten of
us, including Dick, at the fore. It was as we were crossing the ford that
we heard the clash of steel ahead of us.

"Dick, ride back to the main party and warn them of danger. They
are to stay there until one of us returns!"

"Aye father!" The sight of the slaughtered guards at the
Archbishop's palace had had a chastening effect on Dick and he no
longer questioned any order.

My archers strung their bows, and we drew swords. Without an order being given my archers split into pairs and rode off to the east and west of us while I led my men at arms north up the bank. It was when we reached the top, we saw the battle. Two men were back to back in the centre of the road. Around them were bodies and the two men were being attacked by what looked like ten or twelve men. They, too, wore the white surcoat with the diagonal red cross of the Nevill family. Who were the ones we ought to defend and who were we to attack? The surcoats convinced me, and I spurred Destiny. Even as we galloped, I saw one of the two men fall and as the other turned I saw it was Calum of the Isles! I now knew who to fight.

One of the attackers turned and held his shield before him. He shouted something and it was in Norse and they began to run towards us. Two others turned as Calum had his leg hacked into. His companion had managed to slay one of the attackers before he fell. I rode directly at the three men. Knowing that they were Norse helped me. They would not flee but would fight to the death, and so I stood in my stirrups as I made Destiny jump over them. The three had expected to be able to use their swords and hack at Destiny's head but all that they struck was fresh air. My sword came down and smashed into the helmet of the man who was in the centre. I saw arrows slam into the men who had been fighting Calum. He lay on the ground with blood gushing from his wound. After landing I leaned forward and as one of the killers raised his sword to end Calum's life, I hacked my sword so hard into his back that my arm jarred when the blade hit his spine. I was now amongst the last three men but before any of them could harm me four arrows hit them and then another four for good measure. My archers were taking no chances.

I leapt from my horse's back and ran to Calum who still held his sword in his right hand. I took in that his companion was dressed as he was and was obviously another Irishman. The gaping, open wound at his throat told me he was dead. Blood was still pumping from Calum's thigh. I tore a length of cloth from my tunic, but he said, in a voice I could barely hear, "I owed a debt and it is paid, I am sorry Sir William but…" with that he died.

"You died well Calum of the Isles and your death is worthy of a tale for it was a warrior's death!" My men rode up and I turned, "Are any left alive?"

Alan shook his head, "No, Sir William, and they were too good to risk trying to wound them. I am sorry."

I looked at Erik, "Aye, lord, they were Norse and Danes." He saw Calum. "And the fact that Calum is dead tells me that they were good warriors."

Alan began searching the bodies, "Did he tell you anything, lord? Do we know who is behind this?"

I shook my head, "I think he was going to. He died with a sword in his hand."

Erik nodded, "The old ways are still there with some warriors, Sir William, it is how I wish to die." He suddenly knelt. "Lord, look at his left hand, it grips something." He prised open the fingers and there was a ring. He took it and handed it to me.

It was a ring with a coat of arms upon it. I recognised it for I had seen it on one of the knights who had escorted King Alexander to Oban. It was the de Balliol coat of arms. Had I found the head of the snake? I stood, "Keep the knowledge of this ring to yourselves. There are plots and plans here which are more entangled than a skein of wool. Carl and Idraf, ride ahead and see if there is any more danger. They must have had horses, find them. Tom, fetch the others and say nothing other than we have foiled an ambush."

Erik said, "The other looks like one of Calum's kinsmen. Will we ever know this tale?"

I nodded, "Before he died, he said he had paid a debt. I know that he left us because he thought all of his shield brothers were dead. I am guessing that the man with him is the last of them. He must have found the men we hunted and rescued his friend. The question is, did he follow these men here to try to stop them or were they hunting him?"

We discovered the answer when Carl and Idraf brought the horses and ponies they had found. We had to speak quickly for the royal party was approaching the ford. "Sir William we found all but two of the animals less than four hundred paces from here. They were hobbled. The other two were four hundred paces further away and were tied to a tree."

I nodded, "Then we have our answer. He followed them and hearing us approach tried to warn us." I looked at the body, "If the debt was to me, Calum of the Isles then you have paid it and more. I shall honour your memory." I nodded to the bodies. "Put them on their horses. We will dispose of them in Stockton. Wrap Calum and his shield brother in their cloaks and put them on their horses."

My wife looked shocked when she saw the bodies. I knew that she had not recognised Calum for we had covered his head with his cloak. Queen Margaret was also terrified by the sight, but the Queen Mother remained impassive. King Alexander knew that he too had to be stoic and as he had killed, probably, his first warrior the previous night, he was somewhat prepared for the sight of blood.

Alan Durward reined in and said, "Was this intended for us?"

I nodded, "Possibly a backup plan but one of the men who served with me at Kilmartin foiled it." I lifted the cloak so that he could see Calum.

He nodded, "I remember him, now, the wild Irishman." He looked around, "Why here?"

"This is the last place before Thornaby and then the ferry across the river. Had we taken the Yarum road then Calum and his oathsworn might be alive."

Erik was about to load Calum's shield brother onto a horse, and he shook his head, "The sisters, lord. This was *wyrd* and Calum died well. These two were the last of the band. Do not fret about it. You could do nothing. This was meant to be."

Somehow the pagan thought was comforting.

It was getting on to dusk when we reached the ferry. Had we not had the interruption of the skirmish then we would have reached it by mid-afternoon. We were spied from the walls and I knew that my mother would throw herself into the preparation of rooms. She would have seen the royal standard! My father would be more philosophical about it all. Sir Petr and Folki came down with some men at arms to help unload the ferry. The first ones off apart from me were the royal party, the senior lords and my family.

As we stepped ashore Sir Petr nodded towards the body laden horses, "Trouble, lord?"

"An ambush just five miles from here! Calum died." I saw the question form, but I shook my head. "There will be time for questions later. Help unload the ferry and I will take King Alexander and the Queen to my father!"

The royal couple hurried through the gates, as did the Queen Mother. The dead bodies were a painful reminder of what had nearly been their demise. My father bowed, "Welcome King Alexander, my house is yours."

"Thank you, Sir Thomas. It seems we are continually indebted to you and your family."

My mother appeared and curtsied, "If you would like to follow me, I have chambers for you and I can arrange for a bath if you…"

The Queen Mother gave a thin cold smile, "That will not be necessary, Lady Margaret. We will not stay overlong. This journey has been a trial."

The Queen Mother did not know all the details of the attack in York, but she knew that something had prompted our sudden departure. The bodies at the ford had also been a warning. I knew that she was close to the Comyns and as much as I disliked Comyn himself, I could not see him risking his ally by attacking us on the road. I was desperate to speak with my father for he knew the politics of the north better than any. If the de Balliol clan was behind this attack, then he might give me an insight. I would not tell Sir Alan and the others for I needed proof and Alain de Balliol had ridden with both Sir James and Sir Patrick. I needed proof. The signet ring was the start but that was all.

There was too much going on for me to be able to talk. My wife joined with my mother to help organise rooms. The knights and men at arms, not to mention the servants would all be housed in the warrior halls. It would be a tight and cosy fit. I also sent a rider to Durham to warn the Bishop and to ask for an escort to meet us. We could mount a strong guard, but we had foiled two attempts and our enemies might use a larger band for a third and final attack. The first opportunity to actually sit and think was when we sat down to dine. It was a small gathering; only Sir Petr and my father ate with the royal party and the rest of the men and knights were fed in the warrior hall. The meal had been hurriedly concocted but that was the last thing on anyone's mind. My mother was superb for she managed to bring the conversation around to things which were far removed from violence and death. She asked about the wedding. She inquired where the couple would be living. She commented and praised the dress of the Queen and the Queen Mother. She was ably aided by my wife so much so that I even saw the Queen Mother smile. The three senior knights and my father and I had to bite our tongues. We could not speak that which we wished. The ladies had to be away so that we could dissect the two attacks. I had said that we were sworn to secrecy but that would not involve my father.

My mother was a wise woman and she rose when the food was finished. She nodded to my wife who also rose. "Ladies, Your Majesties, it has been a long day and from what I can gather, a traumatic day. We will take you to your rooms and there you will be safe for the walls and corridors are well guarded."

The Queen Mother nodded, "You are right Lady Margaret. Come for the men will need words to plan a safe route home through this barbaric land." It was an unnecessary insult which she softened a little, "Thank you, Sir William, for you made the journey as safe as you could manage and for that I thank you."

Dick tried to press himself close to the back wall, but my wife said, "And you, Dick, can escort your mother to her room!"

When they had gone, I said, "Sir Petr, would you ensure that the watch is set?"

I saw the disappointment on his face, but he nodded, "Yes, Sir William."

My father dismissed the servants and the squires, and we took our chairs to sit before the fire. Alan Durward was blunt, "Sir William, you learned something at the ford. You are no dissembler and I saw it on your face." I glanced at my father and the Lord Hostarius smiled, "If we cannot trust the Earl then all is lost. Sir Thomas, there was an attempt on the life of King Alexander in York. Your son believes that it was Vikings masquerading as the men of Sir Geoffrey Nevill."

My father had seen too much in his life to be shocked and he nodded, "Speak, William, for in silence lies doubt and mistrust."

I reached into my purse and took out the ring. Holding it before me I showed it to the other four. The firelight made it glint. All were silent until Lord Dunbar spoke, "It belongs to the de Balliol family." He turned to look at me, "You think John de Balliol is behind this?"

Sir James Galloway shook his head, "He is in his lands in France. He was invited to the wedding, but he could not attend."

Alan Durward was a clever man, "That does not rule him out. He might have gone to France so that he was not suspected of treachery if it went wrong. Do you not realise Sir Patrick, that had Sir William been less vigilant then we would now be dead for it was only the arrival of Sir William and his men which saved us?"

"Aye, but we would have taken some with us."

"And when we and the King and Queen were dead then other lords would have died. Had John de Balliol been there and survived the slaughter then it would have pointed the finger towards him. I do not say it is he who is behind this and his absence from the wedding is no proof."

I nodded and said, quietly, "And there are two sons, Hugh and Alain." I looked at Lord Dunbar.

He caught my eye and nodded, "You take your role as protector seriously, Sir William. That is good."

Alan Durward looked confused, "What am I missing, here?"

Lord Dunbar smiled, "Alain de Balliol was with us when we went to Oban with the King." He turned to me, "He was not my choice but King Alexander's."

Sir James nodded, "Sir Patrick is right. King Alexander brought six knights with him whom he said he wanted as his household knights."

I closed my eyes as I tried to picture the knights who left after the battle of Kilmartin, "Tell me, Sir James, how many of those six knights survived the battle?"

"I can not recall. Let me think."

Sir Patrick and Sir James looked at each other and it was Sir Patrick who spoke, "Just Alain de Balliol! Then it must be he who is behind this!"

My father spoke for the first time, "Do not be hasty. The de Balliol family is a powerful one and such an accusation, if untrue, might drive them into a potentially rebellious camp. The warrior who died warning you of the ambush took the ring as a sign to my son, but he did not get the chance to give details. We are senior lords, gentlemen, and we cannot act like errant knights desperate to please a lady." That made them smile for it was a good analogy. We need proof and it seems to me that the proof will lie in Barnard Castle."

Alan Durward agreed, "You are right, Sir Thomas, and I would have the King and Queen safely in Jedburgh before we take action."

I asked, "Jedburgh and not Edinburgh?"

"The Comyn family has powerful connections in Edinburgh. What I have learned from this whole journey is that we need to find somewhere secure and safe. I feel both here and I am sure that Durham will be equally protecting. Jedburgh is close to Dunbar where the Mormaer has men he can call upon and far enough from both the de Balliol and Comyn heartlands to put distance between us."

My father asked, "And the de Brus clan?"

"Annandale and Dumfries are further west. Jedburgh is safe from them too."

We each stared into the fire until I said, "Then why did de Brus not aid the king when we fought the MacDougall, clan?"

Alan Durward gave a thin smile, "And there you have the politics of Scotland, Sir William. We have always been happy to join together to fight the English but there the feudal ties end. I cannot answer you, but I think I agree with your father. We cannot fan these embers of rebellion by acting hastily. King Alexander's untimely death has put his son in a precarious position. We three senior lords are all that we can trust, for the moment. Our quest is to make the new king safe and then to begin to build alliances against all that would threaten him. Your quest, Sir William, if you will accept it, is to discover where this warband of warriors resides for they have shown to me that while they are few in number, they are a clear threat."

"Of course I accept, for I swore an oath. The question is how do I discover the truth?"

My father was always the strategist and the planner. His eyes had been closed while we had spoken, and I wondered if the others thought him asleep. I knew he was not and when he spoke it showed that he had been planning. "You need to visit Barnard Castle, son. However, you cannot take a large conroi of men. I would suggest you take just twenty or so, an escort if you like. We need to involve Sir Petr and we need to be less than truthful." He smiled, "Sometimes a knight must be a little dishonest for the greater good. Alain de Balliol was with you at Kilmartin although as no one can remember him fighting he was not at the fore. You say that you are passing through Balliol lands to return to the land of the Campbell clan for Sir Petr wishes to make peace with Sir Cailean before Sir Petr returns to Sweden."

"Does Sir Petr wish to return to Sweden, father?"

He nodded, "Someday, but not until he has made enough money to buy back the family lands." He was a patient man and not irritated by my interruption. "This gives you an excuse to cross through to the west. I do not believe for one moment that the Nevill family is involved and the attempt to divert attention to them is crude and obvious but let us pander to our hidden enemies. When you leave Barnard Castle you can head north and return home through Stanhope and Raby. Both are the heartland of the Nevill family."

Sir James, whose lands were close to both de Brus and de Balliol shook his head, "That will not work for several reasons. If we are right, then Sir William will be putting his head in a noose and will be either incarcerated or killed. If we are wrong, then will the de Balliol family not be suspicious when they head north rather than to the north-west?"

My father smiled patiently. Had Sir James played chess with my father he would have known that he worked out moves ahead. "One problem my son might have will be the roads. At this time of the year, the passes are often closed. This warband cannot move until Spring. Word will reach the de Balliol family that my son is heading towards them. If they are innocent, then there will be no men in the castle and my son will be welcomed. When he leaves then the bridge across the river heads north for a while in any case. If they are suspicious and follow, then that is confirmation of their guilt and the warband will be hidden elsewhere. If they are guilty then they will shadow him and assume that we have swallowed their bait, but we will know one way or another." He saw Sir James open his mouth, "And if my son does not return then we know they are guilty!"

Sir James shook his head, "You would use your son as bait?"

"For the very reason that if they harm him in any way it is proof positive of the family's involvement."

Alan Durward smiled, "And if there is no warband at Barnard Castle then that tells us that Sir William was wrong about the destination of these mercenaries and that they were making their way to MacDougall."

All eyes were on me, "I know that one of the de Balliol family is behind this. The death of a brave warrior and the message he delivered told me that. I am happy to undertake this quest. I shall leave at the end of February. Let our foes wonder what has happened and let them fret about what we will do. I take it that you gentlemen will be preparing men to thwart this threat?"

"Of course."

"Then all will be well!"

Chapter 15

Into the Lion's Den

My father's men with Henry Samuel, Sir John, Sir Mark and Sir Petr leading them escorted the royal party north. That the Bishop would meet them halfway ensured that they would all be safe. We did not leave early for many reasons. My father wished to speak with me and, more unusually, mother also asked to have a word before we left for Hartlepool.

My father was concerned lest he was seen to be callous and uncaring, "I said what I said last night, not because I am reckless with your life, but I genuinely believe that you will be safe. Of course, what happens when you find this warband is another matter and I would not relish the prospect of fighting a warband made up of such desperate men."

I smiled, "I know, father. That is another problem, and I will wrestle with that when we have the truth. It is this uncertainty I do not like. Calum pointed us in the direction of de Balliol at the cost of his life."

"Aye."

He smiled, "Good, I am pleased. And how is Thomas? I know you did not take him with you; was there a reason for that?"

"Accommodation and I thought he might learn more from Geoffrey. He was a good squire. I am aware that I am training him to be a lord of the manor."

He waved a hand around the hall, "And one day you shall be lord here. Thomas will, hopefully, need a manor of his own soon. You have done enough service for King Henry to warrant one."

I laughed, "There would have to be something in it for King Henry to be so generous."

"Aye, you have the right of it. When will England have a good king once more?"

"Edward has potential," I told him of what I had seen of the prince.

"But he suffers ill-health?"

"He does."

"Then I pray that God spares him." He stood, "I will bid farewell to your wife and your son. You are lucky to have such an understanding wife. I was lucky too."

He left me and I finished the ale the servants had poured. My mother came in and her face was serious. I wondered what was amiss. She gestured for me to sit, "You know that Eirwen is with child once more?"

I nodded. Their first child, Alfred, had been born a year after they had been wed. "It is good for he is a good father. It is a shame my brother could not have seen how well his children have grown."

She smiled, "Mathilda shows the joy Alfred would have enjoyed. Since she moved in with Henry Samuel and Eirwen she has become younger! It is good."

"Is that why you wished to speak with me for your face was filled with signs of ill omen?"

She sighed, "No, it is the old wives' tale, William, you know that one child comes into the world to replace one who is leaving."

I held her hand, "You are not..."

She smiled, "Bless you no. It is your father. Have you not noticed that he is losing weight?" I had but I shook my head. I know not why I did so unless it was to somehow make what I knew my mother was going to say to me to be in doubt. "Then have you not seen how he eats little?" Again I shook my head. She sighed again, "Men, you are all the same! It is women who notice such things. Mary commented on the state of your father's health! He is dying. There is something inside him which eats away at him. The doctors can do nothing. I told Mary last night."

"Why did..."

She held up her hand, "This is hard enough for me as it is, my son. He wished no one to know. That is his way but if you are to continue to put your life and health in danger, I thought you should know. None of us knows when the end shall come. We take each day at a time. When I wake the first thing I do is to see if he lives. Each time I wake and before I go to sleep I tell him how much I love him, have always loved him, in case he does not see another dawn. He has had a good life and a longer one than most men but when he is taken, whenever that is, it will be too soon."

I am a warrior and I have watched men die but at that moment I felt tears welling up in my eyes. I had thought he would live forever. Suddenly the prospect of riding off to find this warband seemed irrelevant. I should spend every minute that I had with my father. I owed that to him. I was his last son and heir. Suddenly his words about the manor became clear!

"I shall not go on this quest. I will stay close to Stockton."

Her voice was suddenly commanding, "No! He would hate that and blame me for telling you! You cannot let him know what you know. He is a clever man, and you will speak to him differently. He will know that you know but he will not wish sympathy. You know the way he is. He has always faced up to his problems and he is doing so with this. Allow him the dignity he deserves."

"Then I shall pray for him three times a day. I will make a donation to the nunnery in Hartlepool. I will enlist the help of God!"

She smiled, "And I spend every moment I can on my knees in the chapel of St John. Perhaps God will hear us. Surely all your father's work as a crusader should be taken into account."

Just then Dick and my father came in. They were laughing and Dick was holding a sword in a scabbard. Dick did not sense the tension in the room. He said, "Grandfather has just made me a gift of his sword. Now can I begin to train as a squire, father?"

My father said, "I will not be going to war again and it is a good sword. It has served me well." He suddenly frowned, "I am sorry, did you want it? I…"

I shook my head as I tried to keep my voice level. I did not want it to break, "I think it is a wonderful idea and yes, Dick. This day is the day you begin to train as a squire so that one day you shall be a knight. Hopefully, you will be as great a knight as Sir Thomas of Stockton."

My father waved a hand, "I was just lucky! I am happy that you are not upset, son, I would not hurt you for the world."

"Nor I, you." I went to him to embrace him. I cared not if he now knew I knew I had to hold him. I felt his bones as I put my arms around him. I held him longer than was normal and I saw my wife and mother both wipe away a tear. Dick was engrossed in the sword and did not notice. When I felt his fingers move, we parted.

He looked in my eyes, "Do not be a stranger for I would like to be involved in the planning for this visit to Barnard Castle. I have knowledge which may help you."

I had control of my voice once more and I said, "Then I shall visit every few days. The ride will be good for Dick and Thomas, eh? We shall have to find you a courser."

My father's face brightened, "If I do not need a sword, I will certainly not need a warhorse. Take Dragon. He is a good horse if you think you can manage him."

My son showed his increasing maturity, "I will lead him this day and when I ride it shall be on the sands at Seaton Carrowe! If I fall it will be a soft landing!"

His words set a happier mood on the way home. Mary and I kept silent as Dick chattered on about his new horse and sword. We would speak in our bedchamber. None could know for it would hurt my father. I saw that in his eyes. To be honest I was so busy when I returned to my hall for I had much to tell Sir Geoffrey, the squires and my men at arms that I had no time for melancholic and maudlin thoughts. I told them of Calum's death but not the de Balliol connection. I spoke of that only to Geoffrey and Thomas. Now that Dick was to be a squire three squires were waiting on us and Thomas was able to speak to me at the table.

When the food was finished, and my wife went to see to Matthew and Margaret, I sat the squires down with Geoffrey and me. "We have a short time here and then we will ride to Barnard Castle. This may be dangerous, but I do not think it will be life-threatening. However, I have been wrong before and you should know the dangers before you agree to follow me. I will say the same to the men we choose but I want all of you to use this night to make your decision." I saw Dick begin to mouth his agreement and I said, "On the morrow, Richard!" The use of his full name ensured his compliance. "From now on we are on a war footing. The training of the squires will be from dawn until dusk and each evening before we eat, we will review which men we might take. We cannot take too many and yet the ones we take must be the best."

That night Mary lay in my arms and sobbed. She loved my father as much as she had her own father. Her tears kept my face dry. It made us both more determined than ever to be as good a pair of parents to our children as we could.

The four weeks soon passed, and the news of my father's illness made them pass even quicker. I went with Dick and Thomas every three days. If Thomas and Dick wondered why they said nothing and as Henry Samuel was also present then there were no awkward questions for he knew nothing of his ailment. My father seemed to enjoy having three of his grandchildren around and I caught him looking at them when they bantered and joked with one another. It was almost as though he was drinking them in to savour when they were not there. I know that my mother was grateful too and would often find excuses to join us as my father told me of roads and paths in that part of England.

We had decided on the twenty men at arms we would take at the end of the first three or four visits. I spoke to all my men. My father and I had planned everything as carefully as we could. The enemy had shown great cunning and we would need to be equally as devious. Henry Samuel insisted upon accompanying us. "Our names, uncle, are always linked because of Elsdon. They will not see anything untoward and I know more of the Scots than either Geoffrey or Petr. You will need an extra pair of eyes and," he looked at the two of them, "you will need the experience of another border knight."

Neither Petr nor Geoffrey took offence.

163

As the day neared for our departure, Matthew began to pester me to accompany us. There was no chance I would allow him to, but I promised him that when I returned, I would make him a page and that seemed to satisfy him. My father's illness had also affected my wife who whilst she had always been loving and attentive was now even more so. It was as if she had seen my mortality looming large.

The three Scottish lords had sent messengers to me. They chose men I knew, and the messages were not written. They merely asked my plans and told me what they had learned. I thought that this was still a risk as the enemies of King Alexander could intercept the messenger and force the information from them. I merely said that I would be riding west soon but gave no further details. Even the men at arms I was taking did not know our destination. We left just forty days before Easter. That too afforded us a story. It was the start of Lent!

The night before we left, we held a small celebration. All my visits since learning of my father's illness had been during the day. This time we would be staying in the castle. I now noticed how much thinner he had become. Previously I had just thought his thinness was down to old age. I was able to observe for myself that he did not eat much, and he drank sparingly. I also saw the signs that he was in pain. He did his best to hide it from me, but knowing to look for it, I saw. He smiled and laughed whenever he was the centre of attention, but I could see that it was an act. I regretted my promise to go on this quest. I did not fear for my life, but I worried that my father might die while I was away, and I wanted to be there at his side.

Our squires did not have as much to do this time for there was just a handful of us. My father said when they had brought in the platter of fowl, "Come and sit. Let me speak with you! We do not have such large appetites that you need to be up and down all the time. I would talk to my grandsons before they leave this hall." I knew why he did this. He was making the most of every moment he had.

They were happy to do so but I saw Thomas frown. He had begun to ask questions about my father's health. He was clever and astute. Dick was still caught up in the thrill of becoming a squire. It was he who was questioned by my father.

"How are the horse and the sword?"

"Dragon is everything you said he would be, and he is well trained."

"That is the result of Alan Horse Master. He is retired now but his sons have learned his skills. That is what good fathers do for their sons. They pass on what they have learned so their sons are even better than they were."

My son nodded, "The sword has taken some getting used to. I am still growing, Grandfather, but Erik and Alan say that using the sword now will make me an even better swordsman when I gain the strength."

Henry Samuel nodded, "But do not forget, cousin, that you will be wearing mail and that will sap your strength too."

Thomas picked the last of the meat from the bone he had been eating and, after wiping his hand on the cloth which was draped over his left shoulder said, "I doubt that, even if we fight, you will have an opportunity to wield the sword for it is you who will carry your father's standard."

Dick nodded, "I know, and I am aware of that honour."

My mother looked up and flashed a sharp look at me, "I thought this was a peaceful quest. There should be no need for any to draw a sword!"

My father smiled, "Margaret, do not fret. It is a peaceful quest, but they know not what they might meet on the road. They need to do this."

"I know but they are my family, and I would not have any of them in danger."

"Ah, you would imprison them here in my castle then?"

"I did not say that! Do not put words in my mouth!"

"But that is what you are saying for as soon as any leave this castle, they are in danger!"

It was a mark of my father's illness that my mother stopped arguing and I changed the subject to less contentious issues. "So Henry Samuel, when is your new child due?"

"The midwives think three months. I am lucky for Eirwen had an easy first birth. The women think this one will be as easy, God willing."

Once we were talking about babies then my mother was happy, and she went through all the names which might be suitable for the next child. I saw that my father looked content. His line would continue. It had begun with Ridley and the Warlord and soon there might be eight boys to carry on the family name.

The next morning I was up well before dawn, but my father was up before me. I could see that he was waiting to speak to me. He had the servants bring me breakfast. I noticed he just had some mulled and buttered ale. "I meant to give you this, William. I should have given it to you before, but it slipped my mind. I think that giving my sword to Richard brought it to the fore." He brought out a blue stone which was fastened to a leather thong. "This was the Warlord's, and he went to Constantinopolis especially to fetch it. I think it was the pommel stone of some sword. I know not if it was ever attached to a sword, but my father had it around his neck when he died, and I have worn it ever since. Your brother would have had it but…" I nodded. "Wear it now to keep the tradition going."

I took it and hung it around my neck, "It should go to Alfred's son next, Henry Samuel."

He nodded, "And when you are head of the family that will be your decision. I know you will make the right one for I hope I have done my best and brought you up well. I pray that my father and his would be proud of me."

I felt my voice thickening up, "They could not do other."

He nodded and we looked at each other. The moment was broken when Sir Petr entered, "I am ready, Sir William. I feel that since Kilmartin I have done little to thank your family for rescuing me!"

My father clapped him on the back. I saw that the effort pained him, "You owe us nothing for I was a friend and shield brother to your father. Had I not gone on crusade with your father I would not have met Lady Margaret. Do not feel that you need to do any more."

"Yet I do. I hope you do not mind that I leave Sven here. He wishes to come but…"

"Say no more. I enjoy speaking with someone who is closer to my age than any save Ridley the Giant and I see little of him these days. It is good to speak with Sven about your father and the crusade."

The others entered and I knew that the goodbye I wished to give to my father would have to wait. My mother was tearful, but my father just looked thoughtful as we headed west towards Hartburn. We did not need to cross the Tees. We had just twenty-seven miles to travel and even with shorter days we would reach the castle before dark. We were all well mounted and we had sumpters with us carrying supplies. We stopped to water our horses and tighten our girths at Sadberge, just six miles down the road. I used the time to explain to the men at arms our true mission. It says much about the men that I had chosen that none were surprised. There was no worry on their faces just determination.

"We are looking for signs of those men who landed at Hunter's House. If they are in the castle itself then we have our answer, but I think that even if they are there now, by the time our banners are seen they will be spirited away. We play the innocent, but we keep a good watch. Say nothing while we are in the castle but when we are on the road to Stanhope, then will be the time for debate. Be vigilant! If anything happens to my son, we will all have to answer to Lady Mary and my mother, Lady Margaret!" That made them smile and we rode west.

I knew that those in the castle would know we were approaching. You cannot hide a conroi of mailed men, even one as small as ours. It felt strange to be riding without archer scouts ahead. We had to play the part of a conroi of men at arms who were travelling without thought of war or ambush. I knew that the enemy would be watching. If they had been surprised at our arrival then I would have doubted that there were enemies close by. However, the fact that, as we approached the castle, not only was the drawbridge down and smiling faces to welcome us but also there was neither sight nor smell of a Norseman told me that they had enjoyed plenty of warning of our approach. The warband was hidden; the welcome told me that they had been watching and that reeked of treachery. When we had visited Raby Castle Sir Geoffrey had been surprised at our arrival.

Alain de Balliol himself was there to greet us with a smile as broad as a summer sunrise, "Well met Sir William and you too, Sir Petr! I have chambers ready for you. My brother, Sir Hugh, is master here at the moment while my father and younger brother are abroad. I shall take you and your knights to meet him." He gestured to the steward, "Angus here will show your men to the stables and then the warrior hall."

They had rooms ready and knew we were coming. They had riders watching for us.

We dismounted and followed the Scottish lord towards the keep of the mighty castle. "I hear the wedding went ahead as planned."

I nodded, "It was a happy day, and the two kingdoms are now joined. It will make for a peaceful border."

"And for that we are grateful. Just because we are Scottish living in England does not make us immune from border raids."

"And yet this castle looks impregnable. Who could take it?"

"You would be surprised. Know you that the MacDougall family is still supporting the Norwegian King?"

"I heard."

"We have suffered attacks because many Norse and Danish warriors have been making their way across the spine of this land to join them. None have died but some have lost animals!"

I said nothing for I was now convinced that the men we sought were close by. The story he had told was to create a mist into which he hoped we would not look too closely. We entered the keep and went to the Great Hall which put my father's to shame. I saw that there were more than a dozen knights within and even had I not been suspicious before that would have made me so. It was too many knights. Added to that was the fact that they were not the actors that Alain de Balliol was. There were no smiles, in fact, there was a tense air of animosity in the hall. We were not welcome! His brother too, Sir Hugh, did his best to appear happy to see us but the smile was not in his eyes.

"Sir William, my brother has told me of your great deeds on the battlefield and I assume from his livery that this is the Swedish hero, Sir Petr! I look forward to hearing your tales tonight as we feast!" He added apologetically, "Of course, as it is Lent then it will not be as grand as normal, but we can make up for food with your story!" He waved a hand to the four servants who awaited us. "Until it is time for us to eat, gentlemen."

We followed the servants. I could almost cut the tension in the room. The fact that none had smiled was ominous. Had our arrival upset their plans? I began to fear that we might have made a mistake and were forcing the de Balliol family to act earlier than the Spring we anticipated. The roads to Barnard had been snow and ice-free. Our plans had been made on the assumption that there would be no rising until the spring offensive! Was I wrong?

The four of us and our squires had discussed how we would behave in the castle. We spoke words we had practised back in Stockton. We chatted about the castle, the weather; we spoke of our families and we smiled. There could be hidden listeners anywhere in the castle. When we were summoned, we dressed well, and we smiled. That was the day I admired mummers for it was harder to keep a false smile than it was to be honest. Sir Alain was obviously their actor for he chattered away like a magpie. He asked about the royal wedding and it was as he did so that I saw that Sir Hugh was studying my face. They were looking for the inconsistency in my story. I managed to speak of the wedding as though it was a joyous event and that our departure north had been planned.

When Sir Hugh eventually spoke the mask which Sir Alain had worn cracked a little for he was unhappy with his brother's words. "Sir William, was the journey from York to Stockton a hard one? We have heard of many travellers who were ambushed and robbed upon that road."

I smiled, "We had a good escort, Sir Hugh, and once you pass Mount Grace Priory then my father's protection is surety against ambush." I feigned a frown, "Have you heard of such robberies? I pray you to tell me where and when I return home, I shall ask my father to increase our patrols."

Sir Hugh shook his head, "No, Sir William, it is just rumour, you know? We are remote here and perhaps our visitors seek to enliven their tales by exaggerating. Your stories are much more entertaining."

That was the last he spoke, and the strained atmosphere lasted the whole meal. I was relieved when we all retired. Dick and Thomas slept behind the door. If any tried to enter, they would have to shift two bodies. I did not think it necessary, but Thomas and Dick took the potential threat seriously. When we rose and I glanced out of the door I saw that our corridor had been guarded. There were de Balliol men at each end.

When we breakfasted Alain de Balliol was more serious than the night before, "My lord, the road twixt here and Innis Chonnell is a dangerous one. Cannot I persuade you to let me provide an escort of my men?"

We had rehearsed this, "I have brought so few men for this is not a martial visit. We left Sir Cailean with ill words spoken and Sir Petr and I would like to make peace before Sir Petr returns to Sweden."

"I understand. You will be safe until you have passed Carlisle for the Sherriff keeps the roads between Penrith and Carlisle well-guarded and until Penrith you ride de Balliol land." He shook his head, "You have picked a strange time to travel, my lord."

I smiled, "We are not fools, Sir Alain, and while the weather may be inclement we are hardy men and the lack of leaves on the trees makes ambush harder but I thank you for your concern. When summer comes you must come to visit my manor at Hartlepool. It is an interesting place."

"I am sure it is."

When we left, we headed down the road which twisted down to the bridge over the Tees. The bridge was fortified and being overlooked by towers and walls would daunt any attacker. Once on the other side of the river, the road twisted up and around. My father and I did not think an attempt would be made to attack us this close to the castle, but we were still vigilant. It was here I missed my archers. The road appeared to be deserted but we waited until we were a mile up the road and hidden by the trees of Deepdale Beck before we stopped, ostensibly to check our girths. The road was empty of travellers but there was a screen of thin trees.

Henry Samuel sent two men up the road to watch for any who approached while I sent two more back down the road. "Well, what did you find?"

It was Erik who spoke, "There had been warriors there, my lord, and they were Norse. They had cleared out the warrior hall of all signs of them, but I found this." He held up a small bone carved hammer of Thor.

Folki nodded, "And when we fetched food from the kitchen, I spied the crispy remains of seal meat. The Norse, especially those from the islands, enjoy the rendered fat as a delicacy." He smiled, "I could smell them but they were not there."

"Then the warband was here, the question is, where are they now?"

Even as I spoke the words, figures rose from behind the scrubby trees, "They are waiting to ambush you, my lord, four miles down the road on the far side of the woods of Lartington, where the road crosses the River Balder."

Hands went to swords as Carl and Idraf grinned at us.

"Then we were right?"

"Aye lord. When we arrived, four days ago we spread ourselves out around the town. There are many woods. When you approached it, the warband evacuated the castle and hid themselves in Lartington Woods. There are more than two hundred and fifty of them. Not all are Norse or Danish, but the majority are. We went close to their camp and heard them speak. There are Franks as well as Englishmen and Welshmen. I would say that a quarter were Scots."

Idraf nodded, "They have a dozen or so Welsh archers. Last night a rider came from the castle and the warband moved to where they will ambush you."

"You have done well."

Henry Samuel looked angry, "You thought not to tell us of this, uncle? For shame! Do you not trust us?"

"Of course I trust you, you would not be here otherwise, but I knew not your acting ability. This was my father's idea. Carl, Idraf and the others were, are, our secret weapon. The enemy know not that we have archers with us and the rest of you gave nothing away which might have suggested we had men hidden." Henry Samuel nodded his understanding. The fact that it was my father's plan helped. And now we must move before they realise we are on to them. Which way Idraf?"

"Our horses are just a mile along that track which heads north. There is a ford across the Tees a mile further north. Horses can cross but men on foot would struggle."

The archers ran and led us to their horses. Once mounted we made good time. The river was higher than it would be in summer and almost impassable. Our archers had chosen well but we barely made it across safely. Dick almost fell from Dragon's back, but he recovered and regained his stirrup.

I knew that Henry Samuel was brooding about the apparent lack of trust and so I rode next to him. "Do not let this sour you, Henry Samuel. You have played chess with your grandfather. Have you ever beaten him?"

"No, but this is not a game of chess."

"Isn't it? It is like an opening. We had to keep hidden our plans from all. Last night you all played your parts. The de Balliol family would have sensed our tension and when we left, I saw that even Erik and Alan Longsword were looking over their shoulders as we left the castle. When we rode up the road you were looking around for an ambush and the watchers in the towers would have seen that. If you and the others had known that we were protected by our archers, you would have been more relaxed. I am sorry I did not tell you, but I would do the same again." I shrugged, "As far as I am concerned that is an end to the matter!"

Chapter 16

Viking Scouts

Stanhope was a mere fifteen miles up the road and we soon made the small castle. There was a real contrast here with Barnard Castle for it was clear we were not expected. Sir Geoffrey himself came to the gate when he had been summoned by his guards. This was his home, and he liked the cosy village and relatively tiny castle. I could understand that. Raby was as big as Stockton. He looked relieved when he saw me, "Sir William! This is unexpected. I pray you enter but I fear that your sudden arrival has caught us unawares."

I nodded and dismounted, "I am sorry for the unexpected nature of this visit, but I have questions I need to ask which must be asked directly so that I may see your face. I am sorry and I cannot explain fully but know that I have the authority of not only my father to ask these questions, but also the Archbishop of York, not to mention King Henry." I had been given the written authority of King Henry to ask questions before the attack but that was just a detail. It did not diminish the intent.

Sir Geoffrey Nevill gave a happy nod, "Then I am intrigued, and you have already lightened the tedium of this time of year." He gestured towards his hall. "Come let us get in from the cold. I fear food will take some time to prepare but I have some good ale and a hot poker to warm it through. Cedric, take the archers and the men at arms to the warrior hall and the stables. This is a small castle. Raby has much better accommodation."

"Fear not Sir Geoffrey, we are not on a progress; we seek answers, and any hardship will be acceptable."

Once in the hall, his servants poured the ale and then warmed it with a poker. "Now, what are these questions?"

"Thomas."

My squire opened the hessian sack he was carrying and took out the blood-stained tunic. I said nothing and allowed Sir Geoffrey's eyes to widen as he realised that it was one of his.

"I do not understand, my lord. This is one of my tunics but whence came the blood and how did it come into your possession?"

"Men wearing tunics just like this one attacked a party of travellers just five miles south of Stockton. It is your surcoat is it not?"

"It is and you say there were a number of them?"

"At least twenty."

"The men who wore them?"

"Dead!"

He looked relieved, "Then they are not from the Nevill family for we have lost not a warrior this last year."

"But they are yours."

"They look like it." He cupped his hands and shouted, "Cedric!"

His steward, having taken our men to their quarters, rushed into the room, "Yes Sir Geoffrey?"

Sir Geoffrey held up the surcoat. "Twenty or more of these were used to lay blame at our family's door, Cedric. What do you know of this?"

I saw the old man's eyes widen with fear and then realisation dawned, "Six months since, my lord, do you not remember? We had sent to York for such surcoats. Your father wished to take men to the royal wedding and wanted them dressed well. The surcoats did not arrive, and we assumed that the men sent to fetch them had absconded with the payment for them."

Sir Geoffrey nodded, "Now that you mention it the memory becomes clearer. Do you think, Sir William, that the carters we hired sold them to these killers?"

I shook my head, "They were, I have no doubt, killed and this was an attempt to blacken your name and throw suspicion upon your family." I could not tell him about York, but he deserved to know of the plot.

He became angry, "And do you know who did this? If so let me have his name and I will end his and his men's lives."

Until I spoke with Alan Durward, I could not give him the details and so I gave him a version of the truth. "A few months ago I discovered that there were Scandinavians, Norse and Danish mainly but including English, Welsh and Scottish warriors, landing on the beach close to my home and making their way west. We have stopped the trade, but I believe that these men were up to mischief. I have reason to believe that there are two hundred and fifty or more of them. I confess that, at this moment, the identity of the men who planned this deception is not entirely clear, but I will discover it for I lost men to this treachery. What I would advise is for you to watch your borders as though we were at war. Question any who you do not know. When I discover whence this threat emanated be ready to come to my aid."

"That I will, and I will send a rider to advise my father too. Does the Bishop know?"

"The Bishop knows, and he keeps a good watch too." He nodded. "Tomorrow I will ride to Elsdon. I need to speak to the lord there and see if he has any news."

"A hard ride, Sir William."

"It will be a harder one if war comes!"

The next day I led my men not south and east back to our home but north and west. I needed to speak with Alan Durward for I feared that our visit to Barnard Castle might have forced our enemies to strike sooner rather than later. I sent Sir Geoffrey, with a good escort of four men, back to my father. I wrote a letter detailing what we knew and relying upon his good judgement to make the right decision. We would head to Jedburgh. I intended to stay at Elsdon or Otterburn. Sir James and Sir Robert were both good knights and Sir James had been given the manor of Elsdon when I had been elevated to Hartlepool.

We were nearing the ford at West Woodburn where we had fought the battle against the French and the Scots all those years ago when my scouts found trouble. The village was still deserted and the ones who had farmed there had moved to East Woodburn. It was a depressing sight for the village had been a happy one. Idraf and my archers were watering their horses when we reached them. We did not have far to go to reach Elsdon and, I suppose, we were more relaxed. The one who was ever vigilant, however, was Carl the Betts. While his horse was watering and before any had crossed, he waded across the ford and when he reached the other bank he stopped and knelt.

Idraf frowned and I said, "Is anything amiss, Idraf?"

He nodded, "Carl's nose seems to say that there is." He turned to his archers, "String your bows!"

As soon as they did my knights and men at arms did as I did and pulled their coifs up in preparation for donning helmets. Carl disappeared from our view and when he returned, he was holding something. He held up a carved bone comb. It was well carved, and he walked up to Erik and threw it to him. Erik examined it and then said, "Norse."

Carl said, "Fifteen of them and lightly armed. They were not mailed for their boots did not sink deeply into the soft mud. There are the remains of a fire yonder. They are ahead of us."

It was getting on to late afternoon and Elsdon was five miles away. It was just three miles to Otterburn, and we could ford the river close by. The tower guarded the ford. I said, "Carl, how do you read these tracks?"

"They are scouting and must have left Barnard Castle before we did, or else we would have caught them. They only have one pony, and I am guessing that carries what they need to cook. They are going in the same direction we are and that means they are heading for Jedburgh." He looked at Erik, "How fast would they be travelling?"

Erik looked at the sky, "The days are still short, and they would wish to avoid attention. That means they will avoid the roads where they can. Perhaps ten miles a day, perhaps more."

Idraf and I knew the area better than the others and he looked at me, "There is a wood, lord, in the bend of the River Rede. It is close to the road, but the nearest houses are the three farms at Rochester. They could push further north and that would put them close to the houses of Cottonshopeburnfoot."

"Then we will push on and see if they are close to Rochester. I would take these scouts. If they are not there then we ride to Otterburn and, after spending the night there, take Sir Robert's men to catch them at Cottonshopeburnfoot." I turned to Idraf, "You know the area well and Sir Robert knows you; ride to him, with Dick and warn him of the situation."

"Aye lord, Carl, take charge of the archers."

We mounted and headed north along the road. Darkness soon came to the road for the river cut through a valley whose sides shielded the water from the sun at this time of day. I made sure that Carl and his archers were well ahead of us. They would make even less noise than us and their noses and ears would detect a fire and the smell of Norsemen. We were on a Roman road and as it was cobbled we tried to ride on the earth on either side of the roadside ditch. Once darkness fell, we had to use the road and I knew that sound would travel. Once we crossed the Rede again, we found we could travel on soft earth and grass once more. I wondered if we had taken too much of a chance for we had to ride for another hour before Carl stopped and dismounted. We used hand signals and Carl indicated the wood ahead. He pointed to his nose and sniffed. He could smell their fire and he held up a thumb to confirm it. I pointed to the four squires and the horses. Even in the dark, I could sense their disappointment. We could not afford to lose our horses. I then gestured for Alan Longsword to take the left flank and Henry Samuel the right. I pointed to Sir Petr. He would be next to me for I still knew little about him in a fight. My men at arms filled in the gaps and, after we had drawn swords I nodded to Carl. He and the rest of the archers nocked an arrow and headed for the woods which lay four hundred paces from us across rough scrubland. Had it been daylight we might have seen signs of the scouts. I knew that this might not be our prey for other travellers, innocent ones, might use the woods. At this time of year, there were often sudden downpours. A wood afforded protection from the worst of it.

When we entered the woods then what little light from the sky there had been disappeared. I was ten paces behind Carl, and I kept looking at the ground to avoid stepping on to a branch or a twig. I could not smell the woodsmoke nor hear the murmur of conversation. When I heard the pony whinny I stopped, as we all did. The pony had heard us or smelled us and our horses. Would the warriors react? I knew now that this had to be the warriors we sought for the murmur of conversation we heard as we moved closer, was too loud to be one or two people. It also told me that we were close. I waited until Carl had moved off before I followed. My eyes had adjusted to the dim light and I could see, in the distance, the glow from the fire. Alan Longsword was next to Tom and Erik was next to Henry Samuel. Both were experienced and along with the archers before them would know to begin to make a half-circle so that we could surround them. I needed a prisoner. I could now make out words as voices were raised. Perhaps there was an argument. A voice silenced them and I recognised that it was a Norse one.

Carl turned to me. The question was clear when he drew back on his bow and I nodded. We needed prisoners but we needed their numbers thinning first. He gave a signal to the other archers and the seven of them moved closer. They knew their business better than I. I gestured for Sir Petr to move closer too. I was impressed by the way the Swedish knight moved for what we were doing was unnatural for a mailed man and yet he was not making a sound. I was learning about the new warrior.

The first noise we heard was the thrum of the first arrow followed by the buzz of another six. We moved more quickly then for there was a shout as the first sentry was slain. Then there were more cries as they realised that they were under attack. Carl sent another arrow at the camp before I reached him. I continued past him. There were six men with arrows in them and they were lying on the ground. I saw another three wielding weapons and they were also stuck with arrows. I heard the sound of a pony and knew that one, probably the leader, had mounted the animal and was trying to flee. It was at that moment that the Viking with the long sword and round shield ran at me. I just had my sword and a dagger. The warrior took me by surprise and I almost paid for that single moment of inattention with my life. What saved me was the tree. The Viking not only swung his sword but punched with the boss of his shield. The edge of his shield caught a branch and twisted so that I was able to use my sword and dagger to catch the sword. Even so, the top of the blade caught my helmet and I saw stars. He was a strong man and I started to tumble backwards. As with all battles, others were fighting all around us but this one was restricted to the length of a sword and was a deadly duel to the death.

He cursed me but it was in Norse. I was trying to wrest the initiative back from him. He punched again with the shield and this time he broke the branch and the shield hit my sword and my shoulder. I felt myself tumbling backwards again. Rather than fighting what I knew was a losing battle I allowed myself to be pushed to the ground. He could not stop himself and he too began to fall. It is a natural reaction to put your hand out to stop yourself and the Norseman did so with his right hand. As he fell his body struck my dagger and he drove the long, narrow blade into his side. I felt warm blood begin to flow. He raised his head, as he was lying on top of me, to headbutt me. I angled my head so that he did not strike my nose but the edge of my helmet. Once more my ears rang but I knew he was hurt more. I rammed my knee up between his legs and pushed with my sword at the same time. The combination made him slip to the ground. Too close for a blow I punched with the hilt of my sword. I caught the bent nasal of his helmet and was spattered with the blood from his broken nose. I punched again and again. It was as he tried to raise himself on to an elbow that I was engulfed in his blood. The dagger wound I had inflicted had wounded him worse than I had thought. He lay still.

I jumped to my feet and shouted, "I need a prisoner!"

I saw Sir Petr fighting a Norseman and he was trying to incapacitate the man and obey my orders. As Erik later told me, that was easier said than done and when the Norseman used axe and dagger to land a flurry of blows to the Swede's head Sir Petr just reacted, and his sword rammed up under the chin of the Norseman. It was the final blow.

"Are any left alive?"

Henry Samuel shouted, "There is one here, but he has not long to live!"

"Erik!"

Erik Red Beard ran to the warrior who had been gutted by Henry Samuel's sword. Erik knelt next to him and spoke. Their heads were close together and the dying warrior shook his head. He was still trying to hold in the writhing snakes that had been his intestines. Erik said something else and then handed the warrior his sword. It was a risk for the man could still kill but the warrior merely smiled and held the blade. A few heartbeats later the sword fell from his dead hand. Before I could question Erik, Tom of Rydal arrived leading a pony with a warrior on its back.

"Did any escape?"

Tom shook his head, "They fought well but they died."

Alan Longsword said, "And we lost none, my lord. We were lucky!"

"Well, Erik?"

"They are scouts for the de Balliol family. They were supposed to find out where the King of Scotland had gone. There is an army coming for him. The camp at Barnard Castle is just one of three. They are coming."

I nodded, "But we know not when!"

By the time we reached Otterburn we were exhausted, and I knew that we would not be able to leave early the next day, not unless we wished to kill our horses. Sir Robert said, when I told him what had happened and what I had planned, "I will take my men tomorrow and recover the bodies."

I was dead on my feet, but I knew I had to give advice to the young knight, "Tomorrow, you had also better send to Sir James and warn him. It may well be that we need to defend against an attack sometime soon."

He frowned, "From whom, we are at peace?"

"And there are those who profit from war. I pray that I am wrong, but I fear that I am not."

I was too tired to eat and after my squires had helped me to take off my mail I collapsed into a deep sleep.

Younger men can ride all day and survive on just an hour or so of sleep. I had a son who was training to be a squire and for the first time in a long time, I did not rise at dawn. Others were already up when I descended to the small hall where the food awaited us. My knights were there already, and Thomas fetched me an ale.

"Sir Robert and Sir James left at first light to collect the bodies, uncle, and to see if any had survived the attack."

I nodded, "And the hurts our men suffered?"

"Tended to. They will not slow us."

"Good then while I eat have the horses saddled and the men readied. It is now imperative that we get to Jedburgh as soon as possible. You should have roused me, Henry Samuel, for I fear we have begun the rocks sliding down the mountain and they are now unstoppable. If there were three camps, then that means we face not a warband of a couple of hundred but an army of a thousand or more. Alan Durward can counter that number, but it will take time to raise the army. It is still winter here in the north." As I gobbled down the food and washed it down with the ale, I wondered what my father would do. The message Sir Geoffrey had given was that we had found the camp, but the numbers would not have alarmed him. Nor would he have known of the urgency. I could spare no more men and it would be the handful I had with me and whatever Alan Durward could conjure up which would have to face these hired killers.

We met the two northern knights on the road north. The news they had was not good, "I am sorry Sir William, but it looks like two of the enemy escaped. We found their tracks for one was wounded; he had been struck by an arrow. We found the arrow close by a bloody stain on the grass. We lost them when they crossed one of the becks which criss-cross this land."

I smiled, ruefully, "As you know, Sir James, I was lord here and know that too well." I pointed south, "There will be three large warbands heading north and they may use this road. Keep men watching for them and when they are spied then rouse the land, send to Rothbury, Prudhoe and Morpeth."

"These warbands, lord, who commands them?"

"I believe the de Balliol family and they seek to end the life of King Alexander and claim the throne of Scotland. It is a bold plan."

"And you, my lord?"

"I go to warn King Alexander and then honour a promise I made to a dying king!"

My tardy start and the need for caution meant it took all day to travel the twenty-six miles to Jedburgh. The prisoner had not lived long and had we had the chance to question him more we might have discovered if there were other scouting parties looking for weaknesses. My scouts sought signs of danger as we inched our way north. The delays afforded me the opportunity to speak with Henry Samuel and Petr.

"Jedburgh is a palace and not a fortress and it would be hard to defend. Walter Comyn has denied them Edinburgh and Traprain Law has fallen into disrepair. The only castle left to the Scottish King is Dunbar which is fifty miles further north."

Henry Samuel said, "Or Berwick which is closer."

I had forgotten that, and I nodded, "Aye, then there is hope for Berwick is less than thirty miles away. Well done, nephew, that is hope unlooked for."

Sir Petr was the one who did not know the area nor the customs of the men who guarded the border, "I am sorry, Sir William, but surely there must be enough men who live along the border to defend King Alexander. Even if there are three warbands there cannot be more than a thousand men."

"Sir Petr, when we went west with King Alexander, we had a handful of knights. Remember Kilmartin? There we had even fewer. The Scots are a divided nation. A Scottish king has to win over his people to fight behind his banner. The reason de Balliol is making a move now is that the young king is seen as weak and with three others who have tenuous links to the crown then the gamble might pay off. The only lord with men who are close by is Lord Patrick of Dunbar. Sir James' home is in Galloway and Lord Hostarius in Atholl. King Alexander will be lucky to summon four hundred men to defend him, let alone the thousand he would need."

My heart sank when I found just the royal couple and twenty knights. Alan Durward and the Mormaer of Dunbar were absent. Sir James and his bodyguards remained. I saw, on Sir James' face, concern as I dismounted, "Your arrival, Sir William, does not bode well. You appear as a harbinger of doom!"

I nodded, "My suspicions are confirmed, my lord. De Balliol, or whoever controls the clan at the moment, has raised an army and they are on their way north. The night before last we surprised and killed their scouts. They were less than twenty miles from here. There may well be others closer by and if this is all the men you have then we are in great danger." He nodded, "The royal couple? I saw the royal standard."

"They are in the palace with the Prior."

"And the Queen Mother?"

There was a pause, and he shook his head, "She is in Edinburgh with Walter Comyn and her relatives from France."

It all became clear to me, "So we cannot flee there for then King Alexander would be under the sway of the Comyn family."

"He may be young, but he knows his own mind. He does not trust Walter Comyn. He and his mother had words when she suggested seeking sanctuary there."

"Then that leaves Berwick. We must leave on the morrow for…"

He shook his head, "Robert de Brus, 5th Lord of Annandale, is a claimant to the throne too. Some would say that he has the better claim of those who seek the throne."

I nodded, "I know the man. He claims the manor of Hartlepool even though it was given to me by the Bishop of Durham. What has he to do with it?"

"It is his man, Sir Adam Jesmond, who holds the castle." He shook his head, "I fear that Robert de Brus, 5th Lord of Annandale, will, in all probability, be appointed Regent."

"But it is you, Lord Patrick and Lord Hostarius who have protected the king thus far!"

"And of the three of us, it is likely that only Sir Alan will be a regent. De Brus and Comyn, along with the Queen Mother will probably be the others."

I had made a promise which it was unlikely I could keep. My father had taught me never to give up and we would have to make the best of this. "Sir James, you need to send to Sir Alan and Sir Patrick. Men will have to make up for the lack of walls."

He nodded, "I will do so." He smiled, "Ironical is it not that the Bane of the Scots, Sir William who was of Elsdon, is now Scotland's hope!"

Chapter 17

Enemy at the Gate

The next day I rode with my knights and Sir James to examine the defences of Jedburgh. It was a depressing journey. Riders had been sent to summon help, but we had to plan as though the guards at the palace and the knights of Sir James were our only defence. Idraf and my archers had left at dawn to watch the routes from the south. There were many ways to approach from that direction as the River Red could be forded in many places. The fortresses of Prudhoe and Carlisle would be avoided and as this was an irregular army of disparate men they could travel on smaller roads and cross through forests. They could melt away and then rejoin closer to Jedburgh. Jed Water would be no obstacle to such mercenaries.

"In the absence of a decent wall, Sir James, we need to use the two streams to channel the attackers. They have to come from the south and that is our only advantage."

He nodded, "I will have men begin to dig a ditch and embed stakes; if we join up the waters we will have a watery defence. The townsfolk of Jedburgh will have to defend their king!"

The day passed without a sign of the enemy but none of us relented. Even knights laboured to make a ditch which might slow down the enemy. Erik and Sir Petr both told us that our foes would have bows. The only archers we had were the handful I had brought. There were crossbows but they were not the same. It was not as though we had a castle to defend. A castle was the place to use crossbows. It was as we ate that night that we spoke to the king. He showed me, that night, that he was a king in the same mould as his father. He did not bemoan his fate nor seek to blame any. He was remarkably detached from it all.

"But you do not know for certain, Sir William, that the de Balliol family is behind this, do you?"

"You are right King Alexander, and these men may well be something to do with the war in the west. Whoever is behind it, the threat remains; there is a mercenary army heading north and who commands it is largely irrelevant. Had we not found the scouts just down the road then there might have been doubt about their destination. Having seen how thinly you are defended then I am convinced that in the next few days we will be fighting for our lives."

He nodded, "I could negotiate."

Sir James shook his head, "Sir John de Balliol and his youngest son, John, are both abroad. It is Hugh de Balliol who is behind this. He is a gambler and gambles that one throw of the dice wins all. He will come and the only talk he might consider would be if you either gave him the crown or allowed him to rule in your name."

"Then we fight!"

I smiled for he would not be fighting but I sensed that if we asked him to don mail and hold a sword then he would. His father had been a brave man and his son was cast in the same mould.

Hope arrived the next day when Lord Dunbar led in twenty of his knights and four hundred men. We had more than doubled the defenders. Whilst it was true that only the knights were mailed, Lord Dunbar's men were loyal. As well as the good news we also had the bad. Idraf rode in to say that the warbands led by knights, were less than a day away.

Sir James said, "Knights?"

"Aye, my lord, we saw their spurs, but they wore no livery. The banners they carried were the standards of Scotland."

Sir James shook his head, "So even if we defeat them, we cannot hold any to account. This is a clever plot, Sir William."

"And has been a long time in the planning. Even before we went with King Alexander to Oban men were arriving at the sands and travelling across the land. It was like water dripping from a leaking pail. It is hard to spot but is inexorable!"

Idraf said, "There is one thing more, Sir William." I looked at him. "I said we saw no liveries but that is not quite true. We did see liveries, but they were not Scottish ones, and they were not worn by knights. We spied ordinary spear and swordsmen wearing liveries, English liveries."

"English?"

"Aye, Sir William, including your father's, yours and the other knights of the valley. Others I had seen before, but they all belonged to English lords."

Sir James shook his head, "Surely that cannot be, Sir William."

I saw the cleverness in an instant, "Men serving my family have died in battle and we have not always been able to recover the bodies. Suppose someone took not only the swords and the weapons but the liveries too? This way there will be suspicion amongst Scottish lords. And surcoats are not difficult to make. When the battle is over they will not see the de Balliol banners, but they will see dead Englishmen! We have to win if only to clear the names of those men whose liveries are used."

183

The extra men were put to work for the last hour of the day. At least we would be able to give a better account of ourselves when the battle was joined. We had men camped by the defences and it was they reported the sounds of riders coming from the east. We stood to and I was relieved when Alan Durward led twenty of his own knights and a further twenty knights and men at arms as well as fifty spearmen from loyal burghs in the north. While his men were fed, we told him all that we knew.

He looked downcast, "I fear I have more bad news. Firstly, King Hákon of Norway and the rebellious MacDougalls have renewed their attacks in the west. There will be no aid from there and it seems there is a move to have me replaced as regent and replaced with de Brus, de Balliol and Walter Comyn."

"And does the king have no say?"

"The king has no say." He looked at me, "If things were not looking so parlous here, I would ask you to ride to your king. If King Henry were to use his power, then it might be that I could keep my place as regent."

"King Henry likes you and has given you manors in England. Aye, that might work but, once again, the plotters have outwitted us. I am pinned here by this Norse threat while others move castles and bishops into position."

Lord Dunbar smiled, "Let us deal with one problem at a time. Sir James, we have many more times the men you and Sir William had this morning. You know the defences well. Can we hold?"

"Until we were reinforced then I would have said no but now it is in the balance."

"Then let us take a little rest and then improve our defences on the morrow. There is little point in bemoaning what we do not have. We trust in God and fight with what we have to hand." Lord Dunbar, every bit as much as Alan Durward, was King Alexander's best hope.

The scouts were sent out again before dawn to warn of the moment the attack would begin. Their first reports were a mixed blessing. The enemy warriors were besieging Elsdon and Otterburn. Farms had been looted and animals slaughtered for food. It meant we had a day of grace to finish our defences.

Sir James became hopeful as we spoke of what this meant, "It will take some days to reduce those two strongholds." He shook his head, "I know for I tried many times."

Henry Samuel was with us and he had a clever mind. Of all my father's children and grandchildren, he was the closest in every way to my father, the earl. He had played chess with him more than any other and it showed in his warning, "This may be a ploy to draw us away from our defences or even to assume that they are the real target. The rest of the castles in the Coquet Valley will now bar their gates and wait. They will not ride to our aid nor Elsdon's. If my uncle is right and the target is King Alexander, then this is a trick!"

"I will ride to Otterburn and see for myself."

"We need you here, Sir William! It is too great a risk."

"And it is a risk I must take. I will ride with just my men at arms and Sir Petr. Henry Samuel, you take charge of the remainder of my men. I will ride only until I can see if you are right. I am the only one who can do this for I lived through sieges here on the borders and my practised eye will tell me if these are in earnest or a trick!" I saw my son grinning, "And you, Richard, can help your cousin. Folki and Thomas will suffice." His face looked crushed, but he nodded.

In the end, none could dissuade me and no one, not even King Alexander, had authority over me. I took just six men as I did not intend to fight, just observe! I was not a fool and I planned on using my local knowledge. If I was right, then the leaders of this attempt to seize the crown were not local men. They would not know that north of Otterburn was the Durtrees Burn. The valley was steep-sided and the farm at the bottom was long abandoned. There was a place just over a mile from the tower of Otterburn where I could observe the attackers.

We spied their sentries on the road close to where the Roman Road crossed the Rede and joined with the road to Otterburn and Elsdon. We were walking our horses in the trees which lay at the top of Durtrees Valley. Had they looked up they might have seen the movement, but the twenty men were watching the road. I knew that we were hurting our horses for the round trip would be almost forty-four miles, but we had to see.

When we reached the end of the valley, we left our horses with four of my men and hung our helmets from our cantles. We used the cover of scrubby shrubs and spindly trees to reach a vantage point. The moment I saw the siegeworks I knew that they were not in earnest. This was a trick. Firstly there were, so far as I could see, less than forty men surrounding the tower and the village. I could not even see the rest. If Sir Robert had so chosen, then he could have sortied and hurt them. Secondly, they had not dug a ditch. If they were trying to starve the garrison out, then it would take until Easter to do so!

I turned, "I have seen enough. They are trying to draw men here and away from Jedburgh."

We hurried back to our horses and remounted. The journey back was every bit as tiring as the outward one and perhaps that tiredness made us careless. We were near to the bridge over Jed Water close to where Willowford Burn joined it when we suddenly came upon thirty men. Some were on the far side of the burn and river while more than half were on our side. They were watering their ponies. As they had not been there when we had headed south, they had to have arrived since and it begged the question, '*what if more were further north?*' They saw us as soon as we saw them and I just reacted, "Charge!"

I drew my sword and spurred Destiny. Although tired, not to say exhausted, he was a warhorse, and he did his best. The ones who were watering their horses did not all react the same way. Some drew weapons but more than half of them tried to mount their horses or simply stood and stared. That gave us a chance and my sword hacked into the chest of what looked, from his plaited beard, like a Dane. Thomas and Sir Petr were just behind me and both struck the men who ran to them. One man managed to mount his horse and, as I splashed through the burn, I rode at him. He had a pony, and I had a warhorse. His pony baulked and I slashed across his arm. He tumbled from his horse into the water. Two riders bravely charged me holding spears like lances. Once more I saw signs that they were Scandinavians and I gambled that they had never used a spear from the back of a horse. They were confirmed when the one who reached me first rammed his spear at me. It struck my mail and was painful, but he held his spear too tightly and the strike knocked him from his saddle. The other missed my body and clanked off my helmet. I lunged with my sword and hit his shoulder. And then I was on the other bank. I whirled Destiny and saw that none of my men was unhorsed although Alan Longsword looked to be wounded. I waited until the last had passed before I turned Destiny to head back to Jedburgh.

There were enough of them left to mount their horses and to pursue us. Their horses must have been as tired as ours for they struggled to catch us. Perhaps we had slain some of their friends for they did not give up. Ahead I saw the fires cooking the meals at our camp and smoke rising, then suddenly Idraf and my archers appeared from the high ground to our right and a flurry of arrows hit two men and a pony. The rest fled.

"Well met and timely!"

"We were returning from the scout when we heard the noise of the horses." He pointed behind him, to the east, "There is a warband five miles in that direction."

"And what are they up to?"

"They were camping when we spied them." What were they doing there? Perhaps they were there to cut off any further help from Dunbar.

While Alan was seen to by the healers, I told the other leaders what I had learned. "They will attack us, and the sieges are there to confuse us. We need to keep working for this time tomorrow we will have to draw a sword and defend the king and his town!"

We continued working until dark and by that time we had the defences finished. We even manage to break through to the river and the beck so that the ditch, whilst not a moat was wet and muddy. Any who crossed it would be slowed down and, more importantly, would not be able to charge us.

My few men and knights were camped in the abbey grounds. King Alexander and his three leaders were inside the abbey. Hindsight is a wonderful thing but, looking back, I can see that was a serious mistake.

Chapter 18

The Battle of Jed Water

The guards who had been watching the ditch and the stakes all died quickly and most died quietly as skilled killers slipped over the ditch and slit their throats. The guards were unused to fighting Norse and Danish warriors. These were the ones who did not wear mail but were both fearless and skilled with knives and swords. The first that any knew was when a scream rent the air. I was awake in an instant and I jumped up, "Quickly, to arms!"

Idraf shouted, "Come archers! We buy our knights some time!"

Having two squires made life much easier for me but every moment of delay meant it more likely that we would lose this battle before it had barely begun. I could hear the clash of steel as the sentries fought with the enemy. The attackers had chosen their moment well for it was a moonless night and our men were tired from working all day; their reactions were slow. I was dressed first and, after donning my helmet I drew my sword and followed my archers who were just a hundred paces from me but were already, despite the light from our fires, shadows.

Erik must have slept in his mail byrnie for he was just two strides behind me. As he ran, he said, "If nothing else this tells me that the attackers have Viking blood for this is just the sort of attack we relish!"

I cursed myself for I had known when I had viewed the apparent siege that they had some trick planned and this could have been anticipated. Erik and I ran into the first three killers who had broken through. Once more that showed their courage and unpredictability. An English attacking force would have waited until they had enough numbers before venturing into an armed camp. The three Norsemen who ran at us were fearless. Their war cries told their race even though they were wearing English surcoats and English helmets. Behind me, I could hear shouts as men were roused and urged to get to the ditch. I drew my dagger as the first enemy raised his sword and then jumped in the air. Erik had locked swords with a second warrior, and I did the only thing I could do. I dropped to one knee and held my sword horizontally over my head. The Viking sword smashed down on to mine, but my dagger was driven up into his thigh. The flood of blood told me the wound was mortal and I was able to flick the body over my shoulder just as the third Norseman tried to swing his long sword two handed into the side of my helmet. I spun on my right leg as the sword ripped

188

through my surcoat, the edge rasping on my hauberk. As I came around, I allowed my sword to swing into his back. Beneath his surcoat, he had a brigandine and a gambeson, but my blade hacked through both. Henry Samuel, Sir Petr, Thomas, Geoffrey and the rest of my men at arms arrived as Erik slew the Norseman. We had bought time but we had to get to the front line where more of the enemy were pouring across the watery ditch.

Henry Samuel was not happy, "If any of us had rushed off like you two then we would have been chastised."

I gave a mock bow, "And now that you are here, what do you suggest?"

"A wedge?"

"Form wedge."

With Petr on my left and Henry Samuel on my right, the others took their places with the four squires at the rear. Each of them held a spear. We began to run. I saw bodies impaled by arrows and recognised Idraf and the archer's work. The line of sentries and those camped by the embedded spears had been breached but our sudden attack might have thwarted their attempt to kill the king while he slept! We met the line of warriors just as they broke through the embedded stakes. We were helped by the fact that they tried to rip them out and so when we hit them only half had weapons in their hands. Two tried to wield the embedded stakes like a spear or a club but Tom of Rydal slew one and Sir Petr the other. Our wedge meant that any who tried to attack us had to face at least four weapons and we were able to make progress through the hole made in our stakes. Added to that was the fact that we all wore mail so that the glancing blows with spears and swords did little harm.

Behind us, I heard Lord Dunbar's war cry as he led his men to avenge those who had been killed in the initial attack. When I heard the thunder of horses, telling me that Alan Durward and Sir James had mounted their knights, then I knew that this night attack had failed. We still had much work to do but the almost suicidal strike force was spent. The guards at the stakes had paid a price for their lack of vigilance but they had died buying us time to stem the flood. The killers sent into the night to wreak havoc had almost succeeded.

The Scottish knights halted at the line of stakes. In places, they had been torn out and before we could face the whole of their army, we would have to replace them.

"Hold firm!" I looked up, as Alan of Durward's voice shouted out his command. "We were lucky, Sir William. They almost had us. Those

189

three you slew were just two hundred paces from the chambers used by the king and his queen. Do you think they intended murder?"

I sheathed my sword and knelt. I ripped off the surcoat and the English helmet. The tattoos on the face told their own story. I nodded, "These men are renegades and mercenaries. They would not be daunted by regicide. They would lose no sleep over the murder of two children. I think this attack with a small and reckless force had a number of purposes: to test our defences and to weaken them and then, if possible, kill either the three of you or the King and Queen of Scotland. Your rooms are adjacent to theirs and had they got inside I would not have given much for your chances." I looked at Erik, Folki and Sir Petr, "You know these warriors better than most what do you say?"

Erik nodded, "These men were as berserkers and they did not care if they lived or died. I have heard of such men who bite their shields and throw them away. It is said that there is a drug they lick from the shield and that makes them fearless. They would not fear men in mail."

Sir Petr said, "I thought it was an old cult but when I watched them run at Sir William it made me think it had been revived."

"A story comes to mind, Sir Alan. The father of the Warlord who was my great, great, great, grandfather fought at the Battle of Stamford Bridge when the Conqueror came to England. The tale was passed down from generation to generation how three of Hardrada's men went berserk and stood, naked, on the bridge holding off the whole of the Saxon army. They were cut and wounded but held out until men went beneath the bridge and skewered them. I believe Erik and it is a lesson for us. We are not fighting a traditional enemy. This warband has been procured for the simple purpose of wresting the crown from King Alexander's head."

"Then tomorrow we will have to stop them." He cupped his hands, "Replace the stakes, take away our wounded and bring me an accurate number of our losses."

"And the enemy dead?" Lord Dunbar was a practical man.

Alan Durward licked his finger and held it aloft. "The wind blows towards our enemies. Make a pyre here in the centre of our line and burn them. Let them smell the burning flesh of their dead and make them have to fight across the still-warm ashes of their corpses."

Alan Durward had a hard side and that boded well for the Scottish crown. If any tried to take it from Alexander, they would first have to tear it from Alan Durward's dead hands!

We remained in position while the defences were repaired and then the fire of the bodies was begun. The smell of burning human flesh and hair was nauseating but the wind took the worst of it to their comrades.

190

We could not see them, but we knew that they waited in the dark. What was their plan? As dawn drew close and the defences were inspected food was fetched by the priests and monks from the abbey. While we ate the abbot and his priors began to pray for deliverance from this enemy. If the enemy had hoped that we would believe that these were hired English and Scottish swords, the bodies we had burned proved the lie. However, the identity of their paymaster was still obscured. Our guesses were just that, speculation with no proof at all. Geoffrey had time to fetch a whetstone and sharpen my sword while Thomas brought my shield and spears for us. We had not had time to grab them in the dark, but we would need them now.

It was when the sun finally rose in the east that we saw the size of the enemy army. There had to be fifteen hundred of them. We had counted a hundred enemy bodies when we had piled them on the pyre but we had lost more than that in the attack. Already outnumbered now it seemed that it would be a matter of when we were defeated and not if. The enemy appeared to be made up largely of foot soldiers and they were formed in a semi-circle between the river and the burn. I saw forty horsemen and recognised them as knights by their spurs. As Idraf had said, none wore Scottish livery, and their standard-bearers held the standards of Scotland. Their horsemen were behind the foot soldiers. Although our men had been absolved for we had all been shriven in the dark, the enemy did not appear to have brought priests. The other unusual thing was that there was no attempt to hold talks. They all waited.

We were almost lulled into a false sense of security for when the attack began, we were not quite ready. The night attack and the wait for the real attack had done that. The men in their front rank had shields but the ones behind must have been archers. Suddenly hundreds of arrows soared into the air. My men all had their shields ready and we held them up, but many others were slow to bring up their shields and I heard the thud of arrows followed by cries as they slammed into flesh. The battle had begun, and the enemy had gained the initiative. Already outnumbered we had lost forty men to the arrows and the enemy none!

I shouted, "Stand firm. When the arrows cease then they will cross." I heard the enemy banging their shields and chanting. The words were a cacophony but a rhythmic one and their beat was almost hypnotic.

Sir Petr, standing next to me said, "They will do this to help them keep in step when they cross. They will come soon."

Idraf and my archers were behind my line of men. We were a little knot of Englishmen amongst the many Scots but I knew that we were a strong band and we would hold when others might flee. My handful of archers were picking off the enemy archers. Our bows had a greater range and we had plenty of arrows. The enemy missiles were not bodkins and at the range they were being used could not penetrate shields and mail. Even the ones which rang against our helmets merely gave us a ringing in our ears. Idraf and the archers were nocking arrows whilst pressed into the backs of my men at arms and squires who held shields above them. When they stepped back to loose arrows they had a good view of the enemy. Idraf shouted, "They come!"

The one Scottish formation I had come to respect when I had fought them was the schiltron, the forest of long spears which could hold off either horses or mailed men. The arrows had decimated the schiltrons but now the three Scottish lords began to reorganise them as the mercenary army began to move across the ditch towards us. The schiltrons were solid blocks of men and between them, the Scottish knights and men at arms formed perilously thin lines to join them. We were between a line of Lord Dunbar's knights and Alan Dunbar's. Being at the centre we would bear the brunt of the fighting. When the rain of arrows first diminished and then ceased, I risked lowering my shield and I saw the wall of men advancing towards us. Their knights were hanging back. If you have hired barbarians to do your fighting for you then you let them bear the casualties. There would be fewer men to pay. If I had brought all the archers of the valley then we would have been able to slaughter them as they stepped into the muddy water of the ditch. It could not be crossed quickly even if they were in step. We could have made it run red with blood. As it was the paltry number we had merely made the ones who would attack us weaker for we had bodkin arrows and Idraf and the others were good enough to aim at mailed men and to kill them. Wading through waist-deep water is never easy and the men who came at us had to negotiate bodies in the bottom.

However, there were so many and so few arrows being sent at them that they were soon at the embedded stakes. We had replaced the ones which had been torn out and that broke up the enemy lines. We were twenty paces from them and stood behind the blackened pile of still warm, in some places glowing, ash. You could see, now that the sun was up, unburnt pieces of bone and metal. The ones who came knew that their elite warriors, the ones sent at night lay there. It would not change the outcome of the battle but it would madden some and unnerve others. There was one thing I had learned in my years of fighting; men's minds could make good warriors weaker and poor warriors stronger. The problem was predicting this.

I had my spear braced against my right foot and Thomas' and Richard's poked out to the left and right of me. My extra squire meant that my three knights were protected by four spears. Idraf's archers' arrows continued to find flesh and each time a warrior raised his sword and screamed a command he was signing his own death warrant. It was strange to see men dressed in English surcoats but shouting in Norse and Danish, Welsh and Scottish! The arrows stopped the ones to our fore forming ranks, and they gave up and simply ran at the men who fought beneath my banner. The one who first reached me had a large two-handed axe, a sure sign that he was a Dane and behind him were two men with spears. They came directly for me. The archers had struck the four who had followed them but the three came straight for me. The problem with a war axe such as the one which was swung at me is that it is hard to time the swing whilst running. The warm ash over which they had run must have also been somewhat disconcerting. Thomas and Dick rammed their spears forward and I held my shield so that I could block any blow which came my way. If the man with the axe connected then my shield would be badly damaged and despite the padding, my arm might well be broken. It was Dick's spear which gouged a line in the warrior's cheek, but it was my spear which killed him. He was so distracted that he failed to notice my unmoving spear and the axe fell from his hand as he impaled himself upon it.

The two spearmen with him rammed their spears at me. Thomas' spear took one but the other hit my shield and glanced off towards Dick. The dying warrior who had dropped his axe now tried to wrest my spear from his body. I saw that more men had now emerged from the ditch and passed the stakes. I let go of the spear and drew my sword just as the warriors ran at our little line. There was one of the original three men facing us and as he drew his bloody spear back to strike at me, I lunged with my sword and ripped into his throat. In that heartbeat between his death and before the next wave struck us, I wondered whose blood was on the spear.

Carl shouted, "My lord, your son is wounded!"

"Take him to the healers!" Every part of my being wanted to pick him up in my arms and carry him, but I was a warrior and knew what I had to do. We would be not only one spear light but there would be one archer fewer. The battle fates were conspiring against us. I felt cold rage creep up my body. The stroke I used to swing down towards the warrior who led the next group of men had hatred and anger behind it. I knew not if Dick lived or died but I would ensure that everyone who came within a sword's length of me would die. If the de Balliols came then there would be no ransom. They would die! I blocked his sword with my shield and while he managed to bring his shield up you could see that he was used to a round Norse shield rather than the narrower longer ones we used. He did not manage to cover his head and my sword drove into his helmet, crushing his skull beneath. He slipped into a silent death to join the other bodies before us. I realised that the mercenaries came at us in groups led by one man. It was in the nature of the warriors. With the leader dead the rest tried to avenge themselves on us and their attack was furious and frenetic. I, too, was angry but this was the cold anger of one who is determined to succeed. I was also comforted by the two young warriors standing next to me. Henry Samuel was as good a warrior as ever wielded a sword and Sir Petr, despite the shortcomings of his nature had shown that he was a more than competent warrior. Even when four men ran at our tiny wedge our bloody blades found flesh and our mail proved its worth. We would be battered and bruised when this was over, but we would, God willing, be alive.

All around the lines were joined and they ebbed and flowed as men fell and others advanced. The schiltrons were doing their job but the mercenaries we fought were fighting for pay. This would be their last chance to make money and they would either win and walk away rich men or they would die. They were professionals and the Scots they fought were farmers. Gradually the forest of spears was hewn down. It was then that the enemy leader, I assumed Hugh de Balliol, launched his masterstroke. He knew that when the hedgehog of spears broke then the men would flee. There was a wail from the left of our line. Idraf shouted, "Another warband, lord! They are attacking our left!"

Alan Durward must have seen them too for he shouted, "Men of Atholl angle left!"

Even as I slew another mercenary, I knew that this was the warband Idraf had seen to the east. I knew from his description that it was not a large one, but it would be enough for we now had one flank which was no longer secure. That it was part of a larger plan became clear when, as we slew the last of the mercenaries who had attacked us, we heard horns from the enemy and the knights who had waited for this moment began to move towards us. We were the thinnest part of the line. Our spears were now shattered, many of the stakes had been destroyed and the knights would simply charge us and ride us down. When there is little hope then you snatch at whatever you see.

I shouted, "To the stakes! Stop them at the ditch!" Looking back it seems a wild idea but as I ran I was grateful that not only my men but also those of Lord Dunbar and Sir Alan who were close to us, followed me. There were still men on foot running towards us but none of these had mail. These were the ones who were not as bold as those who had attacked in the night or had made the first charge. Nor were they expecting to be charged and I ran one warrior, by his curses a Hibernian, through with my sword. It came out of his back. I put my foot against his body and pushed it from my sword. The warrior behind stumbled as he crashed into the falling body and I hacked my sword through his back. He was half in and out of the water. I kicked his body back in to make a more treacherous footing for the first horse.

"Hold them here!" I knew that while we might lose the rest of the battle the stakes we had embedded would give us some protection. The knights would not be able to ride boot to boot. We would take more of them with us and our deaths might be worthwhile.

Sir Petr was laughing next to me, "This is how I hoped my life would end, in a glorious battle! My ancestors would be proud!"

Henry Samuel shouted, "Do not be so keen to consign us to an early death! My uncle leads and so long as we live then there is hope! There is always hope!"

The first of the knights was already in the ditch and he discovered that his mail was no defence against bodkin arrows. Three of them slammed into him and knocked him from his saddle. His horse just stood in the middle of the ditch, an equine obstacle to those which followed. The horse was a warning to the rest and as they approached the edge of the ditch they slowed and raised their shields. They had lances and I saw them enter the water in a line. It was then that I recognised Hugh and Alain de Balliol. They were in the second rank and I also saw that they were coming for me. This would not be easy but as Henry Samuel had said, while there was hope we would fight! I knew that even beyond the ending of hope my men would fight.

The knights came at us as fast as they could, but you cannot gallop over a ditch. Some tried to jump but the bodies at our side of the ditch caused their horses to slip and their riders slid into the ditch where they were easily slain. Of course, on the flanks, there were just schiltrons and the Scottish warriors, bravely though they fought were being forced back by the mercenaries now augmented by horsemen. As I had learned long ago, you fought the battle to your front and did not worry about how others fared. Three squires and our archers watched our backs, and I knew that we could rely upon them. The first lances were delivered at the halt and were easily deflected. The wood was soon hacked into kindling and that left the horsemen with their swords. The problem was that, as our spears were shattered, we could not get at the riders. It was as the knights and men at arms attempted to climb the ditch that a solution was found. Erik had picked up the two-handed war axe dropped by a Dane and he stepped forward and hacked into the side of the head of the nearest warhorse. He then backhanded it in to the next one. As the two knights fell into the water so Sir Petr and Henry Samuel used their swords to execute the prostrate mailed men. A warhorse is expensive and the deaths of the two horses prompted the knights to urge their animals up the slippery bank.

I chopped my sword into the side of one courser's head. It was not a killing blow, but it maddened the horse which threw its rider and then the badly wounded horse ran back across the ditch. The enraged knight waded towards us with his sword held in two hands. I vaguely recognized his face from the hall at Barnard Castle. He cleverly swung his sword at my legs. I had the wit to jump and when I landed, he had to halt his sword for the reverse swing. I hacked sideways into his head which was conveniently at my waist height. The sword crushed the metal and then drove through bone. It was at that moment that Sir Hugh de Balliol took his chance. He used the dead knight's body to clamber his horse up on to the bank of the ditch. His brother followed and the two horses knocked Sir Petr to the ground. Folki still had a spear and he came to his master's aid. He rammed the spear into the chest of Sir Alain's horse which tumbled backwards, depositing the traitor in the now bloody ditch.

I had my own battle to fight as Sir Hugh's spear was rammed at my face. His horse had his forelegs on the bank. I flicked up my shield and deflected the spear, but the head caught under my helmet and tore my helmet from my head. I chopped down on the spear and cut it just behind the metal head. As he threw away the stump and drew his sword I lunged at his leg. My sword sliced along the side of the horse and the tip penetrated his mail just below his knee. Unlike some knights he was not wearing poleyns to protect it. He roared, not in pain but in anger as his horse tried to move away from the sword and stepped back into the water. It was his shield which faced me and so I did the unexpected, I dived at him and became a human spear with my sword held before me. It was not an elegant dive but with the weight of my mail and shield, I drove my sword into his shoulder and knocked him from his horse. We both landed in the muddy, bloody, watery ditch. He was trapped not only by his horse but by my weight too. I pushed hard on his face as I held him down. I tried not to breathe but I knew he was trying to gasp for air which merely accelerated his demise. When his horse freed itself and we both rose to the surface, he was dead.

"Uncle, beware!"

I turned, just in time to see Sir Alain de Balliol wading towards me. Four other knights were heading for Sir Petr and Henry Samuel. Thomas was trying to get to me, but the press of bodies between us was too great. My dive had killed the enemy leader, but it had also put me beyond aid. The guige strap on my shield had broken and was floating in the ditch. I held my sword two handed as Sir Alain came towards me with a war axe and a shield.

"You have interfered enough, Englishman, now it is I who shall become King of Scotland and not my brother. Already you are surrounded. You may have killed many of our men, but Alexander is a boy, and he will die! The victim of men hired by the Norwegian King!"

My father had often told me that there was little point in talking while you fought. It was a waste and dulled your reactions. He was right and I swung my sword, not at his shield, which he held above the ditch water, but at his thigh, just below the surface. Delivered with two hands I cut through mail and into his leg. When his left leg collapsed a little, I raised my sword to strike down at his head. He barely managed to block the blow with his shield, and he was forced back. With a weakened leg, he struggled to keep his balance. I was aware of other rebels trying to get at me, but I had to finish this before they finished me. I would have paid my debt of honour and kept my word. Alexander would be safe. I brought my sword down diagonally across Sir Alain's body. This time his axe, which he held across his body, could not save him and my blade chopped through the haft and ripped across his chest. The blow itself was not fatal but the blood which poured from his thigh was. His head fell back into the water.

He coughed up a mouthful and said, "One day my younger brother will be King of Scotland!"

I lifted my sword and said, as I drove it into his throat, "But not you!"

Their leader dead, the knights who remained all began to wade towards me. I turned to face them. Thomas, Henry Samuel and Sir Petr were hurrying to get to my side. I would not die alone. I wondered if Dick was dead or alive. Just then arrows flew from behind me. This was not the half dozen or so from my archers but thirty or forty and even as they slammed into the knights in the water another forty followed.

Idraf shouted, "It is Sir Richard of Hartburn! He leads the Earl's men! The men of the valley have turned the tide!"

As four Scottish knights fell before me, I turned and saw the banners of Sir Geoffrey, Sir Richard, all the knights from the valley, even Sir Fótr! The tables had been turned! We had won but my thoughts were on my son. Leaving others to pursue and slay the remnants of the mercenary army I waded back to the bank and, after sheathing my sword ran to the abbey. To my great relief, I saw that Dick was not only alive but helping the priests to tend to the other wounded. He was alive

197

and the arrival of men sent by my father had turned certain defeat into victory.

Sir Richard led the reinforcements to chase the survivors towards Otterburn where Sir James and Sir Robert were waiting to ensure that none escaped. I saw Lord Dunbar brought in. He was badly wounded, but he lived. Sir James alas was dead, but the charismatic Alan Durward lived.

He came over to me, "Scotland is in your debt, my lord but I fear few shall know of it. This battle never happened! King Alexander needs to be protected from others who might try to emulate the de Balliol family. I need to build alliances!"

I nodded, "I have kept my promise, my lord, and that is all the reward that I need."

He left me to go to the royal couple.

I had lost but two warriors. Alan and Erik lived as did all the archers. I had kept my promise and I could go home.

It was when my former squire, Sir Geoffrey approached me with a face as black as the night that I feared we had lost knights in the pursuit. He simply dismounted and, dropping to one knee said, "It is Sir Thomas, my lord, your father is dying. He may be dead already! He was on his death bed when he sent us."

I had kept my word but at what cost?

Epilogue

Hearing the news we just grabbed our war gear and mounted our horses, thankfully well rested, and the men who had been with me during this adventure and with my wounded son we headed south. I was anxious to leave quickly and urged those who would be coming with me to hurry. Sir Geoffrey came with us, leaving Sir Richard of Hartburn to return south with the rest of the Cleveland lords when they had rested.

I knew that it would be physically impossible to travel the ninety miles in one day. To do so we would need to have relays of horses. We would break our journey in Newcastle. While we rode Sir Geoffrey, my former squire, told me all that had unfolded. When he had reached Stockton my father had already begun to deteriorate and was in his bed. Sir Geoffrey had been unwilling to speak to him for he did not wish to make his condition worse and instead rode to Hartburn and told Sir Richard. It was to my old friend and Eleanor's husband that I was indebted. He had been lord of Otterburn and knew the land better than any. It had taken just half a day to begin to gather the men by which time my father, ever attuned to the movements in the castle and its rhythms rose, against the doctor's orders. It was he who had commanded his archers and men at arms to follow Sir Richard. I had smiled when I had heard that he shouted, "The townsfolk can defend my castle! I want my men to defend my family!" The effort had been too much, and he had collapsed. None of us knew if he lived or died. I prayed that God would let him live. Even Sir Fótr who had given up on war came with his son to help us. I was humbled that none spurned the opportunity to come to the aid of four of the Warlord's heirs.

The attack of the men of Cleveland had been planned by Sir Richard. He knew that he had less than one hundred men to influence a battle where we would be outnumbered. A visit to Otterburn told him that. The sieges had been lifted and Sir Robert had captured a besieger so that he knew the plan. Sir Richard rode from behind the warband which had outflanked us, and he had caught them unawares. Not one man escaped as our archers rained death upon them. I saw now that the crucial moment had been when Sir Hugh fell. That meant their plan was largely in tatters but as Sir Richard's attack was unleashed even as the traitor was dying then all was well. Dick's wound made him pale but my son showed on that ride from Jed Water, that he had the steel of the Warlord in his body.

199

When we ate with the Sherriff, John de Vesci, in his castle on the Tyne we told him what had happened. I omitted the de Balliol name for the last thing we needed was unrest in the north of England. When time allowed, I would need to speak with the Bishop and I knew, as much as I did not relish it, that I would have to visit with King Henry. This was treachery at the highest level. It says much about the flawed King Henry that I had no idea if he would punish or reward the de Balliol faction! I knew from the brief conversation I had with Alan Durward as our horses were being prepared for the ride south that the battle might be disguised as a raid by Norsemen. There was enough bad blood in Scotland as it was and by turning from the de Balliol family to the Norwegians might regain the isles for King Alexander. When I had mounted my horse, the king had rushed from the Abbey to clasp my arm and thank me, "I am in your debt, Sir William, and your family's!"

The thirty odd miles we galloped from the Tyne to the Tees was the fastest ride I had ever endured. Some men's mounts went lame and they had to be left but nothing would stop me. We reached the castle as darkness was beginning to fall. I threw myself from my horse and with Thomas, Dick, and Henry Samuel hot on my heels I raced through the Great Hall and up the stairs to my father's chamber. I had prayed all the way south that I would be in time. I spoke to no one. The servants, looking grim merely bowed as we flew past them. When I reached the door of my father's bed-chamber, I flung it open. Inside I saw a priest making the sign of the cross over my father. My mother and my wife were comforting each other while my sisters and sister-in-law gently wept. I was too late.

My mother said, "William!"

At that moment the priest jumped up and said, "Sir Thomas!"

In two strides I was next to the bed and I grasped his thin, bony and icily cold hand, "Father, you live!"

All around was total silence but I just had eyes for my father. I could smell death upon him but he opened his eyes and gave a weak smile. "God is kind and has given me but a brief moment. I knew you would come if you could and I thank him."

My words came out in a torrent. I had so much to say and so little time, "Father, do not go. I have much to say. You know that I love you?" He nodded. "I have tried to be a good son and to make up for the one who was so murderously taken."

"And you have and more. Aye, I know you love me but it is not in our nature to say such things. Perhaps you can change that. My will is writ and you shall be the new Earl. My home is in good hands. I see Henry Samuel, Thomas and Richard."

They knelt too. Henry Samuel and Thomas took his other hand. I saw tears coursing down all their cheeks. This was not just the death of a man; this was the passing of a legend.

"This is not the way I wished to pass, eaten from within by some worm but a man cannot choose his own end." He saw Petr, "Your father would have wished to go with a sword in his hand. If God is willing, then when I see him in the afterlife I can look him in the eye and tell him my debt is repaid."

Suddenly his eyes closed, and he gave a sigh which I knew from the warrior's deaths I had seen was life leaving him. Bowing my head I prayed that God would welcome this warrior who had fought in two crusades and defended the weak and the poor from a rapacious king. I was the new earl but I was not fit to clean the boots of the man I was replacing. I stood and went over to my mother. I said not a word but opened my arms. She hugged me and sobbed, "God kept him alive so that he could speak with you." She pulled back, "William, what will I do without him? How can I live without the man with whom I have spent more than fifty years?"

"You will do so, mother, in his memory. None will ever forget him. He shall be buried next to the Warlord. This family has had two great men who strode like giants through their time."

She smiled, "And in his son, we have a third! The land is safe in your hands, my son! And now we must prepare for a funeral and I must put on a face to meet those who will come to mourn Sir Thomas of Cleveland the hero of Arsuf! The sword for hire who became a confidante of kings!"

She was right and we had to begin our life without him.

The End

Glossary

Cowpon- Cowpen Bewley
Hostarius-protector of the king's property (Scotland)
Østersøen – The Baltic Sea
Sudtune- Sutton on the Forest

Historical Note

This is fiction! As far as I know, there was no battle of Jed Water although there were battles at this time in the western isles. The Campbells and the MacDougalls were enemies and their clan leaders were real. King Alexander did ride to Oban to try to persuade the MacDougall clan to cease supporting the Norwegians. He failed and died of a fever in Oban.

His heir was a child, and he did marry King Henry's young daughter in York in 1251. There was no attempt on his life. Fiction! The three Scottish lords, Alan Durward, Lord James Galloway and Lord Patrick Dunbar were instrumental in supporting the young king.

Hugh de Balliol and Alain de Balliol were the sons of John de Balliol, but they died before 1271. I chose to have them try to gain the throne. Their brother John de Balliol did become King of Scotland although not a popular one. He was placed on the throne by Longshanks, King Edward 1st. The Robert de Brus in the story is not the one who would become king but his father. The de Balliol and de Brus families had equal claims to the crown.

The story will continue if only because I am interested in this fictitious family I have created. I know not where it will end but I hope you enjoy the journey with me!

All the maps used were made by me. Apologies, as usual, for any mistakes. They are honest ones!

Books used in the research:

- The Crusades-David Nicholle
- Norman Stone Castles- Gravett
- English Castles 1200-1300 -Gravett
- The Normans- David Nicolle
- Norman Knight AD 950-1204- Christopher Gravett
- The Norman Conquest of the North- William A Kappelle
- The Knight in History- Francis Gies
- The Norman Achievement- Richard F Cassady
- Knights- Constance Brittain Bouchard
- Knight Templar 1120-1312 -Helen Nicholson
- Feudal England: Historical Studies on the Eleventh and Twelfth Centuries- J. H. Round
- English Medieval Knight 1200-1300

- The Scandinavian Baltic Crusades 1100-1500 Lindholm and Nicolle
- The Scottish and Welsh Wars 1250-1400- Rothero
- Chronicles of the age of chivalry ed Hallam
- Lewes and Evesham- 1264-65- Richard Brooks
- Ordnance Survey Kelso and Coldstream Landranger map #74
- The Tower of London-Lapper and Parnell
- Knight Hospitaller 1100-1306 Nicolle and Hook
  Old Series Ordnance Survey Maps 93 Middlesbrough

Griff Hosker
February 2021

Other books by Griff Hosker

If you enjoyed reading this book, then why not read another one by
the author?

Ancient History

The Sword of Cartimandua Series
(Germania and Britannia 50 A.D. – 128 A.D.)
Ulpius Felix- Roman Warrior (prequel)
The Sword of Cartimandua
The Horse Warriors
Invasion Caledonia
Roman Retreat
Revolt of the Red Witch
Druid's Gold
Trajan's Hunters
The Last Frontier
Hero of Rome
Roman Hawk
Roman Treachery
Roman Wall
Roman Courage

The Wolf Warrior series
(Britain in the late 6th Century)
Saxon Dawn
Saxon Revenge
Saxon England
Saxon Blood
Saxon Slayer
Saxon Slaughter
Saxon Bane
Saxon Fall: Rise of the Warlord
Saxon Throne
Saxon Sword

Medieval History

The Dragon Heart Series
Viking Slave
Viking Warrior
Viking Jarl
Viking Kingdom
Viking Wolf
Viking War
Viking Sword
Viking Wrath
Viking Raid
Viking Legend
Viking Vengeance
Viking Dragon
Viking Treasure
Viking Enemy
Viking Witch
Viking Blood
Viking Weregeld
Viking Storm
Viking Warband
Viking Shadow
Viking Legacy
Viking Clan
Viking Bravery

The Norman Genesis Series
Hrolf the Viking
Horseman
The Battle for a Home
Revenge of the Franks
The Land of the Northmen
Ragnvald Hrolfsson
Brothers in Blood
Lord of Rouen
Drekar in the Seine
Duke of Normandy
The Duke and the King

New World Series

Debt of Honour

Blood on the Blade
Across the Seas
The Savage Wilderness
The Bear and the Wolf

The Vengeance Trail

The Reconquista Chronicles
Castilian Knight
El Campeador
The Lord of Valencia

The Aelfraed Series
(Britain and Byzantium 1050 A.D. - 1085 A.D.)
Housecarl
Outlaw
Varangian

**The Anarchy Series England
1120-1180**
English Knight
Knight of the Empress
Northern Knight
Baron of the North
Earl
King Henry's Champion
The King is Dead
Warlord of the North
Enemy at the Gate
The Fallen Crown
Warlord's War
Kingmaker
Henry II
Crusader
The Welsh Marches
Irish War
Poisonous Plots
The Princes' Revolt
Earl Marshal

**Border Knight
1182-1300**

Debt of Honour

Sword for Hire
Return of the Knight
Baron's War
Magna Carta
Welsh Wars
Henry III
The Bloody Border
Baron's Crusade
Sentinel of the North
War in the West
Debt of Honour

Sir John Hawkwood Series
France and Italy 1339- 1387
Crécy: The Age of the Archer
Man at Arms: The Battle of Poitiers

Lord Edward's Archer
Lord Edward's Archer
King in Waiting
An Archer's Crusade

Struggle for a Crown
1360- 1485
Blood on the Crown
To Murder A King
The Throne
King Henry IV
The Road to Agincourt
St Crispin's Day
The Battle for France

Tales from the Sword

Conquistador
England and America in the 16th Century
Conquistador (Coming in 2021)

Modern History

Debt of Honour

The Napoleonic Horseman Series
Chasseur à Cheval
Napoleon's Guard
British Light Dragoon
Soldier Spy
1808: The Road to Coruña
Talavera
The Lines of Torres Vedras
Bloody Badajoz
The Road to France

The Lucky Jack American Civil War series
Rebel Raiders
Confederate Rangers
The Road to Gettysburg

The British Ace Series
1914
1915 Fokker Scourge
1916 Angels over the Somme
1917 Eagles Fall
1918 We will remember them
From Arctic Snow to Desert Sand
Wings over Persia

Combined Operations series
1940-1945
Commando
Raider
Behind Enemy Lines
Dieppe
Toehold in Europe
Sword Beach
Breakout
The Battle for Antwerp
King Tiger
Beyond the Rhine
Korea
Korean Winter

Other Books
Great Granny's Ghost (Aimed at 9-14-year-old young people)

For more information on all of the books then please visit the author's web site at www.griffhosker.com where there is a link to contact him or visit his Facebook page: GriffHosker at Sword Books

Printed in Great Britain
by Amazon

71582638R00122